Trompe l'Oeil

Trompe l'Oeil

(To Fool the Eye)

By

CAROLINE MILLER

Trompe l'Oeil
Published by Rutherford Classics

Copyright © 2012 Caroline Miller, Portland, OR
All Rights Reserved

Second Edition 2017

Library of Congress Control Number: 2012951932

ISBN: 978-0-9981697-4-3 (softcover)
         978-0-9981697-5-0 (ebook)

Manufactured in the United States of America

Publisher's Cataloguing in Publication

Miller, Caroline

Fiction, 2. Mystery, 3. Suspense. 4. Historical,
5. Psychological, 6. Thriller, 7. France.

What critics say about *Caroline Miller's* work:

"*Gothic Spring* is a fine addition to any fiction collection."

–*Midwest Review*

"*Gothic Spring* is quite delightful to read!"

– *Rebecca Reads*

"Victorine Ellsworth knows something about the death of the vicar's wife...but what? Is she the killer?" Recommended as a good read, April 2012

- *Alan Caruba*

[About Caroline Miller's two novels, *Gothic Spring* and *Heart Land*] "Both novels combine the energy and creativity of Miller's youth and sagacious wisdom of a woman who has seen the world and experienced first-hand progressive change."

-*SE Examiner, October 2009*

"Ms. Miller is a powerful, eloquent writer."

– *Silver Reviews*

Dedication

*This book is dedicated
to the memory of Phil Adamsak,
journalist, scholar, gentleman and friend*

Acknowledgements

I WISH TO THANK LEONA GRIEVE for her inspired work as my editor. Thanks also to Tilly and Philippe Gaillard who were a great help with French terms, plus a special thanks to Tilly who edited for errors. Any errors that remain are my own.

Chapter One

WHY DO YOU GO ON with these questions? I know my story is strange but don't delude yourself. I'm not mad. And I swear to you I am not now, nor have I ever been, under the influence of narcotics— except for the brief period to which I've confessed and for which I cannot be held responsible. That I have survived this calamity is a miracle.

The outward signs of my condition, the tremor in my limbs, my periods of acute nervousness, may be cause for alarm; but given the nightmare I've been through, these effects should be understandable. I began my misadventure in a robust state, but you must understand that my escape from the chateau came at great cost to me.

At the outset, I was unaware my status was that of a prisoner rather than an employee. Who could imagine a setting of such grandeur and proportion was little more than a cell: the vaulted ceilings, the marble halls ending in a sweeping staircase, the chandeliers gleaming overhead? To penetrate the dangers of my predicament from the first would have required sharper powers than my twenty-one years afforded.

Yes, I was a fool to place so much faith on the report of my eyes. But here was a setting of overblown beauty. Although tarnished and neglected, the architecture seduced me with its decadence; its decay so alluring that my usual requirements for restraint and order fled from my mind. How could I know such opulence was a snare? Or that the moment I set my suitcase down upon the marble tiles, I'd unleashed forces that would threaten my life and endanger people whom I came to love.

* * *

Madame de Villiers, the woman who had hired me sight unseen was still in Paris when I arrived at the Chateau l'Ombre outside the small village of Sainte Enimie, an eight-hour drive south of the City of Lights. The housekeeper, Mrs. de Toi, settled me into my rooms but could provide no explanation as to my employer's whereabouts except to say that she had been delayed. Having been specific in my itinerary, I was disappointed to find the chateau empty, except for a handful of servants, too few in numbers to maintain the premises at optimum standards. Still, the rooms to which I was assigned were light and airy, consisting of a bathroom, a dressing alcove and a bedroom with tall windows that looked out upon the winding driveway at the front of the house. Beyond it, an expanse of lawn spread like a carpet into a distant grove of trees, a mixture of deciduous and evergreen.

Mrs. de Toi started to help me unpack while I took a moment to stare from the windows at a flock of birds, specks against a cerulean summer sky. The atmosphere seemed serene.

With a sigh, I turned to ask my new acquaintance how long she had been in service at the chateau. She was a stout woman in her mid-fifties, her hair the color of steel. Her black dress and gray stockings were the traditional garments of a servant, but she wore them with a confidence that suggested both pride and authority.

"For many years, Mademoiselle. Since Madame de Villiers and…" A cloud drifted across her expression but the moment passed almost imperceptibly. She shrugged before continuing. "Since Madame was no more than six years old."

Whatever the thought that had disturbed her countenance, the affection in her voice for her mistress was strong enough for me to remark upon it. "She seems like a daughter to you, then."

"It's true," the housekeeper answered but added nothing more. She headed for the alcove to place a few of my dresses upon padded hangers that exuded a lavender scent. I followed her to continue our conversation. "I haven't brought much. Perhaps there are shops in the village you can recommend?"

"Sainte Enimie is so small, Mademoiselle. You'll find nothing stylish here, especially as fall approaches and the tourists begin to leave. The next time Madame drives to Paris, you might accompany her. She likes to shop and knows all the best places."

"Does she go to Paris often?"

I was eager to learn all I could about my new employer, Odeil de Villiers, a woman completely unknown to me. I'd obtained my position through Mrs. Crofter, the Dean of Students at Mills College, just as I was about to graduate with honors in French History. She'd called me to her office and told me I had an opportunity to live in France for a year to help with research on the history of a place called Chambre l'Ombre. I'd hardly been able to believe my good fortune when I heard her. My parents had died in a car accident two years earlier, and I'd been slow to recover from the shock. The thought of escaping to the romantic setting of the Gorges du Tarn had been more than I could have wished for—a new environment, a fresh beginning—although it struck me as odd that a local French scholar should not have been hired for the job.

The Dean waved my reservation aside. "I know the woman slightly. We met at some antiquities conference. She is a supporter of these gatherings and makes a sizeable financial contribution, though is not a scholar, herself. Anyway, she wrote me about the position and you fit the requirements exactly. You needn't worry about your qualifications. She's interested in putting together something small. Something for the tourists. Nothing academic. You love history and your French is excellent. Why shouldn't you go? You certainly deserve the opportunity."

Whether I deserved it or not wasn't in my thoughts. The truth was my parents had died without leaving a will, forcing me, their only child, to go through probate to obtain my small inheritance.

In the meantime, I'd had to earn my living expenses by working two part-time jobs on campus. In the afternoons I made salads in the cafeteria. In the evenings, I manned the desk at the library. Fortunately, my scholarship paid my tuition; but after two years of working while carrying a full academic schedule, I was both weary and depressed.

Fortunately, the Dean had apprised my prospective employer of my circumstances and Madame de Villiers had been kind enough to provide traveling expenses and a little pocket money. A week after graduation, I was aboard Continental Airlines flight 905 headed for a new life. The year was 1960.

Mrs. de Toi either hadn't heard or was disinclined to answer my question about the frequency of Madame's trips to Paris. She kept pacing from my suitcase to the closet, attending to the task of unpacking without saying anything more. I decided not to press the matter. For the moment, I was happy to have arrived and to find myself in this lovely setting. In time, I told myself, all would be revealed.

When the ormolu clock on the mantle chimed five in the afternoon, the housekeeper, having finished her task, looked surprised at the lateness of the hour. "Madame should have arrived by now," she frowned. Then she headed for the door, pausing long enough to inform me that dinner was at eight.

Once I was alone, I sauntered about my rooms, admiring the striped gold and white wall paper, the ladderbacked chairs with embroidered seat covers and the large mahogany four-poster bed that stood to the left of the fireplace. The hearth was stacked with kindling and logs, waiting to be lit. Despite the summer season, the room was chilly so I struck a match from the crystal jar on the mantle and ignited the paper beneath the kindling. Soon the wood began to crackle and send warmth throughout the room. Setting a ladderbacked chair beside the fire, I sat amazed by my good fortune and gloating a little that my classmates back home were probably pounding the pavement in search of jobs.

I confess I hadn't arrived in France totally ignorant of my future circumstances. The college library provided me with some information. I knew the chateau crept along the ridge of a high embankment that overlooked the Tarn. The river was not a large tributary but it stretched like a blue vein across a landscape dominated by scrub wood and rocks.

As to the design, the chateau had been the work of the Italian architect, Girolamo della Robbia, who also designed the Chateau Madrid and who lived during the reign of Francis I (1515-1547). His concept, unlike anything else in French construction, called for unusual height, decorated with external galleries running between turrets. This chateau, like the Madrid, featured a high-pitched roof and a true loggia, decadent grandeur that had been allowed to fall into disrepair. Nonetheless to my eye, the construct was fresh and magical.

The hour of eight o'clock came and went and when Madame de Villiers still had not returned, I was obliged to have supper in my rooms. After that, I retired early, anxious for a new day to begin. I slept fitfully and awoke the next morning in a groggy state when Mrs. de Toi threw back the blue velvet drapes from the windows. Although the sky was bright and clear, the housekeeper looked worried. She confessed she'd had no word from the mistress and wondered if I'd mind joining her in the kitchen for breakfast. Naturally, I agreed and dressed hurriedly.

The room in which I found her can only be described as cavernous. It was warmed by a great fireplace and a pair of ovens in which bread was baking. Once I'd seated myself at the oak table, the cook placed a mug of rich, dark coffee in front of me, together with a plate of fresh rolls and a quantity of strawberry jam.

There could be little doubt the kitchen was the hub of the chateau's working community for Mathiam Fourbe, the groundskeeper, soon appeared. He was a shy man, somewhere in his sixties with grizzled hair and calloused hands that testified to years of labor. After being introduced, he settled himself at the table several chairs away. If he was short on conversation, he was enthusiastic about his food, tackling with gusto the sweet rolls and tea Mrs. de Toi set before him. I found him difficult to watch as he smacked his lips appreciatively and occasionally poked a finger between his lips to extrude bits of food that had caught in the spaces where his teeth were missing.

Mrs. de Toi, apparently, saw nothing lacking in his manners. She seemed protective of him, in fact, perhaps because they'd been employed at the chateau at about the same time. When he left us that morning, she appeared comfortable enough in my company to confide that Mathiam labored harder than was right for a man of his years but had to do so as few people from the village were available to work the grounds.

"Mathiam does his best with the landscape as do I with the rooms, but young people aren't interested in service anymore. They flee to the cities to make their fortune…or, so they think. Of course, it's true we can't compete with city wages, but there isn't much expense to live here, either. Anyway, where's the pride in honest labor anymore?" She turned to me for corroboration and, although I was a child of flight myself, I assented to her opinion, eager for us to become friends.

Satisfied with my response, she sliced off another wedge from a loaf fresh from the oven and dropped it on to my plate. "You could use a little meat on those bones," she said with a degree of affection.

For the better part of the morning, having no assignment, I lingered in the kitchen, helping where I could. A couple of girls came up from the village, and I listened while they were given their instructions before they drifted off, giggling. They weren't more than fifteen or sixteen and were apparently doing odd jobs for the summer. Mrs. de Toi looked disdainful as they headed for the upstairs bedrooms to change the sheets. "Good thing Analeese is upstairs waiting for them. She'll sort them out."

Analeese, I discovered, was a young woman, about my age, who had married a year earlier and was several months pregnant.

Mrs. de Toi busied herself with preparations for evening supper. She was making a stew and I decided to help with the cleaning and chopping of vegetables fresh from the garden. She seemed to enjoy my company and talked freely about her background. She'd had a brief marriage that ended badly; but that was all she said about the experience. She preferred to talk of her family, a sister who lived with her husband on a farm just outside of Valence. She had two nieces and a nephew she saw seldom because her duties at the chateau took priority but she spoiled them with parcels sent by post as often as she could. Christmas was the one holiday she never missed at the farm and from the glow in her cheeks, one could see she looked forward to that time of year. Of course, she assured me, her affection for her relatives did nothing to diminish her devotion to Madame de Villiers, whom she'd raised since infancy, nor for Mathiam who was a lifelong friend.

Curious about her relationship with the gardener, I asked if he had a wife and she confirmed that he once had, a woman named Cloutilde, whom he'd loved to distraction. Regrettably, she'd been killed by a bomb that had landed in the village during World War II. She'd been four months pregnant at the time, and the loss of both wife and child was a tragedy from which Mathiam had never fully recovered.

With the stew simmering on the stove, Mrs. de Toi turned to the task of making a pie, while at the same time she began to reminisce about her early days with my employer. From the way she kept looking in the direction of the hall, as if expecting the front door to open at any minute, I knew she was worried about her mistress. Talking seemed to calm her and I was eager to listen. I sat warming my hands around my third mug of coffee as the cook, covered in flour, told me about the family she'd come to serve as a young woman.

"The boys were in their teens. Robert at fourteen was the oldest. Henry was a year younger, and then there was Madame de Villiers, a brown-eyed nymph of six. The boys teased her mercilessly as boys do with little sisters. I'm afraid I coddled her to make things even. I say 'coddled' so as not to be mistaken for spoiled. She had such a sweet nature. She could never be spoiled." The pride in Mrs. de Toi's voice was evident. "Not like her mother," she went on. "There was a pampered woman if ever there was one. Always off to one health clinic or another to indulge herself. Her husband became quite lonely so it's natural that he had a wandering eye..." Mrs. de

Toi put down her rolling pin to look at me. "You know what I mean. It's not good to leave a man alone so much of the time."

"Was there no love between the husband and wife, then?"

"There might have been. What I do know is that theirs was an arranged marriage: a merger, if you like, between two prominent families. On the paternal side was money. On the other was impoverished aristocracy."

Mrs. de Toi went on to say the marriage might have lasted many years, if only for convenience, except for the war. Monsieur de Villiers, unfortunately, thought it his duty to join the resistance. His attempt at espionage proved unsuccessful. He was captured and executed by the Germans. Mrs. de Toi crossed herself before going on.

"He died well, they say, singing La Marseillaise before a firing squad. But the wife? She had no courage. She was afraid she, too, might be suspected, so she locked herself in her rooms, leaving the care of the family to me."

"And where are they now? The boys, I mean."

"Dead. Like their father, they joined the resistance."

"Both of them?"

The cook nodded as the tears she could no longer control rolled down her floured cheeks. "Only Odeil, my sweet one, survived."

"What became of the mother? Did she die, too?"

"She emerged from her rooms when the Vichy government was dismantled, behaving as if nothing had happened. I thought then that her mind had snapped. Fortunately, her husband had had the foresight to make arrangements with his Paris attorney for his family. Monsieur Larouche was the attorney's name. He's gone now, too, as he was old even then; but he drafted a document that left the family well provided for and gave my little one a good education. Of course, part of the fortune was stolen by the Germans, but the de Villiers family had more than most when the war was over.

"I understand you've been hired to help Madame write a little history of the chateau. She wants to make the place a tourist attraction and use the profits to restore the estate."

"Yes. I hope I can help." The cook's remark brought me up sharp, my thoughts having drifted back to what I imagined the place might have looked like during the war. "But you didn't say what happened to the mother? Where is she now?"

Mrs. de Toi shrugged guiltily. "Apparently, she was not the hypochondriac I supposed. She died of a blood disease not long after peace was declared."

"So, Madame has no family?"

"Like you, my little bird, she flies solo."

"You know about my parents?"

"I heard something about your loss, yes. But you'll find a new family here. Madame is so kind. She'll be more like a sister to you than an employer. There isn't much age difference between you, is there? Maybe ten years? Being young women, you'll find you have much in common."

Despite Mrs. de Toi's happy prognostication for the future, her prediction proved untrue with regard to the weather. The day that had begun with a clear, blue sky brought an afternoon of unhappy rain—a downpour that seemed to dig its fingers into the earth as if eager to upend every shrub in the gardens. Even the trees, less vulnerable to the downpour, were threatened by flashes of lightning. I decided to retreat to my room with its cozy fire.

The ormolu clock on my mantle had struck four and I was standing at my window when a Peugeot threaded its way along the gravel driveway. I watched it stop beneath my window, the storm pelting its black exterior. I should have had a clear view of the driver but what emerged from the car was a black umbrella, beneath which I glimpsed a pair of red stilettos. Madame de Villiers, I surmised, had arrived.

Footsteps could be heard scurrying along the hall. Mrs. de Toi, clucking like a mother hen, apparently, had opened the door, for what I heard next were squeals and peals of laughter. To get a better view, I abandoned my room and hurried toward the top of the staircase. Looking down, I saw the housekeeper hugging the woman I presumed was my new employer.

With her bags retrieved and her wet outer garments removed, I had a good look at the new arrival—a woman with a trim figure dressed in a form-fitting black suit. She looked up as if sensing my presence.

"Can this be Rachel? Rachel Farraday?" Her voice reminded me of crystal wind chimes and, as I descended the stairs, she held her arms out to me. We embraced rather than shook hands, and I was delighted to find her so warm and unpretentious. She made me feel as if she had known me my whole life.

"I'm so happy to have you with us at last," she said stepping back to look at me. "I'm sorry I was detained, but I'm sure Amelia...that is, Mrs. de Toi, made you comfortable?"

I nodded, feeling a bit shy with both women now scrutinizing me as if I were an unfamiliar painting. Yet, I confess, I did the same.

Of Madame de Villiers it can be truly said she was a work of art. Nefertiti came immediately to mind, for in the face of my new acquaintance I saw the same almond-shaped eyes, the arched brows and long curve of the neck that identifies that long ago queen. Every manner, every gesture, spoke of her aristocratic breeding although, as I've said, nothing in her manner was aloof.

As we stood taking one another in, I discovered we were of equal height, both tall and slim. We probably could have exchanged wardrobes with ease. As to complexion, however, we were in marked contrast: she was fair, almost the color of a lily, with auburn hair that she wore in a chignon. I was still tanned by the California sun and my black hair was inelegantly pulled back in a ponytail. As to her age, my employer looked younger than her thirty years but exuded an air of confidence appropriate to a woman twice her years. In sum, I liked her and felt certain that ours would be a happy collaboration.

Mrs. de Toi returned to the kitchen to make sandwiches and a pot of cocoa while the two of us headed for the sitting room where a roaring fire awaited. Even in summer, I was to learn, a fire in this cavernous place was a necessity.

The room my employer and I entered was large and vaulted, its ceiling ornamented with a host of mythical figures. Although the paint had faded, the beauty of design needed no improvement. Rich, too, were the pomegranate walls and the dark woodwork. It was a perfect burrowing place.

After the cocoa had been served, Madame leaned back in the upholstered chair that seemed too large for her, and sighed. "It's so good to be home. I am never really happy unless I am here. I hope you will find it so, Rachel, if I may call you that?"

I nodded.

"And you must call me Odeil. I hate 'Madame,' it makes me sound so old."

"You are hardly that." I smiled.

"Sometimes...sometimes," she insisted, "I feel much older than my years. There's so much to be done." Her eyes wandered about the room with that same look of appraisal with which she had greeted me. As if satisfied all was as she'd left it, she sighed again. "Forgive me. I've not asked if you're comfortable in your rooms. Has Mrs. de Toi seen to your needs?"

She did not wait for my reply, but answered her own question. "Of course, she has. She's a darling and she likes to make a fuss, does she not?"

"She's been very kind to me," I agreed. "She does seem to anticipate my needs."

"Yes, she has that knack. I couldn't do without her. And she manages the day servants so well."

"I noticed she seems to be the only one in residence. She told me her husband is no longer about."

A pale hand waved through the air in a dismissive gesture. "The man was a drunkard and unreliable. He ran off with another woman years ago. Mathiam is the only other permanent employee. He sleeps in the carriage house. The rest of the workers, as you've noted, are day laborers from the village."

"Mrs. de Toi said it's difficult to keep servants?"

"True. I'm afraid no one cares to be in service these days. Most of the young people leave for the cities as soon as they can. A few stay on the family farms or work in the local shops. But yes, there seems to be a perpetual turnover. And of course, these young people expect to be paid the earth. But I have plans and I'm confident, with your help, I shall breathe life into the old place." She glanced about the room with a tender expression as if looking through a family album.

"I understand your hope is to make the chateau a tourist attraction."

"If I can. That's why the work you and I will perform is so important. We must advertise the place, create an interest. Then people will come and workers will come and I'll have enough money to renovate the estate."

"That's a pretty tall order coming from a piece of writing."

Madame leaned forward, her eyes shining in the fire's light. "Yes, but we can do it. I know we can. Dean Crofter, from your college, spoke so highly of you. And I'm relying on you to set the pace. I'm one too easily distracted, so you must be the taskmaster."

"I'll do my best," I said, uneasily. "When do we begin?"

"Tomorrow, if you feel up to it. I don't suppose you've had a chance to see much of the chateau. Why don't you wander around this afternoon and we'll start early in the morning, say nine o'clock?"

Amused that she would think the hour of nine was early, I assented.

"Good," she went on. "Then after our tea you must excuse me. It's been a long drive and I'm feeling tired. Dinner's at eight. Did Mrs. de Toi tell you? I'll probably have something in my room so I'll see you in the morning. Enjoy your self-guided tour and when we have a sunny day, Mathiam can show you the grounds. They're quite lovely."

"I've done some exploring already. The rose garden is gorgeous. I've never seen so many varieties."

"Yes, Mathiam has a good eye for mixing colors, doesn't he? I never begrudge his requests. Money spent on flowers gives a handsome return, I always think."

Madame and I parted soon after her observation, leaving me to amuse myself however I chose. Not wanting to disturb Mrs. de

Toi, I wandered up to my rooms to read. A cheery fire greeted me while outside the tempest continued to flay the landscape.

Once I'd seated myself in a comfortable chair with an afghan tossed over my knees, I was so cozy I managed to turn only a few pages of my novel before falling asleep. The rest of the afternoon was spent in a luxurious cycle of dozing and reading and dozing again. Once or twice I rose to add a log to the fire but that was the extent of my exertion for the day.

When Mrs. de Toi brought my supper tray that evening, she found me asleep with the book dropped on the floor beside me. The delicious aroma of the bowl of stew she was setting in front of me woke me. She'd added a glass of red wine, crusty bread, some grapes and a generous wedge of camembert, as well.

"I've no doubt you're hungry," she said, stepping back with her hands folded in front of her to view with satisfaction the meal she had provided.

"This looks wonderful," I said and I began eating hungrily.

Pleased with my approval, she pulled the curtains across the windows and instructed me to leave the tray outside my door when I had finished. She then headed for the door but not before reminding me that breakfast was at eight. Now that Madame had returned, I was informed, I would join the mistress in the dining room.

An hour or two later, my eyelids were so heavy I crawled under my comforter and turned off the bedside lamp. For a time, I lay listening to the rain pounding impotently against my windows. Not since I was a child asleep in the arms of one of my parents had I felt so cosseted.

The morning landscape, washed by the earlier rains, greeted me the next day as I pulled back the drapes from my windows. Without glancing at the clock, I knew the hour was early, as the sun was barely above the horizon. The fire in the hearth had gone out and, as the room was chilly, I was about to crawl back into my bed when a day girl entered with morning coffee. Noticing the chill, she busied herself with relighting the fire. As she did, the ormolu clock chimed the hour of seven.

Before leaving, the servant informed me, it being a fine day, breakfast would be served on the rose terrace instead of the dining room, and that Madame de Villiers was already up and dressing. Surprised, I hurried to do the same but despite my best effort, I found my employer seated at a wrought iron table when I arrived.

"Good morning," she said cheerily, looking up from a letter several pages long that she held in her hand. She'd been so preoccupied with it, she hadn't seen me until I was upon her.

Seating myself across from her, I was delighted by the array of fruits and rolls and cheeses in front of me. As yet, Madame de Villiers had touched nothing.

"I hope I haven't kept you waiting," I apologized. As I spoke, I couldn't help admiring the classic cut of her cashmere outfit— camel colored pants and a plum colored sweater set off by an expensive pearl choker. My cotton skirt and nylon pullover left me feeling shabby.

"You're not late in the least," she assured me. "It's just gone past half past the hour if I heard the hall clock correctly. We're both up early. I hope you slept well."

"Very well, thank you. In fact, I slept through most of yesterday afternoon, too."

"Jet lag, no doubt. You mustn't feel guilty. The rest has done you good. Your cheeks are positively rosy."

She poured me a cup of coffee from an ornate silver service while I reached for a croissant and a triangle of camembert. Her attention drifting back to her letter, I luxuriated in my pleasant surroundings. The morning was the complete opposite of yesterday and, with the sun at my back, I began to feel almost too warm. I might have been tempted to doze off again, but when a frown clouded the porcelain complexion opposite me, I had to ask if anything was the matter.

My employer looked up and folded her letter into a tight square, which she tucked into her pants pocket. "No, nothing of significance. Some dreary correspondence from my lawyer, that's all. Unfortunately, I shall have to return to Paris."

My face must have reflected my disappointment for she was quick to reassure me. "You needn't worry. I don't have to leave right away. We'll start our project first. Then, once you're occupied, you'll hardly notice I'm gone. I won't be away long in any case."

Our breakfast ended, we proceeded to the library where we were to begin our work. A fire was already blazing in the hearth but much of the room lay in shadows. The color of the walls appeared to be a faded gold although little of it could be seen, the three walls being occupied from floor to ceiling by shelves crammed with books. A bay window opened to a view of the eastern lawn and the grove of trees. My room, directly above it, had the same view, although it provided a deeper vista that included the road winding up to the front of the house.

My employer stood beside me, taking in the scene. "It's a lovely landscape, isn't it? Sometimes I'm so distracted by it, I've been known to stare out the windows for hours... But the books, they have their fascination, too, do they not?" She pulled one slim volume from a shelf and read aloud a few lines from the *Rubaiyat* by Omar Khayyam.

> *We are no other than a moving Row*
> *Of magic Shadow-Shapes that come and go*
> *Round with the Sun-illumin'd Lantern held*
> *In Midnight by the Master of the Show.*

Her voice was sonorous, perhaps even sad, but that impression passed like a puff of wind once she smiled again.

"When you have time to acquaint yourself with the collection, you will find it unique, Rachel. Most of the works have been handed down, some from centuries past. I suspect there are sources here one won't find at the Bibliotheque."

Her pride of ownership was reflected not only in her voice but in the care she lavished upon the space. In this room there were no ceiling cracks, no dust left to settle in corners. Her cavernous desk was freshly polished and appointed with appropriate writing tools. An electric typewriter stood nearby, and even the leather chairs with their inviting pillow shapes gleamed as if they had been oiled.

"I'm surprised all these treasures survived the war," I said, taking in the room. "One would think the Germans would have looted everything. So much art and antiquities were lost that way."

"They never found our important treasures." Madame's eyes sparked with triumph. "We were able to hide most of them…but not all. We had to leave something for the looters or they'd have grown suspicious."

"Hide them? Where? Not in the chateau, surely?"

"Ah, that's a story for another day. First, I'd like you to acquaint yourself with the materials we have on hand that pertain to the chateau's history. If we need more, make a list and I'll look for resources when I return to Paris."

I had seated myself on the window seat and was looking into the room. She joined me. "All this knowledge recorded and sent down to us through the ages. It's a wonder, isn't it? Some of these histories, like those of Thucydides, were written over a thousand years ago. Yet, in 1960 we can share his thoughts, see the past as he saw it. Is that not time travel?"

I smiled in sympathy with her meaning. "It's true, Madame. Historians write for unborn generations, don't they?"

My employer gave one of my hands a pat. "There, I knew we were kindred spirits. I was sure of it the moment I set eyes on you. We're going to become great friends, you and I. And please, call me Odeil, not Madame. If we're going to work together, we must work as colleagues."

I nodded to her request and didn't feel uncomfortable with it. In the short time we'd been together I, too, had formed an opinion, and mine was that Madame de Villiers was a person too far above the ordinary, too ethereal, to be treated as an equal. As a consequence, in the days that followed I took pains to avoid any form of address rather than treat her casually.

But at that moment, closeted together in the library, Madame seemed satisfied with my response. What remained for us to decide was how to begin our little venture.

"Have you made any notes or assembled any source materials as yet?" I asked, answering her question on how we should begin with a question of my own. She looked crestfallen when she heard me.

"I-I'm afraid I've done nothing, yet. I was hoping you would show me how to start."

"Oh, I see." I took a moment to stare into my hands. "Well, let's start with an inventory of materials. How is your library organized? Is there a history section?"

Madame stood and waved in the direction of the three walls. "I'm afraid not. Everything's a bit scattered, I fear. My father never took the time to organize his possessions and I've been negligent, too, I'm afraid. I'm sure there are histories on every shelf in every corner of the room."

When I realized the enormity of the task before us, my heart sank, although I endeavored to sound cheerful. "Then we must take stock of items shelf by shelf, organizing as we go along. Does that seem reasonable?"

"Yes." My employer smiled at me. "That will keep you well occupied while I'm away."

"Certainly, and before you leave, you might look among the papers your parents left you. A legal description of the property would be helpful. Do you have that?"

"I'm not certain where, at the moment." A frown appeared on her porcelain forehead, again. "I'll have to ask my attorney for a copy when I'm in Paris."

"That would be a start. In the meantime, what about diaries? Did your family leave any that you can lay your hands on? That would be a help."

The frown deepened. "Father told me a few anecdotes about the place, but I don't think he wrote anything down…"

"What about your grandparents, then? Didn't they leave any records?"

"My grandparents?" Madame's eyes grew wide. "They had no connection with the chateau. It was a wedding gift from my father to my mother…though he was more enamored of the place than she was, I think."

"Then, this isn't a family estate?"

"Dear me, no. My mother's parents were titled but there wasn't any property. The money was on my father's side. He was renovating the place when war broke out. Because of him, we have decent plumbing and lighting. He'd gotten that far, at least. My dear foolish father would probably have impoverished himself if it weren't for Hitler. What you see is the dwelling as it was when my parents occupied it. Nothing more's been done, except to maintain it. Mother took no interest in the buildings, and with no one to manage them…well…" Madame shrugged as if there was no need to finish the sentence.

"May I ask how your father made his living?"

"He was an investment banker. The war took away a good amount of our wealth, but not all. We inherited a bit from other branches of the family, those who were killed off in the violence. As to survivors, if any exist, my mother lost track of them. She was never any good at staying connected with the family once her parents died…"

Madame's eyes drifted toward the windows as her thoughts returned to the past. Then she pulled herself back to the present as if she were a leeward boat righting itself. "But you mustn't worry about finances," she said, as if reading my mind. "My father was very clever about that. Trusts were arranged in Swiss banks; that sort of thing. We shan't starve. Still, although the old girl has good bones, an estate of this size needs a lot of capital."

"Have you never thought of selling? That might be a solution."

Madame de Villiers threw back her head and emitted a light laugh. "I'm a romantic like my father. The thought never entered my head. Besides, it's the only home I've ever known. And what would become of Amelia or Mathiam? I couldn't sell the place out from under them."

"It might be difficult, as well, given its current condition."

"Oh, don't think I haven't had offers," she corrected me. "Of late, I've had several persistent ones, but I've rejected them. I have other plans."

"To make this a tourist destination?"

"You sound dubious. Does the idea strike you as foolish?"

"No, not at all. The area attracts tourists. The chateau's gardens alone would make it a destination."

"I was thinking about guests, actually. We have so many rooms."

"A bed and breakfast, you mean?"

"Yes, why not? We could refurbish a few spaces at first and build from there. If the accommodations are comfortable, I should imagine people might like to stay at a historic chateau, even if it is a bit crumbly."

"I'm sure they would. I love it here already."

My employer looked at me from where she stood. "You give me such hope, Rachel. I know we can make a go of it." Suddenly, she made a little twirl and clapped her hands. "Oh, I'm so happy, I could sing."

I looked at her in surprise.

"Don't worry." She smiled. "I won't subject you to my voice."

We were sharing a laugh over her joke when Mrs. de Toi entered with morning coffee. The pot, the same one used at breakfast, had been refreshed with a darker, more aromatic blend than before. As I observed its heavy, silver ornamentation, it occurred to me that, if sold, the silver coffee set alone could fetch enough money to refurbish a room or two.

The housekeeper set the tray down on the small table near one of the leather chairs and poured the thick, black liquid into china cups.

"I suspect the pair of you need a break from all your work this morning. This coffee will perk you up." She handed us each our drink as she spoke.

Madame, I noticed, took hers with a liberal lacing of cream and sugar. She took a sip and seemed to savor the experience. Then she shared our plans with the cook, who'd been standing with her arms crossed as if expecting a report.

"Rachel agrees we might make a go of a bed and breakfast at the chateau. And given your considerable talents in the kitchen, Mrs. de Toi, I suspect we'll make our reputation with the cuisine, alone. Of course, we'll have to solve the problem of reliable help; but we'll work on that when we come to it. First, we must get our little piece written so tourists will come flocking to our door."

"Don't forget there's the job of getting the grounds ready for fall planting. Mathiam needs a number of supplies. He's given you a list. I trust you've had time to look at it?"

The crispness in the housekeeper's voice led me to know that although she was a servant in this establishment, hers was no ordinary relationship with her employer. In effect, she was the mother-inresidence.

Madame's guilty look assured me it was so. "Of course, you're right, Mrs. de Toi. I've no intention of ignoring Mathiam's needs. But I don't know where I've put the list. Perhaps you might ask him to give me another?"

"I will, if you promise not to lose it again? Maybe it would be best if you allowed him to order for himself. You know he won't be frivolous."

"No, of course, he won't. Tell him to go ahead, then. We can't have him short on supplies."

"Very good, Madame." The older woman left us with a smile on her lips.

Madame winked once we were alone again. "She won that round, didn't she? But then, she usually does."

That night, I went to bed especially happy. The day had fled by turning the hours into minutes. My employer and I had talked about refurbishing the rooms and, more importantly, we had laid out a plan for the development of our history. In the morning, I was to begin by making sense of the library.

Whether it was from a surfeit of wine at dinner or from the excess of conversation during the day, I don't know, but soon after I'd turned out my light that evening, I fell into a sleep which brought me the first of several vivid dreams that would occur over the course of my stay at the chateau.

What I recall, initially, is hearing music emanating from the hall below. I rise and make my way to the balcony over the stairs. There, I'm greeted by a scene of masked dancers, couples in formal wear, weaving in and out of the various rooms which are brightly lit. The women flash by as ribbons of color, their gowns twinkling with multicolored ornaments. The scene is mesmerizing and, as I stand above them in my flimsy nightgown, my mind fills with questions.

Who are these people? What are they doing here? Madame de Villiers said nothing about a party.

The moment my dream touches upon this point in reality, the music stops. The maskers look up. Discovered, I attempt to run away but am held back by a figure in a black cape whose face, like all the others, is hidden behind a mask. Instantly, I realize I am transformed. My hair no longer falls about my shoulders but is piled high upon my head and the gown I'm wearing is silk, the color of pomegranate. My hand reaches up to touch the glittering ruby necklace that hangs about my throat. Even without a mirror, I know I am beautiful.

The stranger and I descend the stairs while the dancers below break out into gloved applause. As we enter a great hall, the musicians strike up a waltz. Unimpeded, my partner and I begin to glide across the room and are soon followed by the rest of the party. The dancing figures cut elaborate circles around me, their eyes following my progress. I am troubled as I have no idea what their intense interest means.

Chapter Two

"COME. I HAVE A MAGNIFICENT idea." Madame de Villier's voice shattered the stillness and my tranquility where I sat in my chair in the dining room.

A moment before, I'd been gazing out at the grounds thinking…thinking what? I couldn't remember.

"Forgive me," I said. "I seem to have been lost in a daydream."

"That happens to me often," said my employer, who by then had taken me by the arm to lead me away from my cold cup of coffee. She wore a blue jersey dress that skirted the floor. "Perched so near the river, the clear air becomes intoxicating. That's my explanation, at least."

Together we walked toward the library. "What's your idea?" I asked, without much enthusiasm. I was having difficulty shaking off the malaise that had visited me for the past several days. Perhaps Madame de Villiers was in its grip, too, for each day seemed to begin like this one, with a spurt of energy which faded, leaving us with little or no progress to show for the time that had passed. Both our minds seemed filled with thoughts that pulled us first in one direction and then another, so that our little history drifted aimlessly like a paper boat upon a small pond.

Sometimes our conversations wandered far afield, as might be expected between strangers curious to learn about one another. I discovered early in our acquaintance that Madame was deeply religious. When I was forced to admit I had none, she'd looked surprised. "But surely you cannot look at all the beauty and variety in the world and not wonder how it happened. You must believe in divine creation?"

"Not everyone agrees with the notion. There are those who argue that given enough permutations and enough time..."

"Ah, time. That's your agent. But there's a flaw in that approach, isn't there? Time has only one direction while thought and memory escape this limitation. Through them, we glimpse what is eternal."

"That's a little too poetic and not convincing to me, I'm afraid."

"Do you never dream, Rachel?"

"Quite a lot, at least since I've been here."

"Then you must agree that dreams are timeless and bound neither by the laws of nature or of man. Do you not think of them as a peek into the infinite?"

I gave no answer but let my expression speak for itself. She challenged me a bit further but did not pursue the subject to the point of putting me on the defensive, I'm glad to say. My point in recalling the conversation is to make clear these divergences of opinion never diminished our appreciation of one another—although they did account for our lack of progress on the history.

I'd decided not to struggle against the tide of her thoughts and so was surprised that morning when she initiated a conversation that touched upon our work.

"Perhaps a straight history will prove too boring for tourists," she began. "I was wondering if we might include a bit of folklore."

"About the village, you mean?"

"Oh," she paused. "I hadn't thought of that. That might be a good idea, also, if it doesn't take us too far afield. But no, I was thinking of a story Mathiam used to tell about a monk who was buried alive in one of the tunnels beneath the chateau..."

"Tunnels? Buried alive? Here?" I sat staring at her with an owl-like focus.

"Yes. Don't ask me why the holy man was silenced because I don't know. I never found out. Mrs. de Toi got wind of these stories and put a stop to them...but not before giving Mathiam a tongue lashing for frightening me into thinking the chateau might be haunted. I remembered it last night and thought the tale might add cachet to the place. A haunted estate is bound to attract tourists, wouldn't it?"

"Possibly. And what about the tunnels? Are they real?"

"I believe so, but to be honest, I never went looking for them. I was a nervous child and, unlike you, I believe in an afterlife which includes ghosts."

"Did your parents never talk about them? Or your brothers? Surely they would have been willing to explore."

"If they knew they existed, they never said anything to me. Maybe they feared I might wander off and get lost."

"Well, I think you should ask Mathiam about them. For all you know, your father might have hidden some of the family's valuables there during the war."

My employer dismissed the idea out of hand. "I'm sure they'd be too damp and musty. Artwork certainly would be damaged. Anyway, I'm pretty sure Mathiam brought everything out of hiding once the war was over."

"But how can you be certain until you've looked?"

Her dark eyebrows came together in a frown. "To be honest, I wasn't thinking about the tunnels when I raised the issue. I was thinking about the ghost. But as you seem enamored of their existence, feel free to investigate. Ask Mathiam to help. He's used to bugs and dirt…that sort of thing." She gave a little shudder as she spoke.

I told her that I would do as she suggested, and after that we let the matter drop.

Unfortunately, the season made it difficult for me to find Mathiam at a time when he wasn't busy. The gardens and grounds were at their peak, and he was forever fretting and giving direction to the local itinerants. What's more, Madame delayed her trip to Paris so we could become better acquainted, which meant most of my time was spent with her in what passed for research.

I confess, I had no complaint about the pace of things. The days drifted by in a pleasant malaise and, in what seemed no time at all, the deciduous trees began to show a tinge of color. Seeing the splashes of yellow and red, Madame sighed. She could not put off her trip any longer. She would have to leave for Paris before winter set in.

I began to see less of her as she made preparations for her journey. She made frequent calls to her attorneys and was engaged in personal paperwork in her rooms. During these intervals, I was able to plunge myself into earnest work, and it was during one such morning that Madame found me, seated at her desk behind a pile of books. My head was bowed over one of them so I failed to hear her approach.

"You've found something?"

Startled, I looked up and noted she was wearing a gray suit with a green scarf tied about her neck. "Are you leaving, already?"

"No, not quite yet. I came down to ask your opinion of this outfit. I bought it when I was last in Paris. Now, I'm not sure about it. What do you think?"

She walked to and fro like a runway model while I looked on. "The scarf is absolutely necessary," I told her. "Otherwise, there wouldn't be enough color. You don't usually wear gray, do you?"

"Almost never. I prefer color. I don't know why I bought this outfit. The wool is very fine, of course." As she spoke, her fingers caressed the line of the jacket as if enjoying its tactile quality. Then, suddenly, she came forward her neck craning a little to see what had been occupying my attention.

"Ah, 'The Sacrifice of Isaac.' It's a favorite of mine, though the subject's somewhat grizzly isn't it?"

"Very. I was sitting here wondering why God would want a father to kill his son."

"A test of loyalty, surely."

"But doesn't He already know Abraham is loyal? Isn't God supposed to know everything?"

Madame reacted to my blasphemous comment with a faint smile. She settled herself in the chair opposite me and crossed her elegantly long legs. "But will Abraham know the extent of his love for God unless he's tested? That's the question, isn't it?"

Her answer didn't satisfy and I couldn't hold back my feelings of skepticism. "Yes, but wouldn't it be easier for all concerned if God just had a chat with Abraham? Why create a situation which strikes terror in the hearts of a father and his child? I call that cruel, don't you?"

"Ah, now you're asking me to know the mind of God, Rachel. Something quite impossible." She gave her delicate shoulders a shrug. "In any case it is sometimes necessary to be cruel to be kind. Didn't some philosopher write that once?"

"Kierkegaard, I think."

"Yes, well there you have it. Sometimes what seems a dark deed has a reason which we may not always understand at the time."

"I can't believe you're saying that. You're arguing that the means justifies the ends.

"Am I?"

"Yes, and I don't believe what you're saying for one moment. You'd never be cruel or hurtful for any reason. It isn't your nature,"

"I'd prefer not to be placed on so high a pedestal, particularly so early in our acquaintanceship. No one fully knows what they are capable of until the time comes. If the stakes are high enough, even you, Rachel might find yourself capable of intrigue."

"I doubt it, but even if it's true, does that make it right? God orders the destruction of a family; should that be a lesson to us all? What lesson? I don't understand. What good can come of it? I need reasons for why things happen. I need to understand. I can't just shrug my shoulders and chalk it up to God's will."

My employer paused and seemed to observe I had taken our discussion more personally than she'd supposed. "Like the death of your parents, you mean?" she asked quietly.

Until that moment, I hadn't realized it but, yes, that was exactly what I had meant. The truth, being unexpected, stabbed me through the heart. My jaw dropped and I didn't know what to say. My cheeks were glowing with the heat of my emotion.

When she saw my struggle, Madame reached across the desk and took hold of my hand. "I'm so sorry, Rachel. I didn't mean to upset you. I should have thought before speaking. But it's true, isn't it? You are still deeply grieved."

I nodded that I was and she tried to console me. "We must find a way to help you heal while you are here. Your parents must be distressed to see you so unhappy. I wish I could help. I wish I could convince you that there are other worlds…"

"Heaven, you mean?" I pulled my hand away, annoyed and afraid I might break into tears.

Madame seemed to take no offense. She leaned back in her chair. "Well, yes, Heaven, of course…"

"Of course. I didn't think you meant Mars with its little green men."

The library door opened before Madame could answer. Mrs. de Toi entered, struggling with a large tea tray. She used the tip of her stout black shoe to hold back the door and, seeing her difficulty, I rose to assist her, glad for the interruption.

The grandfather clock in the hall chimed four in the afternoon. Hearing it, Madame glanced at her watch and rose.

"Dear me, I'd no idea of the time. I must get to the village to wire my attorney with the details of my arrival…"

"Can't you phone him?"

"There's trouble on the line. We can't call out. Haven't you noticed? Well, why should you? Mrs. de Toi and I have selfishly kept you to ourselves."

Madame de Villiers headed for the door. "I'll report the problem when I reach Sainte Enimie. Don't wait on dinner for me. I've several errands and might be late."

When she was gone, Mrs. de Toi looked dolefully at the tea tray which she'd piled high with sandwiches and cakes. "She never eats," she muttered. "I don't know how she stays alive."

"I'll do my best in her absence," I said, sitting down in one of the leather chairs and reaching for a crème cake. "I'm famished."

The older woman smiled and shook her head as she sat her burden on a nearby table. "I don't know how you manage to stay so slim. You're as tiny as Madame but with an appetite. I wish I were young again. Nowadays, if I so much as look at a crème cake, I gain weight."

"I like your looks," I said, biting into the light pastry and allowing the filling to extrude from its sides.

"Yes, but you don't have my knees, do you? You've no idea how they can ache sometimes. I should lose weight, but it's difficult when you're a cook. You have to sample what you're making. I've always said, 'Show me a cook who's thin and I'll show you a cook who takes no pride in her work.'"

Mrs. de Toi moved to sit in the chair opposite me. "Hand me one of those cheese and tomato sandwiches, if you please. That shouldn't do too much damage."

For the next hour, while the rain poured thick as salt outside, the cook and I warmed ourselves by the fire, enjoying one another's company. She was curious about my life in the United States, and I learned more about her younger sister and her niece and two nephews in whom she took such pride. I thought it sad that all these years she'd remained childless; but she didn't seem to regret her lack. She considered herself a mother to Madame de Villiers and, as her love was reciprocated, it was enough.

* * *

The next morning, Madame de Villiers found me at my post in the library. I feared she might renew our conversation of the previous day, for she'd returned late as she'd predicted and had slept through breakfast. This was our first meeting since then. Apparently, she had other thoughts on her mind when she entered the room. The hall clock was chiming the hour of eleven, and I noticed she was wearing a diaphanous gown that swept to the floor. It was a gorgeous floral pattern but unsuitable for fall with its pelting rains. She smiled in her cat-like way as if she could read my thoughts.

"I know it won't get much wear in this season, but it was on sale. Who'd imagine one could find such a garment in Sainte Enimie? I couldn't resist." My employer twirled in front of me so that I could admire how the swirl of color fluttered about her like butterfly wings.

"It's lovely," I agreed. "And you look wonderful in it. But aren't you a little cold?"

"I'll change in a minute but, for now, I'll sit here by the fire. And I won't say anything to disturb you."

A companionable silence fell between us while I continued my work, but it did not last long. Madame looked bored and, by the drumming of her fingers, I knew she wanted to talk.

"I wonder what Mrs. de Toi plans for lunch," she began. "I hope its pot pie. That's the perfect comfort food for a day like this."

"Why not ask her to bake one? I'm sure she'd be happy to oblige."

"Oh, I never bother with such things. She knows best when it comes to the kitchen. Besides, if I started yielding to my whims, who knows what I could do to the budget? Take this dress, for example."

"It was on sale, remember?"

"Yes, but even so, I need to exercise more judgment. There's so much to be done with this place. I simply must live more frugally."

I looked up, hearing the strain in her voice. "I hope my being here isn't a burden. Honestly, if it's a matter of money, I'd work for practically nothing. I can't tell you how happy I've been since I arrived. Between you and Mrs. de Toi, I feel as if I've found a second family."

Madame de Villiers looked gratified. She leaned forward in her chair and spoke through a smile. "You needn't worry, Rachel. I can afford your services. But it's good to know you're happy here. I confess, I've begun to think of you as my little sister and I know Mrs. de Toi is quite taken with you. She's said as much many times. Lucky for you I'm not a jealous person. Yes, I think you've described our little trio correctly: we are a family."

A moment of intimate silence passed between us before she began our conversation again.

"You were raised as a Catholic, were you not, Rachel?"

Bent over a book, I straightened quickly to look up at her. "Yes. How did you know?"

"I noticed the Holy Communion picture on your bureau...the one with your parents standing beside you. How old were you then? Nine, perhaps?"

"About that." I should have been annoyed to learn she'd been in my room without my knowledge but I wasn't. If we were like family, and I felt we were, such wanderings would be natural. Her guileless revelation suggested she assumed our intimacy and I found the assumption flattering.

"Your mother's lovely," she went on, having failed to notice my hesitation. "You look a bit like her with your blue eyes and coal black hair. But I'm inclined to think you favor your father. You have his sculptured features."

Even though the remark was innocent, as it touched upon my parents so soon after our last conversation, tears sprang into my eyes. "I feel like an idiot," I told her as she handed me her handkerchief. "I'm not a child. I should be able to talk about my parents without sobbing. It has been two years since they died."

"You mustn't apologize. I know what you're feeling. I lost my parents when I was young, too young. I wasn't as close to them as you were to your parents, I think. My mother was not a warm woman; but I wasn't prepared to face the world on my own. I suppose that's when I found God."

"And that made you feel better?"

"Yes, it did. Whatever you believe at the moment, I assure you, faith is as true a way of knowing the world as are the laws of science."

"I wish I could believe you," I muttered drying my eyes. "At the moment, what I feel is lost."

"You're not lost." She rose, preparing to leave, her butterfly dress floating around her. "Give yourself time."

* * *

That night, I climbed into my canopied bed feeling drained, glad to pull the comforter over me. The rain had stopped and a placid moon peered through my window, slathering its light over the polished surfaces of the furniture and giving the room the semblance of a foreign landscape. Perhaps it was this strangeness that kept my eyes drifting from one darkened corner to another; but it was also true that Madame's words reverberated through my thoughts and made it impossible to sleep. She had spoken so confidently of her faith and yet, throughout our conversations, I saw whisperings of a haunted expression.

Was she afraid for me? Did she fear for my soul? Or was some other trouble occupying her thoughts?

She'd wanted to talk to me. I'd sensed that the moment she'd entered the library; but my tears had put her off. What had she wanted to tell me?

Thoughts like these so occupied my mind that I tossed and turned well into the night. Not until the wee hours of the morning did the familiar dream come to me, much as it had on other occasions, beginning with the sound of music invading my room.

Hearing it, I rise and join the gaiety in the great hall below. By now, the succession of dreams has implanted their history into my memory and I am fully at ease with the company I am to meet. The dancers part as I enter the chandeliered ballroom, nodding to me from behind their black masks. I nod in response. That is the moment when my familiar guide appears at the opposite side of the hall, dressed in black and red habiliments from head to toe. We approach one another and a waltz begins.

The dancers form a whorl around us, but my eyes are fixed upon those of my escort so that I barely discern their motion. A half mask casts a long shadow over my partner's visible features—the mouth and the chin—making them appear grotesque. I want to pull away but the current around me is too strong.

At the far end of the room, tall doors swing open, drawing my companion and me toward them like leaves being dragged toward a whirlpool. Ahead, the rooms lie in darkness but the sound of a silver bell guides our way. How long or how deeply we penetrate the darkness I do not know, but at last we come to rest before a small light like a candle's flame. If music from the farther room still plays, it is beyond our ears. Here, there is silence, and a pause, as though we've found ourselves before the entrance to a crypt.

A door creaks open. The light becomes increasingly intense so that I'm forced to use a hand to shield my eyes. Nonetheless,

I continue to peer into its brightness, mesmerized by the hint of shapes obscured behind it. In time, my vision adjusts. I am alone listening to the tinkle of the silver bell. Before me stand several towers of treasures. Silks, jewels and gold coins rise high above me. A hundred extravagant lifetimes would make few inroads into these limitless riches. And at the center of this cache looms a silver statue, its head wreathed in a ruby crown. The figure bears a striking resemblance to Mrs. de Toi, although its grimace belies any kinship to her good nature. Even the mouth is thin as a razor's edge.

Her right hand holds a goblet imprinted with a strange crest: two hawks and a white dove in mid-flight, the latter impaled by the talons of the larger birds, its blood coloring its feathers. Even so, the eyes of the predators reflect fear rather than triumph. They seem to understand that the death of one is a harbinger for all.

* * *

I awoke to a dampened pillow. Having left the world of dreams in tears, I entered the conscious world with foreboding. Nor could any of my actions during the day—not even my research— shake the feeling. The rigid spines of the library books I held in my hand, the blank sheet of paper before me, the pen cupped in my fingers, all and each struck me as less real than the dream of the previous night. Time and again, I had to recall myself to my work. Perhaps my dread was aided by the rain that pummeled against the windows and the subsequent shadows that fell in patches over the gold walls and the Persian carpets. The room seemed to be held together more by the dark than by the light. This was a day without edges.

Madame de Villiers joined me in late morning. Her black woolen dress showed no signs of frivolity and she was uncharacteristically quiet as she sat pouring over one book or another. Perhaps, she, too, had slept badly.

Mrs. de Toi interrupted our study just before noon. She was holding an object, or pieces of it, in her right hand. "It's Mathiam's fault," she blustered, her cheeks reddened. "I didn't know he was in the kitchen. I stepped back...and look what's happened!" She pushed the object forward for her employer to examine. "I'm afraid it can't be fixed. There are too many pieces. Oh Madame, I am so sorry. I know it was one of your treasures."

Madame de Villiers looked stricken as she rose to receive the bits of glass. One of the shards cut her hand and a small drop of blood fell upon the carpet. For a moment, the three of us were muted by shock, and then Mrs. de Toi broke into more tearful apologies. "I know I wasn't to meddle with the curio cabinet, but the crystal was becoming dusty. I only wished to give them a good wash." As she spoke, she dabbed at her employer's wound with a clean handkerchief.

"Leave it, Amelia," Madame snapped. "I'm all right. And so would this goblet be, too, if you'd have left the cabinet alone as I instructed." She laid the glass on the desk and reached for her own hanky.

The cook's eyes continued to brim with tears. "I'm sorry, Madame. So sorry."

Her despair was enough to soften her employer's heart.

"I'm sorry, too. It's foolish of me to be upset over a lump of crystal. I'm only glad you weren't hurt. You weren't, were you? Or Mathiam?"

"No, Madame. We're all right. It's just that I know how valuable it was...and you did ask me not to touch anything..." Mrs. de Toi's chin was quivering now. "You can take it out of my wages, if you like. That would be fair."

"I'll do no such thing, Amelia. It was an accident. These things happen. But I do hope you'll do as I ask, in future."

"I will, Madame. I promise."

Both women stood peering uncomfortably at one another until the hall clock chimed. Twelve noon.

The cook stiffened. "Goodness, is that the time? I need to take the pot pie out of the oven."

As she turned to leave, Madame called after her, "Give us a few minutes delay, will you? Rachel and I need to finish something. Then we'll follow."

The cook nodded and, once she was gone, my employer continued to stare at the door through which she'd made her exit.

"I'm afraid I have some hurt feelings to repair," she sighed. "You must help me by making a fuss over the lunch, Rachel. That will cheer her up. I shouldn't have been so cross. But I have asked her not to touch that cabinet and now here's another mishap."

I was standing by the desk, moving a few of the broken pieces about to see if they were large enough to repair. "You should see to that hand," I said matter-of-factly.

"Stop fiddling with those broken bits," came her cross reply. "There's nothing to salvage and you might cut yourself. We can't have two invalids moping about."

"Do you have some iodine or alcohol?"

"Yes, yes. I'll see to this tiny cut, I promise you. But first I want to check the cabinet in case any other pieces are missing."

"This has happened before?"

Madame de Villiers ignored my question and stood gazing down at the shattered goblet. "What a shame. I was particularly fond of this one. The crest is unusual. The origin of its design is one I've never been able to trace. Three birds in flight…"

My heart thumped at my sides when I heard her. Fragments from the dream of the previous night assailed me as if they, too, were shards of glass. "Birds? What kind of birds?"

My employer shrugged. "I'm not a bird expert. Hawks, I think. And a dove if I remember rightly."

The reply left me feeling weak. What I'd heard seemed too much of a coincidence. I wanted to question her further but Madame was too wrapped in her thoughts to allow interruption. "What I do know is that the piece is very old. My appraiser offered me a good sum of money for it which made me suspect it might be worth more. Perhaps I shouldn't have been so greedy. Now, it's worth nothing." She scooped the broken pieces into the nearby waste basket with a sigh.

"Did he tell you anything about it…its history?"

"No. Or if he did, I've forgotten. It was a while ago, six or seven years, at least. I was trying to get organized even then. Obviously, my progress has been slow. A few of the fragile treasures I keep in the cabinet but they seem to attract Mrs. de Toi like a magnet. Tell a person not to do something and see what happens."

"That's too bad. I could have done some research for you. I wonder why she disobeyed your wishes."

Her answer came in the form of a shrug. "She's trying to help, I suppose. But I really wish she wouldn't." Madame sighed again as she continued to stare at the broken goblet lying in the trash. "Sometimes I wonder…"

She bent down, looked at the glass a second time, and then straightened, saying nothing.

"What do you wonder?" I prodded, eager for her to regain her train of thought.

Her expression was blank. She looked at me, almost as if she'd forgotten I was in the room. "Nothing… No, nothing. I've forgotten what I was thinking."

"You said you wished Mrs. de Toi would stay out of the cabinet. Have you a key? Is it possible to lock it? That would solve the problem, wouldn't it?"

"Solve one problem, maybe. But it would create another. Can you imagine how Mrs. de Toi would feel once she discovered I'd taken such a precaution? She'd assume I didn't trust her. I can't have that."

"But if the items are valuable…"

"So is our friendship. Besides, the cabinet is so fragile a baby could pry it open. No, locking things up is a bad idea."

"Then why not move them to another place? What about in your private rooms?"

"Worse. What would I say to Mrs. de Toi? What reason could I give?"

When I persisted in making further suggestions, my employer cut me off with an impatient wave of her hand, the diamond on her ring finger flashing as if it were a warning signal.

"I know you mean well, Rachel, but I'd prefer not to talk about the cabinet any longer. Allow me to deal with my staff as I see fit. That's not why you were hired."

She marched from the room, leaving me with my mouth hanging open. Annoyance was the last thing I'd expected. I was trying to help. Or did she prefer accidents to happen to provide her with insurance money?

No! I had to stop such a thought. She'd been genuinely distressed by her loss. And as for her behavior with Mrs. de Toi, naturally, she wouldn't want to hurt the woman who was like a mother to her.

Even so, the scene which had just passed made me feel like an outsider. Mrs. de Toi had been forgiven her transgression, so Madame allowed her temper to fall upon me. No matter how I tried to get around my feelings, I was hurt.

I decided to forget about lunch. Instead, I plunged into my rain gear and went for a walk. The rain seemed to suit my mood. The harder it pummeled, the greater my sense of injustice. Let it thunder and lightning for all I cared.

I don't recall how long I walked, my boots sinking into the softened turf, but eventually the rains calmed and so did I. With the sweet smell of earth hanging upon the air, my temper left me. Everywhere I looked, the shrubs, the trees, even the grass hung heavy with rain droplets that mirrored the earth like a pointillist's painting. In the midst of such beauty, I fell in love with France again, in love with Sainte Enimie, and in love with the Chateau l'Ombre.

Walking toward the house along the gravel path, I realized my thoughts of quitting my job and scuttling back to San Francisco were adolescent. No real injustice had been done. I was jealous, that's all. I envied the closeness of the two women who had become important to me. I'd never be a part of it if I ran away.

I entered the chateau prepared to apologize and found my employer standing in the hall. She looked as if she'd been crying and the moment I appeared, she ran toward me with her arms outstretched.

"Oh, Rachel, I'm so sorry. Can you forgive me? I'd no cause to speak to you as I did. I was going to ask your forgiveness at lunch but when you didn't appear... I've been so worried, so upset."

We embraced each other and allowed our tears to flow. "I'm the one at fault," I croaked. "I shouldn't have spoken out. It was none of my business–"

Madame took my face in her hands and held it. "Sh-sh-sh. You've done nothing wrong, said nothing wrong. I took my frustration out on you and I had no right. Oh, Rachel, you've brought so much joy into this house. You'll never know how happy you've made me. Please, please don't cry."

She brushed my hair from my forehead and peered into my eyes. "Everything's all right between us, isn't it? You do forgive me?"

Too choked with emotion to speak, I nodded. The answer seemed to satisfy. If anything, the crisis had brought us closer. At last, I felt we were friends.

Chapter Three

THE NEXT FEW DAYS AFTER our quarrel and reconciliation were among the most blissful of my life. The pace of our work continued to suffer, at times almost coming to a standstill. We were too busy exploring our friendship, too anxious to share our inner thoughts to worry about the task we'd set for ourselves. Each morning, if weather permitted, we sipped coffee on the south terrace that overlooked the rose garden still abundant with flowers. Mathiam had cut the stems back in the hope of forcing a last gasp of blooms.

Soothed by the peace around us, it was easy to allow our daydreaming to gain the upper hand, each of us sitting in silence, confident conversation was no longer necessary to maintain our connection. Still, there were moments when Odeil could shatter our serenity with a question that would surprise me.

"Are you afraid of dying, Rachel?"

The question was one I hadn't expected so soon after breakfast. I sat up, not sure I'd accurately heard her. I'd sat idling for so long in the same position, I felt stiff. "Pardon?" I asked, rubbing the spot on one shoulder where it hurt the most.

"I was wondering... Since you don't believe in heaven, are you afraid to die?"

I looked at her, nonplused. How was I to answer a question of such dimension coming at me out of the blue? "I-I don't know. I mean, I haven't given death much thought, actually."

"No, at your age, you wouldn't." Odeil's laugh was without judgment.

"But you're not so much older than I. Have you given death much thought?"

Her hair gleamed in the early light like sparks of electricity. *How would Rembrandt have depicted her, given his fascination with light and shadows,* I wondered.

"Frankly, I don't know what sense I'd make of life without a hereafter. What would be its purpose?"

If she wanted an answer that was profound, I couldn't give it to her. The best I could do was shrug off the question. "Does one need a purpose? Whether God exists or not, the sun still shines, a fine wine is pleasant and friendships are to be cherished. That's all I really know of heaven and all I need to know."

The face of my companion brightened. "Ah, you are a hedonist. Or so you would have me think, but somehow, I don't believe you. You are too thoughtful to accept the here and now in the same manner as a cat or a dog."

"Why not? Pleasure is something we all want, isn't it?" My question failed to evoke an answer. "Don't misunderstand me," I went on. "I do envy your faith. What a comfort it must be to believe you're part of some divine plan..."

"You make me sound egocentric."

"Sorry. I didn't mean to. I'm attempting to explain that faith isn't something one picks from the ground like a flower."

"No, of course, it isn't. But I'm puzzled as to how two intelligent people can hold such divergent views as if we existed in different worlds. Don't you find that strange?"

Observing my employer as she sat relaxed with her feet stretched out on a second chair, I wondered where she was going with this conversation. Certainly, she knew the world was full of learned people who disagreed. Yet, she continued to touch upon this difference between us as if it were a wound.

"I can understand your skepticism. I was near your age when the Second World War ended. The allies had defeated Hitler and his monstrous ideology but at an enormous cost...death on a grand scale. I learned then it's possible to be happy and sad at the same time…happy the struggle was over but sad in the midst of so much destruction. How were we to reclaim our lives?"

A shadow fell across her face reflecting her dark thoughts.

"So, you used religion to make sense of what happened. That is a way of dealing with tragedy. As I've said, I envy your faith."

Odeil picked up her sunglasses that were lying on the table and put them on, almost as if she needed something to hide behind. "I had a dream about death last night, a vivid one. You mentioned having vivid dreams…well, this one was frightening. I woke up in a cold sweat."

She drew her cashmere shawl around her as if she'd suddenly been chilled by a breeze, although the air was still.

"About death? Do you mean yours?"

"Yes," she murmured without looking at me.

"That must have been frightening. But it was a dream, after all."

"Or a premonition…"

"You don't believe that, surely."

"It was very real. And one reads about such things all the time…a man gets a feeling and decides to cancel a trip. Afterwards, he reads the plane he would have taken has crashed. You've heard that sort of thing, haven't you?"

"Pure coincidence, I assure you."

"I knew you'd say that. And you're probably right, but this dream seems different…"

"Of course, it does. You don't dream about your death every night, I hope."

"Jung wrote about the powers of dreams, didn't he?"

"I don't know. I'm not an expert on his theories. But no one's ever proven dreams have any meaning. And premonitions are no more real than fortune telling or reading tea leaves."

"You really believe that?"

"Of course, I do." I leaned forward as if to penetrate Odeil's sunglasses with my gaze. "A bad dream is a bad dream. That's all. In fact…"

I stopped in mid-sentence. My dream about the goblet with the emblem of the birds popped into my head. When Mrs. de Toi had broken one of a similar description, I remembered the shock I'd felt. Could my dream have been a premonition?

Odeil raised her sunglasses to get a better look at me. "Is there anything wrong, Rachel?"

I didn't have time to answer. Mrs. de Toi appeared on the terrace to announce Madame had a call from Paris. My employer left me at once and, by the time she returned, I'd decided to say nothing of my dream.

No matter. Her thoughts had moved in another direction. When she rejoined me on the terrace, her agitation was apparent, and she announced that she'd have to leave for Paris in a day or two. "But before I go, I have something I want to show you." She held out her hand to me and I rose to take it.

As we entered the library, I noticed the oak desk, that was usually buried under a snow of papers, had been cleared away. Lying in their place were a few large sheets, renderings of the chateau's floor plans. The documents weren't old, but the pages smelled musty as if they'd been buried in the earth for a time.

Examining them closer, I could see the drawings were crude, not those of a professional, but the essential landmarks were well documented, showing the floors plans of the chateau as they branched north and south with the front facing east and its back facing west. The structure consisted of two square blocks lined by narrow *salles* or public rooms downstairs, while upstairs the blocks consisted of pairs of apartments, self-contained and accessed by a wide, marble staircase. This arrangement repeated itself throughout the three floors with slight variations until reaching the upper cubicles of the attic, which, in more resplendent times, had been occupied by numerous servants, but were now the sole domain of Mrs. de Toi. Mathiam, as groundskeeper, occupied a gray-bricked carriage house at some distance from the main residence.

Outlined in dark pencil was the room, or salon, one had to pass on the ground floor in order to reach the library. It was called La Salle de Persephone and was quite large, although empty of furniture.

I crossed the space on a daily basis but without lingering, as a fire was never lit in the hearth and the room was always freezing. The only semblance of warmth came from the multicolored window panes that faced east with a view of the front grounds and the distant grove. When light passed through them, a flower-like pattern was cast on the gray and white marble tiles so that, on particularly sunny days, one had the sensation of walking through a garden.

The item of greatest interest in the empty space was the hearth, itself. It was ornamented by a white mantelpiece of considerable size and supported by caryatids, two to each side — stone women wearing sandals and Roman attire with their hair strung up in ribbons. What made them curious were their expressions, each woman being turned toward her companion as though in animated conversation.

Excluded from their whispers, but hanging above the mantle, was an unsigned portrait of Persephone...one that bore a remarkable resemblance to my employer. When I'd first commented upon the likeness, she'd laughed and given me firm assurances that although it was a strange coincidence, she'd neither modeled for it nor had any idea whom the artist was, or the year in which the work was painted.

But on the day in question, the day when we stood together in the library examining the chateau's floor plan, Odeil drew my attention to the depiction of the salon and to one caryatid, in particular, for the four were not identical. My glance followed to where she had pointed and noted the inside figure, the one with the chiseled wink, had a word written beside it: *batil*.

"I think the word's Arabic and means 'void.' "Her eyes were twinkling as she gazed at me. "What do you think?"

"I don't know Arabic. What do you suppose it signifies?"

"I think it's a clue to the entrance of the tunnels. And see those penciled lines drawn over the diagram? My guess is that they're an outline of the tunnels that lie behind."

"So, that's why she's winking," I said, letting out a gasp of air. "She knows a secret. How clever. But where did you find these drawings? Why didn't you tell me about them sooner?"

"I'm embarrassed to say, I forgot I had them. When I found them, you hadn't arrived and I had no idea they might be important. They were in the potting shed, believe it or not, under a sack of manure. I meant to ask Mathiam about them but I absent-mindedly brought them into the house and forgot about them. I discovered them last night when I was shifting things, getting ready for my trip. I'd have told you this morning first thing but I became distracted by my dream."

"But this is wonderful information," I exclaimed. "Now we have evidence the tunnels exist. But how is it you can read Arabic?"

My employer demurred. "I don't do it well. Mathiam's mother was an Algerian *émigrés*, and there are many in the area. It wasn't difficult to pick up a few words."

"Thank goodness you did. Now, we can do a little exploring."

"We?" Odeil looked askance. "I shall be in Paris, remember? This mystery is for you to sort out. But promise me, if you discover how to access the tunnels, you'll do nothing more until I return. Exploring on your own could be dangerous."

"I promise," I said, and I began rolling the diagrams into a neat tube.

We were still congratulating ourselves on our find when Mrs. de Toi found us, her face wearing a harried expression. "I'm having a bit of trouble with the green grocer's son, Madame. He's brought my order but his father says to tell you he hasn't been paid in three months and this will be his last delivery unless what's owed is settled." The cook cast a sidelong glance in my direction, as if she felt embarrassed.

"Not paid? But that's nonsense," Odeil blustered. "I gave you the money to clear the account last month. You settled it, didn't you?"

"You know I did," the cook sniffed. "I left the receipts in the library the day you were to close out the month."

"You did? I don't remember. Rachel, do you remember?"

"She wasn't here. You were alone and I laid several receipts right by your elbow. You can't have forgotten. We paid the butcher and the fishmonger in full, as well." The woman's voice had become a deep whine.

Odeil looked confused and she swept one hand across her brow as if she were attempting to brush away cobwebs.

"None of this makes sense. I remember nothing about receipts. How could this happen?"

"I-if you'd just speak to the lad," Mrs. de Toi pleaded. "I'm sure you can sort it out. He's waiting in the kitchen. I've given him cookies and a glass of milk."

"Oh, all right." Odeil's concession came with a shrug. "I'll have another look here and then join you."

Apparently satisfied, Mrs. de Toi headed for the door. "That's all right, then. I'll tell the boy you're coming."

Despite the fact that we were alone, Odeil's voice was barely above a whisper when she addressed me next. "I'm putting these floor plans of ours in this desk drawer, under some papers. You'll know where to find them when they're needed, but don't say anything about them to anyone, not even Mrs. de Toi. Promise me."

I must have looked aghast but she didn't wait to explain. "I must sort this out with the grocer's son," she said, and hurried from the room.

* * *

Lunch and dinner came and went without any sign of Odeil. Mrs. de Toi served my meals before the fire in my rooms, explaining that Madame had gone to the village and wasn't expected to return until late.

She was right. Not 'til my mantle clock had chimed half past eight did I hear a tentative rap at my door.

Odeil entered looking tired. A few stray hairs from her chignon had come loose and fallen across her face. Slipping off her shoes, she slid into a ladderbacked chair beside the fireplace.

I offered her a cup of tea from the tray on the bedside table. I knew it was cold but thought it might be reviving.

My employer shook her head. "I had something in the village."

The circles under her eyes made her look frail but she was still strikingly beautiful.

"Did you get the money issue sorted out with the creditors?"

"You mean, did I have to pay the bills *again*? Yes. Thank heavens there was enough cash on hand. This time, I've filed the receipts properly."

"Lesson learned, I suppose."

"More than you realize, Rachel. Far more."

The exasperation in her voice was obvious but I asked nothing. I laid the book I'd been reading beside me on my bed and waited. If she had something to tell me, she would do it in her own time. After several minutes of staring into the fire, she began.

"Things aren't always what they seem," she said cryptically. "I feel I owe you some explanation but I don't want to give you cause for alarm."

"That sounds ominous, already," I said, folding my hands in front of me.

In profile, she was such a perfect replica of Nefertiti, I could not take my eyes off her. When she rose and began pacing the room, catlike, I remained mesmerized, certain she was too absorbed in her thoughts to notice me. Finally, she came to settle on the edge of my bed.

"I-I have a cousin," she began. "His name is Christian..." Her voice quavered. "Understand me. Nothing I tell you is meant to detract from Mrs. de Toi. I love her as a mother. You know that, already. Still, relationships are complicated; so you mustn't be shocked when I say I'm not certain I have her undivided loyalty."

I pushed back against my pillows, ready to voice an objection, when she silenced me by raising her hand.

"Hear me out, please. It's important you understand everything and for that I must acquaint you with a little family history. You see, three years before the war, Christian and his family came to live at the chateau. I was ten and my cousin three, at the time. Given our age difference, you will understand we were never close. What we had in common was our nanny, who, at the time, was Mrs. de Toi."

"So, she wasn't always housekeeper and cook?"

"No, those duties came later, after we'd grown."

"So, you're saying Mrs. de Toi has affection for your cousin…"

"Yes, but let me explain. Christian was the son of my mother's only sibling, Denise. The boy was a beautiful child with blonde hair and large, sapphire eyes. Few people could resist his baby lisp and pleasing manners. I won't hide it. I was jealous the moment I laid eyes on him. He could twist people around his little finger while I, a chubby adolescent, felt utterly devoid of grace."

"I'm sure you're exaggerating, especially about the chubby part."

"No, I assure you I'm not. There was no good comparison to be made between us. Christian was irresistible."

"But how did he come to live with you?"

"His parents escaped with him from Holland. Uncle Edvard was a Jew. As he'd made his living as a journalist, he'd followed Hitler's rise to power and early on saw the danger to himself and his family. That's why he came to us, to escape the persecution. But when France was invaded, there seemed no place to hide… especially not here where the Vichy regime cooperated with the Germans. He decided to leave for Paris to assist in the underground, hoping his wife and child might escape the Nazi's oppression. But Denise refused to be parted from him and so she left Christian behind in our family's care. That meant the responsibility for raising my cousin and I fell to Mrs. de Toi. My mother had always been uncomfortable in the presence of children, including me. A boy of three would be impossible for her to understand.

"To make matters worse, my father decided to join Edvard and Denise, and not long after, my brothers followed. That left our nanny in charge of the entire house as mother retreated into herself. Naturally, Amelia, with her warm heart, could not resist tucking a little boy under her wing. She called him her 'little orphan,' and he soon learned how to exploit his position."

"And you felt neglected."

"Of course. He became spoiled. He'd steal into my rooms and lay his sticky, little fingers over everything. He broke my dolls, made a fuss if I didn't let him play with my toys. I complained, naturally, but got no sympathy. Nanny would say, 'He's lost his parents. He's just looking for a little attention.' "

"What did your mother say?"

"Oh, Rachel, if you only knew how funny that question is. My mother was too selfish and too weak to care. In principle, I was an orphan, myself. On the rare occasions when she made an appearance, she was either drunk or woozy from the drugs she took to alleviate her pain."

"She was ill?"

"She was a hypochondriac; I thought...we all thought... We discovered later she really was ill..."

Odeil paused, tracing the pattern on my quilt with one finger. "I suppose I could have been more understanding. But I was a child. I needed her warmth. She was never outgoing, and during the war she became afraid, especially since father had made no secret of his hatred of the Nazis. When they took over the chateau, she retreated to her rooms and the rest of us were left to fend for ourselves. Not Christian, of course. With his blonde hair and blue eyes, the soldiers spoiled him. They never suspected his origins."

'Til that moment, I had thought of Odeil as a gentle person, disorganized and sometimes flighty. Now I had an insight into her courage. She'd survived a terrible war without the protection of a mother's love. Given my close ties to my parents, I could only guess at the strength she'd needed to hold herself together.

"What happened after the war?" I asked, finally. "Didn't anyone come back? I mean, didn't Christian see his parents again?"

Odeil shook her head. "No one came back."

"You're certain no one survived?"

"Legally, they're dead...a court ruling which allowed me to claim the estate."

"And what about Christian? What happened to him when the war ended? He was still a child."

"He continued to live here until my mother died. Then he became a ward of the court until I came of age. After that, responsibility for him was transferred to me and he returned here to live with us. Mrs. Toi is the nearest thing to a mother he's ever known. So, you see what I mean when I say I'm not sure I have her undivided loyalty."

"I still don't understand what you're saying."

Odeil sighed to relieve her frustration. "I don't suppose I've said enough for you to read between the lines so I'll be blunt. I suspect her of siphoning off money from the estate to give to him. The lost grocery receipts, the broken heirloom that proved to be a fake—the original was probably sold..."

"The goblet wasn't the real one?"

"When I examined it closely, I saw it was glass and not crystal. I can't tell you how much the subterfuge upset me."

"I can't believe she'd lie to you," I said, shaking my head. "She loves you. Besides, why would she do it? Your cousin's no longer a child. He must be...what—twenty four or twenty five?"

"He'll soon be twenty-five which means he'll gain control of the trust his parents set up for him and become part owner of the chateau. My mother, in some uncharacteristic moment of concern for her sister's son, left him a forty-nine percent ownership."

"H-he's part owner?"

"That's what I said," Odeil, hissed. "*And* he's a drug addict. That's why I've kept him on a tight leash. Otherwise, he'd run out of money in a heartbeat... and will, once he comes of age."

"So, where is he? Why have I never seen him?"

"Because, I had him committed to a sanatorium." Her voice became louder as if to drown out any harsh thoughts I might have. "I had to try something. He isn't strong enough to kick the habit on his own and I'm not sure he wants to. He seems to enjoy that myopic haze he lives in."

She was becoming so upset, I reached out to touch her hand. "I'm sorry to hear what you're telling me. I had no idea what you've been going through. But do you really believe Mrs. de Toi would send him money to support his habit, if that's what you think the money is for? And how could he buy drugs in a sanatorium?"

"Don't be so naïve, Rachel," Odeil sniffed. "Where there's a buyer there's always a seller. Given my cousin's charm, I wouldn't be surprised if he ran the place."

The expression in those almond eyes had hardened considerably since our conversation began. My friend may be diffident about household matters but where her cousin was concerned she showed a steely will. It made me wonder what her cousin might think of her. If he had any spirit, he would undoubtedly resent being her ward; so it was plausible he might turn to his former nanny for help.

"Trust me," Odeil pleaded, as if reading my thoughts. "I'm not a monster, if that's what you're thinking. I locked him away for his own good. His money is safe. What he's doing, at the moment, is stealing mine. Besides, I haven't told you the worst of it... There's no genteel way to put this so I'll say it outright. He tried to kill me."

Chapter Four

ODEIL DEPARTED SOON AFTER HER revelation to take another long distance call, leaving me with unanswered questions. When she didn't return, I spent half the night attempting to make sense of what she'd told me, wondering how—if it was true—Mrs. de Toi would consent to being Christian's accomplice in the theft of precious objects.

If I'd hoped to learn more at breakfast, I was disappointed. Odeil made no appearance and my attempts to engage Mrs. de Toi in conversation about this mysterious cousin failed.

"If it's him you wish to know about," she said firmly, "you must talk to Madame. It wouldn't be right for me to answer."

Defeated, I returned to my studies but made little progress. My thoughts kept returning to what I'd learned the previous night. Little wonder that I sat dragging myself vacantly through a dull tome when Odeil appeared like an apparition in the shadow-hung library.

A multicolored scarf was wrapped about her head and, from her black attire and high heeled boots, I presumed she'd been to the village. She sank into one of the leather chairs with a sigh and announced she'd spent the morning settling more financial affairs before her departure for Paris, which she'd planned for the next morning.

Stopping my work, I joined her by the fire. "You look as if you could use a nap."

"I could. I really could." She smiled back at me. "But there's so much to be done…" A silence followed; then to my amazement she leaned forward and took hold of both of my hands.

"You're so dear to me, Rachel. I hope nothing I revealed yesterday has lowered your opinion of me. I'm not without faults but I'd never deliberately hurt anyone. You do believe that, don't you?"

Although her outburst was unexpected, I didn't need time to consider. There was no denying I felt a kinship with this woman. I couldn't explain it, even though yesterday's conversation made it clear I knew little about her past. Still, I trusted her.

Without my answering, she sat back and picked up the conversation where she had left it the previous night.

"I want you to understand, I don't care what Christian does with his parents' inheritance, but I won't let him drag down the estate. Mother must have been in one of her stupors when she decided to make him a partner. But her will is sound. I've tested it. So, all I can do is keep him restrained any way I can, especially after his attempt to kill me."

"He did that and you still think Mrs. de Toi would support him?"

Odeil let out a puff of air between her lips. "She doesn't believe me, of course. Her precious Christian? No, on that point she thinks I'm imagining and Mathiam supports her. He would, naturally. He'd never go up against Amelia."

"Then, maybe if you told me, I would understand."

"What can I tell you? I don't understand myself. Somehow he got hold of arsenic…rat poison, possibly. Mathiam keeps it in the potting shed and he can be so careless at times… How Christian managed to put it into my food, I don't know. But he did."

"Were you taken to the hospital? Did the police investigate?"

"Oh, he's not such a fool as that. He gave me small doses over time. At first, I thought I was just overtired, but when my hair began to fall out, I called the doctor. He did a few tests and confirmed what

I'd suspected. I'd come in contact with poison."

"What did the police say when the doctor made his report?"

"Well, he didn't think any crime had been committed. He thought I could be sensitive to the dust Mathiam brought into the kitchen. He wasn't good about washing his hands or changing his clothes when he came in. The doctor told him he had to alter his habit, that's all."

"So, your cousin wasn't suspected?"

"No. In fact the little sneak complained he had symptoms as well...nausea, at least. Well, he would say that, wouldn't he, to throw off suspicion?"

"What about Mathiam and Mrs. de Toi? Did they show symptoms, too?"

"Of course, not. Mathiam works with the stuff and he's as healthy as a horse. So is Amelia and she comes in contact with him more than either Christian or me. No, what happened was deliberate, no matter what the doctor said. In fact, I ignored him and went to the police myself."

"And what did they say?"

"Psh! They treated me like a child. If Christian hadn't burst into the station, furious that I'd taken my complaint so far, I'd have been given a pat on the head and sent home. But he didn't argue his case well when he tried to strike me, so they put him in a cell overnight to cool him down. The next day, they sent him home."

"They let him go?"

"'Yes, a 'family squabble'—that's what they called it, especially after they checked with the doctor who wouldn't corroborate my story. Country bumpkins all of them! No, I got nowhere with the authorities so I did what I could to save myself. I had him committed to Place de la Déconvenue in Mende. There was no denying his addiction. The doctor had seen it, so I was within my rights as Christian's guardian."

Odeil rose to stir the fire, which sent a few sparks flying. "I'm sorry to have to tell you all this, Rachel. I've have no wish to relive these painful memories. But you deserve to know the reason behind my suspicion of Mrs. de Toi. Now that you do, I hope you won't think too unkindly of me...or of her. She means no harm by what she's doing."

As if speaking her name were a summons, the woman in question appeared with Analeese standing behind her. At this advanced stage, the day girl's white apron did little to hide her pregnancy.

"Analeese will be leaving soon to have her baby, as you know, Madame. But she says she has a friend who's willing to take her place if you'd be interested."

Odeil looked up from the fire. "Interested? Of course, I am. Help isn't easy to come by." Letting her gaze fall upon the young woman, she asked if the replacement was someone from the village.

Analeese stepped forward, a pretty girl whose brown hair was twisted into a tight bun.

"Yes, Madame. Her name's Kathrine Bevard. She's very trust-worthy. We were schoolgirls together."

"Bevard? Yes, I recall the name. They run a little sweet shop in the village. Does the girl have any experience in service?"

"Yes, Madame. She's been housekeeping at a boarding house but now that the tourist season is ended, she's being let go."

"You're sure that's the reason. Will her current employers give her a reference? I didn't realize there was a boarding house in the village."

"In Mende," Analeese corrected. "Kathrine wanted to get away from home for a while. Her family's house is so small."

"In Mende, you say?" Odeil glanced at the housekeeper who looked equally surprised. "Well, if she has a reference, I suppose it doesn't matter. Does she want to live in? We can arrange that, couldn't we Mrs. de Toi?" The older woman nodded her assent. "All right then, if her reference is in order, she's hired. She can start next week, if it suits her. That will give you time to acquaint her with your duties."

"Very good, Madame." The housekeeper paused in the door-way before exiting. "By the way, the fire's gone out in the dining room. Shall I have Analeese start a new one or will you take the rest of your meals here?"

"In library, I think. There's no point in starting a new fire when we are so cozy here."

We worked until the clock struck seven with no further talk of cousin's or poison or pilfering. Then it was time for my employer to leave me to make final preparations for her journey.

As we rose to say goodbye, she took hold of my shoulders and kissed me on both cheeks. "You are among my greatest treasures," she murmured.

Her look was so sincere, I couldn't help blushing. A moment later, she was gone. It was the last time I would see Odeil de Villiers alive.

Chapter Five

R AIN SLIDING DOWN THE WINDOWS cast twisted shadow patterns upon the polished floor, animating the La Salle de Persephone. Outside, the wind harried the trees. Their branches knocked against the leaded glass as though pleading to be let in. As it was fall, the colors that spilled through the multicolored panes cast their shapes like phantom dancers.

I was alone in the salon with only a torch for company, my thought having been to do a little exploring. Odeil had left the chateau in the early hours hoping to make good time on her drive to Paris. Madame de Toi was shopping in the village. A shiver of loneliness, as well as the cold, overtook me and yet, despite the absence of company, I felt as though I was being watched. Peering into the eyes of the caryatids, I wondered if somehow these stone figures might have a secret life. Perhaps that's why one of them stood winking at me.

Who were these women with their faded pigments and garlanded hair? Their features, rather than being stylized, were individual. Perhaps these women had been the artist's friends or lovers. Lovers, I supposed, for they seemed imbued with sexual allure, full-lipped and round as plums in form.

By their gazes, they seemed to be aware of one another, expressing, as they did, that look women reserve among themselves when they gossip about men. Mona Lisa wore much the same smile, I thought. Or did those glances provide a clue to a secret they shared? My eye followed the raised hand of the winking vestal and there I found depictions of male genitalia hidden among the flowers of her basket.

Having discovered her secret, I smiled and, almost with a will of its own, my fingers reached up to trace the largest of these configurations. In response, I heard a metallic groan and the caryatids seemed to come to life as the wall, creaking like old bones, moved.

The grinding noise grew for several seconds, then as suddenly, it stopped. I was staring into an abyss—a place where the blackness was so dense, the light from my torch seemed to bounce back at me as if it had fallen upon a mirror.

For some time, I stood on this precipice, the jumping off place between light and dark, honoring my promise to Odeil not to explore the tunnels until she returned. But that would not be for several days. In the meantime, my impatience grappled with my reason. If I were to proceed into the tunnel and suffered a mishap, who would know? Analeese and Kathrine, the new girl, were upstairs making beds. For all practical purposes, I was alone.

I took a few steps forward, just to get a feel of the space. What harm could that do? The door behind me remained open. No spring mechanism threatened to slam it shut and so I gained a little courage. If I kept the light from La Salle de Persephone at my back, I wouldn't get lost. I was still so near the entrance, I could hear the tap, tap, tapping of rain upon the windows.

My only regret was that I hadn't chosen warmer clothes. My wool sweater absorbed dampness from the walls as if it were a sponge and my shoes, kid skin loafers, were unsuitable to the task of maneuvering along the stone strewn floor. But, as my intent was to walk only a short distance, I refused to consider returning to my room to change into more suitable attire.

How long I crept forward I don't recall but eventually I realized the light from La Salle de Persephone had diminished in size. I had traveled father down that worm hole than I realized, a fact that surprised me as I'd found nothing of interest, not even rats, which would have been natural in a place so long abandoned.

No sooner had the thought of vermin entered my thoughts than I heard a rustle behind me. I spun 'round fast enough to lose my balance and must have struck my head on some impediment.

I experienced a sharp pain and felt blood trickling down my forehead. Becoming dizzy, I hit the ground hard and my torch was sent flying into the darkness. I may have passed out for a minute or two, for what I recall next was the sound of voices. Looking about me, I was unable to explain why I was in total darkness. The entrance to the La Salle de Persephone was no longer visible. My only sense of direction came from the whispers—perhaps those of ghosts or even that of the black monk said to haunt these corridors. My heart, too, beat a wild tattoo that was almost loud enough to drown out those whispers.

I sit up slowly and listen. Eventually, it dawns on me I am hearing the cries of children at play, their fluted voices beckoning like sandpipers along the shoreline. Instantly, my spirits brighten. Never questioning who these children are or how they came to be in the chateau, I rise and stumble in the direction of their laughter, noticing, too, that I am being guided by a warm breeze, the source of which remains a mystery.

The closer I get to these voices, the keener my sensory perceptions become. The scents of roses and pine waft around me, pulling me forward until I arrive at a spot in the tunnel illuminated with light; a multicolored swirl of reds, greens and blues, and so iridescent they have to be unreal. Again, I fail to question my eyes. Instead, I step through that portal to find myself in the rose garden at summer's peak. Yet, the landscape is different, somehow. Everywhere, flowers of various sizes and hues dot the horizon, as do several granite statues, caryatids garbed in Roman togas.

And at the center of this composition, encircled by a boxwood hedge, looms a solitary carving, larger than the rest but of a different tone: a depiction of Death with its shroud hung open to reveal a latticework of bones and decay. In its right hand, it carries a battered shield. In its left, a human heart rests, its veins so distended one can imagine it is still beating. The skull gazes down upon this fragile possession with a grim yet curious expression, as if wondering how the object came to be there. "Art contemplating Being," I might have said, if there had been ears to listen.

Happily, these somber thoughts are interrupted again by the children's voices. They come from somewhere behind a myrtle hedge and, when I find them, I see a company of boys and girls richly attired in eighteenth century garments of velvet and lace. The game they are playing is *Blind Man's Bluff* and when they notice my presence, several reach out with their hands, begging me to join them. This I do, enjoying their laughter for a time until, from the corner of my eye, I recognize the companion from my earlier dreams, still wearing the mask and costume to which I've grown accustomed.

Leaving the children, I follow the figure into the grove, allowing the shade to wash over me like cool water. As we move deeper into the shadows, I hear the strains of a distant lute and, eventually, we come to a place where a young man is resting against a tree, singing a melancholy lament for his lost love. He is so young and his brow so smooth, I doubt he's lived long enough to have suffered any such loss; but his voice sparkles like sunlight on a mountain stream and I am refreshed by it.

Others have come to listen, as well, and I long to sit beside them, but my guide beckons me deeper into the grove, a place of dappled shadows where caryatids, freed from their pedestals, dance among the ferns as if movement were natural to them. They greet me with their smiles and again I pause, content to linger and talk with these women who, by their glances, promise to share their secrets with me. Despite my wishes, I am urged forward and, eventually, my guide and I emerge from the trees and find ourselves in the midst of a vast poppy field. The scene is hauntingly beautiful.

A scented breeze greets us as the field of amethystine petals undulate like a calm sea. Ahead stretches a narrow path lined with young poplars. It leads to a hill, the summit of which is crowned by a Roman temple, all in ruins, but burnished by the light of two suns.

I shake my head knowing twin stars so close to the earth are not possible and so the anomaly allows me to comprehend I am dreaming. I've had such dream-awakenings before and usually

I've turned these occasions into a game. Sometimes, I've willed myself to fly or, with the wave of my hand, alter the landscape. This time, I wish to discover the identity of my companion whose face remains hidden behind its mask; but when I resort to all the old, familiar ways of achieving my purpose, they have no effect. The identity of my guide remains hidden and I am unable to alter my circumstances in any way. The poppy field, the hill and even the sky, which I attempt to paint with clouds, remain unchanged. Except for the incongruity of the twin suns, the laws of nature remain in effect.

Confused, I begin to follow the scarlet and black figure as we make our way up the hill. At first, the path is little more than a slope. The dust, gilded by the light of the two suns, rises in puffs beneath my feet—feet that, I notice, wear sandals studded with jewels. I am surprised, of course, but no more so than by my discovery that my clothes have changed, as well. No longer am I wearing a black woolen skirt and matching cardigan but a diaphanous gown like those belonging to the caryatids...confirmation that I am dreaming.

My mood begins to sour as the slope becomes steeper and more arduous. Even the breeze which had been playful, at first, now tugs at my garments with alternating blasts—sometimes hot and sometimes cold. Worse, the abandoned temple that initially appeared near at hand seems to recede into the distance with each step taken. I want the journey to end. I want to rest. My remorseless guide continues the assent, however, pulling me along by refusing to look back or heed my calls. Finally, I sink into the dust like a pack animal with too heavy a burden.

The figure in scarlet and black turns to acknowledge me, at last. Our eyes meet and even behind the mask, I can read importuning. Something is required of me. Some task needs to be accomplished. I have no notion of what it is but being mindful of the obligation, I rise and resume my climb.

How much time passes before we reach the peak, I don't know. I am thirsty and shivering from exhaustion, but on that hilltop I am rewarded by a glorious sight. Before me lays a vast, unbroken horizon, the marriage of earth and sky, and as I stand watching, the scene begins to expand as though reaching out toward some mystical center, the place where infinite possibility and contradictions co-exist: light and dark, summer and winter, life and death. I am being carried like a leaf upon its tide, a journey so peaceful I sense I am drifting toward some universal plane. Call it madness or a revelation, it little matters. I feel I am dissolving into dark matter, the stuff of origin and, as such, I experience both being and not being simultaneously. So many times when I've read religious treatises describing the experience, I've thought it made little sense. But in that moment, I need neither words nor scientific proof. I am drifting in the continuum of all that is or ever could be.

Sensing this insight is fragile, I do my best to hold on to it. But the more I cling to it, the faster the sensation fades. Finally, the moment and the insight burst like a bubble. Just as life's first breath portends its last, so too revelation is the harbinger of dissolution. Like matter and antimatter, I am unable to exist on two planes at once. Nor am I allowed to choose one level of existence above the other. The decision is made for me. I find myself returned to my place upon the hill. Overhead, dark thunderheads have gathered. The wind blows and the sky breaks with rain.

To my horror, I discover my guide impaled above a ruined pillar, a bloodied figure hanging in midair. I cry out and, at that moment, the mask falls away. Seeing the face that lies beneath, I collapse to the ground, covering my eyes with my hands. But no effort of mine can expunge the contorted image of Odeil de Villiers' visage.

Chapter Six

I AWOKE TO THE CHIRPING OF a bird. Its song seemed to welcome the sunlight that poured through my window in the wake of a retreating storm. Confused, I found myself under a layer of blankets. How I came to be in my room, I could only guess. One possibility occurred to me that I was still dreaming. If so, the space in which I found myself was an exact replication of the real one.

To the left of my bed was a blazing fireplace flanked by a pair of ladderbacked chairs, too tall and too stiff for human comfort. Beyond them was a large bank of windows. And opposite me, so that I could see my disheveled hair and wounded forehead, was a row of mirrored doors behind which I would find my modest wardrobe. The cream-colored walls with their gold stripes were probably fifteen feet in height and reflected the incoming light with the brightness of an artist's atelier. Never had that space looked so welcoming.

"Feeling better?" Mrs. de Toi appeared from my dressing alcove, obviously having heard me stir. "Mathiam found you in a dreadful state and everyone's been so worried. What were you doing in the grove in this weather? You've a fever, I can tell you. There'll be no leaving your bed for the next few days. Analeese will bring up the soup I'm making when it's ready. I expect you to eat all of it. In the meantime, I've removed the bandage I put on earlier to see how things look. However, did you get such a gash?"

I was reaching up to feel the damage for myself when Mrs. de Toi slapped my hand away. "No, don't touch it! I've just cleaned it. You don't want to risk a further infection. If that fever doesn't come down, the doctor says you might have to go to hospital."

"Have I been asleep long?"

"Almost two days."

I winced as she applied the new bandage. Gazing once more at my disheveled reflection in the mirror opposite, I winced again.

"What Mathiam and I can't make out," Mrs. de Toi went on, "is why you were outside. It wasn't weather for a walk. I advise you not to wander off without telling someone in future. Good thing Mathiam isn't bothered by rain. He was looking for stones to repair one of the garden walls when he found you. If he hadn't, who knows how long you might have lain out there."

I apologized for making a nuisance of myself but said nothing about the tunnels, as Odeil had sworn me to secrecy. For the life of me, though, I'd no idea how I came to be found in the grove.

Mrs. de Toi stared down at me with her arms folded. I could see she had a list of questions to badger me with. Lucky for me, Analeese entered the room with the promised soup and some crusty slices of bread. Kathrine, the new girl, lagged behind.

She was a small, birdlike creature in her mid-twenties with dark hair twisted into a bun like her friend's. She curtsied when she came forward to fluff my pillows, a gesture which I told her was unnecessary as I was an employee like herself. Mrs. de Toi objected to my characterization and insisted Madame de Villiers and I were as close as sisters. I was to be treated with utmost respect she said.

Naturally, I was warmed by her words but as to the new girl, I'd detected an insolence of manner which led me to suspect she knew full well my position in the house and that her courtesy was a mocking one. My suspicion passed, but in time my opinion of her proved true. In any case, I was glad when she resumed her duties elsewhere.

I had hoped Mrs. de Toi would leave with the two girls but she didn't. She continued to stare at me with eyes full of questions. I fell upon my meal, hoping she would give me a bit of peace. Uppermost in my mind was my ignorance of how I'd escaped from the tunnels.

Despite my wishes, she insisted upon loitering. She fussed with objects on my dresser, settling and resettling my comb and brush while I ate. When the reasonableness of that ploy was exhausted, she swept the area with her finger as if inspecting for dust. If I didn't come up with some reason to eject her soon she might decide to scrub the floor. Mercifully, there came a rap at the door.

"Enter." From her tone, it was clear she eschewed another interruption, and we were both surprised when Mathiam appeared.

Eager to see him, I sat up in bed, wanting a private word with him. But Mrs. de Toi refused to budge. Instead, she stared at the gardener's shoes, as if she expected to find he'd tracked in mud. In this she was disappointed.

"Here to see the patient?" she said after her careful scrutiny of him.

The gardener looked uncomfortable as he came forward and spit out his words. "I was wonderin' if the patient was feelin' better. I heard she was awake."

"You've been gossiping with Analeese, I suppose?"

"T 'was the new girl what told me," he answered without guile. "So I cut these flowers for the room. Japanese Japonica, they are. Thought they might cheer her up."

"Well, don't stand there strangling the poor things. Give them to me. I'll put them in water."

Mathiam did as the housekeeper instructed and she headed to the bathroom for a glass. In the interim, he stood with his plaid cap in hand, shifting from one foot to the other.

"I understand you are the one who found me," I said to acknowledge his rescue. "I'm lucky you did."

"True enough." He blinked at me. "You was soaked clear through. No tellin' how long you'd been lying on the ground. I was sore afraid you might get pneumonia."

"Mrs. de Toi says I was in the grove. Is that right?"

"Yes. And when I seen that gash on your forehead, I wasn't half worried. But I knew if I could get you home, Amelia…Mrs. de Toi…would fix you up. She shoulda been a nurse, that one. She's a remedy for everythin'. I've got to say, you look better than when I found you."

The woman being complimented returned with a glass crammed with Japanese Japonica. She seemed surprised to see Mathiam was still in the room. "Lunch is in the kitchen. You'd best be going down. You can't expect the girls to be waiting on you forever."

Mathiam didn't seem to mind the verbal cuff he'd been given. "Well, I am that hungry, Amelia," he drawled. "A little soup and cheese with some of that good bread of yours wouldn't go amiss." He winked as he tipped his cap to her.

One couldn't help but notice he left with a jaunty air about him.

"Old fool," Mrs. de Toi muttered after he was gone. Her words did nothing to dispel the glow of pleasure on her face, however.

"He's a shy man, isn't he? Today's the most I've ever heard him speak."

"Oh, he can speak, well enough. Never mind that. Around young ladies, he's apt to lose his tongue, but don't think he hasn't got opinions. He has." She was straightening the velvet curtains as she spoke. "He's a good man, all the same. And a brave one. He earned several medals during the war. You might ask him about those, one day. But don't get him started on politics. There'll be no stopping him, particularly if it's about this struggle going on with Algeria. His mother was from there, you know. She married Mathiam's father when he was stationed overseas with the French army. 'Course that was a different time."

"Does he support Algeria's claim to independence, then?"

"Too right. He never stops talking about it. I have to remind him he's a Frenchman, born and bred, sometimes."

"I suppose he has relatives in Algiers?"

"No, not as I know of. His mother didn't have much of a family when she met his father and most of them were old. Probably dead now. Truth is, he's never been to Algeria except for his brief turn as a soldier. He was wounded there in 1944. When he was able, he returned to his job here as head gardener. That's the short of it."

Mrs. de Toi had advanced to the bed to fuss with my pillows and I could see the softness in her eyes as she talked about him. It occurred to me then, there was more to their history than the fact they had worked together a long time.

"So, you've known him since before or after he came back from the war?"

"Oh, a long time. We grew up together in Sainte Enimie. He's older by a few years, but I've known him most all my life."

"How old is he, if I may ask?"

"Not as old as he looks. He turns sixty in a couple of years but life's been hard on him. I'll not speak of that. Truth to tell, we're both getting on. He loves his garden but he can't do as much as he used to. Arthritis you see. But with the help of the workers from the village he gets by. And Madame de Villiers isn't fussy. She never bothers him about the grounds. He'll keep working until he drops, I suppose. Well, he has to, doesn't he? And so do I, for that matter. Neither of us has much put by for our old age, though Mathiam has a little coming in from the army on account of his war wounds. No, I suppose we'll both be working 'til the good Lord takes us."

"Madame de Villiers is lucky to have you both."

Mrs. de Toi stopped fussing long enough to recall her employer's face. "We're lucky, too, Mathiam and me. She's as devoted to us as we are to her."

"I'm sure you're right. But you and Mathiam...has there ever been anything more? You know what I mean."

The cook's cheeks turned rosy. "Romance, you're thinking? No. I might have been willing when I was younger. But his wife, Cloitilde, was the joy of his life. He'd never think to replace her."

"So, friends but never lovers. A pity."

Mrs. de Toi headed for the door, her cheeks still aglow. "If you can fill your head with ideas like that, I'd say you're getting better."

* * *

The moon was a pale wedge of light when Mrs. de Toi returned to my room. Her pinched expression alerted me that something was wrong. I sat up at once, my voice still husky with sleep. "What's the matter? What's happened?"

The moment I spoke, the housekeeper's shoulders began to quake. Tears threatened to cascade down her pale cheeks. I rose without bothering to put on my dressing gown and led her to one of the ladderbacked chairs. The embers in the fireplace were still hot so I added some kindling and a few logs to get the fire going again. Then I pulled up the second chair next to hers. The moment I did, she threw her arms about my neck, clinging to me as if I was a buoy and she was adrift in a roiling sea.

"You must tell me what's happened," I gasped as I pulled away to look at her. "Is there some news about your sister or her children?"

She shook her head and attempted to throw her arms around me a second time. I resisted by taking hold of her shoulders and shaking her a little. "I can't help if you keep sobbing. Tell me what's happened?"

I'd meant to bring her to her senses, but with nothing to cling to she collapsed under the weight of her grief, a Rubenesque figure, sitting with her face buried in her hands. Posed as she was, with the moonlight silvering portions of her body while the rest was erased by shadows, she seemed like some artist's sketch of grief, beautiful in spite of her despair.

Surprised that I could think in abstractions at that moment, I supposed it was because her sorrow had nothing to do with me. I was a mere spectator. Only when she reached for me a third time, her hand squeezing mine with a great force, did I understand she was extending sympathy as well as seeking it. Suddenly, I felt as if I'd been clubbed over the head with a mallet.

"Is-is it Odeil? Has something happened to her?"

The voice that answered was so choked with tears, I intuited rather than heard what she was saying.

"Dead. She's dead. Her car skidded off the road. My child bled alone in the dark. O-oh, when I think of it… When I think of it!"

For her to say anything more proved impossible. Her sobs rent the air and what I remember next was how cold I felt. I was seated beside a blazing fire, but I was shivering. My arms…my limbs were no longer under my control. At that moment, too, my room with its vaulted ceiling and pictures of cherubs painted overhead seemed little more than a sepulcher. Even Mathiam's flowers enhanced the funereal atmosphere. And yet, I could not cry. My mind refused to acknowledge what my body knew.

Emily Dickenson had once written that after great pain a formal feeling comes. That was how I felt in morning's gray dawn—formal, as if I expected Death to appear as a visitor offering condolences for the wrong that had been done; or to leave a card that read, "I will call again."

Chapter Seven

A T MID-MORNING THE SAME DAY, I remained tossing in my bed, unable to sleep or face the decisions that lay ahead of me. As yet, I hadn't fully absorbed the tragedy. It did occur to me, however, that my presence at the chateau was no longer necessary. With Odeil gone, there was no need for a history, or to make plans to take on extensive renovations. I would be obliged to return to the United States, uncertain of my future and no longer feeling San Francisco was my home.

Mrs. de Toi entered my room with a cup of tea and found me staring up at the canopy of my bed trying to silence my emotional pain. Beginning the day with a hot drink felt so ordinary, I might have imagined the horror of the previous night was nothing but a dream...except her red-rimmed eyes assured me otherwise.

I sat up and took the cup and saucer offered me, feeling awkward that this ritual should prevail in the midst of tragedy. Still, I suppose it was duty that gave the woman a reason for getting out of bed. Certainly, I could see she'd taken great care in her toilette. Her dress was fresh, her hair neatly arranged and her petal soft cheeks scrubbed to a polish. But her expression did not lie. She was struggling to keep herself upright.

"There was a telephone call for you from Paris this morning," she said as she examined the bandage on my forehead. "I've written the number down and left it by the telephone in the foyer. You're to call as soon as you can."

"A call? From whom? I don't know anyone in Paris."

"It's all in the message. There's no need to speculate." The housekeeper's face was emotionless as she headed for the door.

"Why didn't you wake me?" I called after her, my voice more petulant than I'd meant to reveal.

The words that answered were caring but the tone was brittle, as if what I said—what I'd felt—didn't matter. "You needed your rest. Besides, Mathiam and I have been occupied with the authorities."

"You mean the police?"

"Someone had to identify the body. Mathiam went with them. I couldn't." The housekeeper shuddered. "And then there were all those questions."

"What about?"

"About her state of mind. Had she been moody or depressed before the accident?"

"They thought it might have been suicide?" This time my voice shook with indignation. "That's ridiculous. They should have talked to me."

"It wasn't necessary. I reminded them you hadn't been here long."

"Five months. I've been here nearly five months."

"That's not long in terms of her life, is it? Mathiam and I can cope."

Her voice was matter-of-fact but her words stung like asps. Again, I was being made to feel like an outsider. But this time, Mrs. de Toil was wrong. A calendar was no way to measure a friendship. What would she have thought, I wondered, if she knew of the confidences Odeil had shared with me, including her suspicions of her housekeeper? Fortunately, despair may have left me bitter but not cruel. I said nothing of what I knew and was actually glad, when I thought about it, to have been spared the ordeal of speaking to the police.

By now, I'd risen from my bed and was throwing on my dressing gown. "Will there be an inquest?"

When she heard the question, Mrs. de Toi turned to look at me, her face registering both surprise and uncertainty.

"I-I doubt you'd be called to testify, if that's what worries you."

"No," I shook my head. "I was wondering if the funeral would be delayed. If I can, I'd like to stay for the service before I leave for San Francisco."

A dam might have broken, given the older woman's reaction to my words. She rushed toward me and flung her arms about my neck as she had done in the wee hours of the morning.

"Oh, Mademoiselle, don't talk of leaving so soon, please. Mathiam and I have become so fond of you...we don't want to face this loss alone. I know you're grieving, too. We must console one another, help one other. You mustn't think of running away. You mustn't."

As she hugged me in those ample arms of hers, my pent up tears began to flow. This was the warmth, the inclusion I needed to thaw my pain. Mrs. de Toi and I had erected walls to contain our separate grief. Now that our need to share had become clear, we shed tears together and were almost happy.

After a time, the housekeeper let go of me and, wiping her eyes, she insisted I return to bed. This I did, and when she had seen me safely tucked in she started clucking about breakfast and admonishing me to eat. I could see it did her good to have some-one to care about, so I raised no objection and was glad to be under her watchful protection again.

She had almost left to resume her duties when it occurred to me to ask about Odeil's cousin. The housekeeper paused in the doorway seeming to choose her words carefully as if she were untangling threads from an embroidery basket. "I believe the au-thorities have notified him of her death. At least, Mathiam and I were led to believe so, though we did not ask the question directly."

"And what about her husband, if he's still alive. Shouldn't he be notified?"

"Husband?" the older woman looked at me with her eyebrows lifted. "Why do you speak of a husband?"

"You always addressed her as Madame, as did I. Naturally, I assumed there was a husband somewhere in her past. She never spoke of him and I never asked. But now that she's dead..."

Mrs. de Toi cast me a look that was full of melancholy. "Madame was never married, not officially. But she loved passionately, once... It was after France was liberated. He was a soldier, an American like you. I thought he was too old for her but he made her happy, deliriously so. Poor lambs, they never gave a thought to what would happen when the war was over. They were like children, grasping at what joy they could find. In time, he was shipped home, of course. A few letters came for a while, but he never returned. Even so, she remained faithful. That's why I called her Madame. She'd earned the right."

Chapter Eight

THE DAY OF ODEIL'S FUNERAL was dark but without rain. A modest group of shopkeepers and the village curious had gathered in the chapel of St. Jude to hear their minister give the eulogy. Neither Mrs. de Toi, Mathiam nor I wished to speak. We were too consumed by grief and avoided glancing at one another for fear we couldn't control our tears. As to the cousin, the only living relative of the deceased, he failed to appear. Perhaps enmity was the reason, or perhaps he was unable to leave the institution to which he had been sent, the Place de la Déconvenue in Mende.

After interring Odeil in the family vault, a brick and iron structure that stood on a hill not far from the grove, those in attendance returned to the chateau for refreshment. Mrs. de Toi had worked tirelessly the previous two days so that when the guests entered the dining room, they were greeted with a buffet arrayed to please the eye as well as the stomach. Mathiam stood by with numerous bottles of early wine from the cellar; and I noted with amusement he was as generous to himself when he poured as he was to the guests. So generous, in fact, that several times, he had to disappear to replenish the stock.

Late to arrive were the two attorneys, executors to Odeil's will. I had spoken to one earlier over the phone, a Monsieur Allaire, who turned out to be younger than I thought—thirty-five, perhaps, with dark brown hair and a pleasing smile. The man who was with him was a founder of the firm and, judging by his wide girth, he made a good living. He introduced himself with a bow that revealed a healthy head of silver hair and handed me his card: William Larouche…younger brother of the co-founder of the law firm, Larouche, Galliard and DuBonnet, I was later to learn. I took the card, although I thought it unlikely I would need his services. Next, I turned to Monsieur Allaire with whom I'd talked on the phone.

"We meet, at last," I said. "And I didn't run off as you feared." I handed him the wine glass Mathiam had generously filled. Then I drew him aside to ask why he'd been insistent upon my staying in France until the reading of the will.

His broad smile caused his eyes to crinkle. "I assure you, Mademoiselle Farraday, my promptings were necessary, as you will soon discover."

"Really? Can't I even have a hint?"

My companion paused to observe if anyone might be near enough to overhear our conversation. "I can only say that during her last visit to Paris, your former employer made a change to her bequests which affect you."

"Me?" I was surprised and about to ask another question but the young attorney sought to fend me off with the wave of his hand.

"I've said too much already. It's not my place to reveal the conditions of her will. I am only a junior member of the firm, though Madame de Villiers did speak with me last. My role here, however, is to assist Monsieur Larouche, who is executor of the estate."

"You mean, at the gathering in the library today?"

"Yes. Four o'clock."

I glanced at my watch. The hour was two-fifteen. "I admit my curiosity is piqued but if you're bound to silence… Not the smallest hint?" The young attorney gave me a quick wink before he drifted away without answering.

Mrs. de Toi passed by me on her way to the kitchen with an armload of empty plates. I picked up a few others and followed. She was standing at a sink filled with soapy water, looking out the window when I found her.

"How are you holding up?" I inquired.

"Such a terrible day," came her reply. "At least, I prepared enough food."

"Enough food to feed the whole of Sainte Enimie," I said, laying my burden on the drain board so I could put an arm around her shoulder. "Never mind, tonight we can sit by the fire and have a good cry together."

The housekeeper reached into the pocket of her black, woolen dress and pulled out a handkerchief. "I'm so glad you're here," she said wiping her eyes. "I-I don't want to be alone. Not now…" Her voice trailed off into silence as she stood staring through the window at the withered herb garden. Her gaze was so intent I asked if she were expecting someone.

"No," she said resolutely, and she plunged her hands into the soapy water and began washing the dishes.

"Can't Kathrine do that?"

"I can do it faster." As she appeared to be determined, I picked up a dish towel to assist her. Keeping busy did seem to help.

By the time the hall clock struck four, the dining room was empty. Kathrine shuffled between it and the kitchen in a lazy attempt to restore order and grew sulky when she learned she would be left alone while Mrs. de Toi and I met with the lawyers.

When we entered the library, Mathiam was already seated in a small chair behind the two leather ones, both of which had been turned to face the desk where Monsieur Larouche was seated. Monsieur Allaire stood beside him, his arms at his side as though ready to run an errand if requested.

The younger attorney smiled when I entered, perhaps to assure me I was about to learn something that would be to my satisfaction. Mrs. de Toi sat down in one of the wing-backed chairs, and I sat in the other. Her eyes kept drifting to the door as if expecting someone. No one appeared.

"Shall I bring some coffee?" she asked, almost as if to delay the proceedings.

Monsieur Larouche, who was shuffling papers, assured her the buffet had been ample. Next, he peered over his reading glasses to ask if everyone was ready.

Mrs. de Toi and Mathiam sat perched on the edge of their chairs and I confess to feeling nervous, too. Nonetheless, the three of us nodded.

Larouche opened his mouth and seemed about to intone gravely, when the library door was flung open, bringing with it a slight breeze. All eyes turned in the same direction and there, standing on the threshold, was a tall figure whose face was hidden by the hood of a voluminous cloak.

"Am I late?" The apparition stepped into the room with a light step and when he was close enough for inspection, I saw a handsome face, wearing an arrogant expression. The nose was Roman and the lips supple, but most striking were the eyes that shone a luminous cornflower blue.

Monsieur Larouche rose with his mouth agape.

"We weren't expecting you, Monsieur de Hess. I think I made it clear in my letter you are not a beneficiary of your cousin's bequest."

"Amply clear, Monsieur," the man laughed as he drew down his hood to reveal a mass of blond curls. He looked about him for a chair and finding only a settee, he gestured for Mathiam to vacate his, which the older man did without protest.

The new arrival sat down and while he removed his gloves with everyone watching, he took an inventory of the room as if to familiarize himself with any valuables it might contain.

Having recovered her senses, Mrs. de Toi started to rise and looked as if she were about to embrace the young man, but his frown and the firm shake of his head dissuaded her. Discouraged, she sank back into her chair, appearing a little bewildered.

Monsieur Larouche cleared his throat as if to register his discontent and repeated his original objection. It had little effect. The younger man crossed his legs and, with one hand resting on his silver handled walking stick, he sat in a relaxed a manner that led everyone to know he intended to remain.

"You mustn't be surprised, Monsieur Larouche, if, as part owner of this chateau, I am a teensy bit curious to learn how my dear cousin has chosen to dispose of her half. That gives me some right to be here, I think."

The attorney scowled, but as he had neither the physical nor legal means to expel the intruder, he conceded, taking a few moments to reshuffle his papers as he attempted to calm himself.

In the meanwhile, Christian de Hess allowed his glance to fall upon me. He seemed puzzled by my presence; although I thought I detected a hint of approbation, as well.

He leaned forward to address me. "You're the American Odeil hired as her assistant, aren't you? I've no idea how well you type, but you certainly have other qualifications."

"It's true, Monsieur," I said, trying to restrain my blush. "I speak French fluently."

His lips were close enough to warm my ear with his breath. "Good. I think I might have use for an assistant."

Speechless, I returned my eyes to focus upon Monsieur Larouche as he began to read the will.

At the outset, the bequests went as expected. There were generous gifts to Odeil's favorite charities and a significant portion of money went to Mathiam and Mrs. de Toi, enough to allow them to retire in comfort. The pair looked pleased and I noted no look of disapproval in the cousin's expression, either. In fact, he patted Mrs. de Toi on the shoulder to offer his congratulations.

His affability soon changed, however, when he learned who was to have controlling interests in the chateau and all its treasures. To everyone's surprise, except the attorneys, that part of her estate came to me, with the proviso that I live on the premises and manage it as a business.

The moment he heard the bequest, the cousin leapt from his chair and began to hurl expletives at the two men in charge. He called them thieves and charlatans and any other name he could think of that described scoundrels.

I listened to his tirade without having had time to fully digest the enormity of my inheritance. The scene he was creating was too engrossing and no efforts on the part of the household servants could calm him. Mrs. de Toi had taken him by one arm and Mathiam by the other, but he was in such a fit of temper, he easily shook them off. For a moment, it even looked as if he and Monsieur Allier might come to blows.

Finally, and as might be expected, he turned his attention to me. But before he got far with a new set of invectives, Mrs. de Toi came to my defense.

"You've no call to blame her. She knew nothing of it, no more than I did. This was Odeil's secret. If she'd have told anyone, she'd have told me and she didn't. This girl's an innocent, she is."

The man addressed backed off but only slightly. Shaking his finger at me he issued a warning. "This won't stand. I'll have justice, by God. This isn't the last word."

The library door was slammed with such vigor when he left that it opened again as if blown back by the wind. Everyone stared at the empty threshold not knowing what to say. Mathiam was the one to finally suggest it was time for a spot of brandy.

Chapter Nine

THE FOLLOWING MORNING, BEFORE THE two attorneys left for Paris, Monsieur Allaire met me in the foyer and handed me an envelope with my name written across it. I recognized Odeil's handwriting and looked puzzled. He anticipated my question by explaining his client had left the letter with him during her last visit. He knew nothing of its contents but had been instructed to give it to me in the event of her death.

I stood looking down at the letter, turning it over and over in my hand, with feelings of trepidation. Coming from beyond the grave, as it were, there was no telling what other surprise it might contain.

Sensing my hesitation, Monsieur Allaire suggested I wait until I was alone to read it. I told him I would and he offered to answer any questions that might arise, if he could. "Just give me a call," he said as he cupped his hands over mine and the letter. The gesture was momentary but I appreciated the warmth of his feelings.

I wanted to tell him how much I'd appreciated the kindness he'd shown me thus far but Monsieur Larouche came huffing toward us with his bags and announced that it was time the men were off.

Monsieur Allaire left at once to collect his luggage from his room, and in the interim, the senior member of the firm handed me a second card. "Take no notice of what happened yesterday with the cousin," he advised. "Once he's consulted his own attorney, I doubt Monsieur de Hess will cause any trouble. Madame's will is ironclad, I can assure you. But if we can be of any service, you know where to find us."

When Monsieur Allaire reappeared, the two men headed for their sedan that was parked in the circular driveway. I received a final wave as the junior partner started the engine and then both men were gone.

Losing sight of them, I couldn't help feeling like a castaway. I would miss their support, particularly that of Monsieur Allaire, who'd been so kind. But, that couldn't be helped. He lived in Paris while I was now the proud half-owner of a crumbling estate, and tied to a partner who'd made no effort to hide his contempt for me.

I closed the large oak door against another gray morning and wandered into the kitchen hoping to find Mrs. de Toi seated before her morning coffee. We hadn't talked much since the will's reading and I was anxious to know her plans and those of Mathiam's. It seemed impossible that I could convince them to stay on, not with their generous inheritances, but I'd have to try, because coping on my own was too daunting. If it was selfish of me to ask them to remain, I would forgive myself, for I not only needed them, but I couldn't contemplate braving my loneliness without them.

I found both of them in the kitchen, seated at the large, oak table, enjoying a cup of coffee together. Mathiam rose as I entered and pulled out a chair. As I seated myself beside him, Mrs. de Toi filled my cup, as well.

"Gone, have they?" she asked, meaning the attorneys. Her tone seemed to suggest she thought their leaving was a good thing.

I nodded they had and then splayed my hands in front of me as if the firmness of the table might give me courage.

"I suppose you've begun to make plans about the future now that you've inherited..."

"As a matter of fact, we have," Mrs. de Toi interrupted. Her face was beaming and, seeing it, my heart sank. "What we've been thinking..." Here she tossed a glance in Mathiam's direction. "That is to say..."

"Please, please hear me out before you make any decision," I cried and threw up my hands to stop her. "I know how hard you've both worked and that you deserve a rest; but I really wish you'd stay on, at least for a while…until I get a feel for managing the place. Would that be too much to ask? Would you consider it?"

My plea was met with a chuckle, which came as a surprise. "That's what I was about to say, if you'd have given me a chance. We'd like to help with Odeil's plans. It'd be our way of keeping her memory alive. Isn't that right Mathiam?"

The grizzled man nodded, barely looking at me.

"What? You'd be willing to stay? In fact, you *want* to stay?" I could hardly believe my ears.

"Of course, Mademoiselle." Mrs. de Toi sat beaming at me. "Where else should we go? This is our home. And now that we have money, you wouldn't need to pay us as much. You could hire more help which would lighten our duties, considerably. Kathrine mentioned her younger sister might like a job, at least until she finishes her schooling. She could work a few afternoons and on weekends. She hasn't much experience, but I'll see she's properly trained. And Mathiam would like to hire another laborer or two, at least till winter sets in. Oh, please, Mademoiselle, tell us your feelings. We've been so anxious to talk to you. Do you think it could work?"

"Work? Of course, it will. I no longer require a salary. That's more money for the pot… Oh, I can't tell you how happy I am. I was terrified you both might want to run off on your own."

When tears of relief sprang into my eyes, Mathiam was left to scratch his head. But Mrs. de Toi understood. She reached over to give me a hug.

"Don't know what you've got yourself so het up about. We wouldn't leave unless you wanted us to. Like I said, this is our home. And don't worry. We'll make this place a going concern. Just you wait and see."

For the next hour, the three of us sat together in the kitchen, warmed by our growing fellowship and making plans for the future. We made lists concerning the necessary expenses which included increased staff and additional supplies. Mathiam asked if we might consider a new mower for the lawns and I agreed. Whatever the cost, I'd find a way to make it happen.

None of us gave a thought to Christian de Hess or any part he might play in our lives. He'd obviously left the sanatorium but no one knew where he'd gone. Besides, given the mood in which he left us, I wasn't anxious to see him anytime soon. I said as much when Mathiam mentioned he was surprised to see the young master at the reading of the will.

Mrs. Toi reached across the table to take my hand when she heard my concern. "You mustn't judge him by yesterday, Mademoiselle. He was in shock. All his life he's never been anything but a sweet boy, I can promise you."

"Sweet boy? I hope you're right about that. I know Odeil didn't feel that way. She told me she thought he'd once tried to kill her."

The housekeeper let go of my hand and rolled back in her chair. "She shouldn't have told you that. There wasn't a word of truth to it. She got sick and blamed Christian for it. She always did that.

Anything that happened, it was his fault. The doctor didn't believe a word of it and neither did the police. Now, you know I loved that girl like my own. But when it came to Christian, there was no reasoning with her. She was against him the moment she clapped eyes on him, a child no more than three or four. Isn't that right, Mathiam?"

"She took it awful hard when her mother gave him half the estate."

"She was after him long before that. And him a poor orphan boy with no parents to see him through that terrible war. Oh, I tell you, my heart went out to him. All he wanted was a bit of affection, poor lad. But Odeil only begrudged him." She turned her eyes in Mathiam's direction. "You didn't see them together like I did. But I can tell you, it used to break my heart."

"But the doctor did confirm poison, didn't he?"

Mrs. de Toi stared at me as if I had spoken a blasphemy. "It was never proved...not that it was done intentionally. We don't know how the pair of them was exposed. Christian had symptoms, too, you know. It gave us quite a scare, I promise you. Since then, Mathiam's been careful to keep his poisons locked up. Haven't you Mathiam?"

The gardener looked a little sheepish. "I try, Amelia. Sometimes, I forget. But I do wash in the greenhouse before I come inside, most of the time. And Amelia makes me leave my boots outside, as well." He pulled one foot from under the table to reveal a white stock.

I couldn't help smiling, although my opinion of the cousin hadn't softened. "But you don't deny he is a drug addict. That much is true, isn't it?"

Both servants nodded, reluctantly, as if their necks were on rusty hinges. "He got into the wrong crowd at university," Mrs. de Toi harrumphed. "Ruined himself, he did."

"He always wanted to fit in. It got him in trouble. No use sugar coating it. Madame was right to put him in that sanatorium. It was for his own good."

Mrs. de Toi gave her friend a hard look and the conversation ended soon afterwards. We dispersed to our different tasks; I, to the library, where I could read Odeil's letter in private as Michael Allaire had suggested.

As I hurried through the Le Salle de Persephone, my heels clicking across the marble floor, I saw the caryatid winking at me and paused to wonder if my experience in the tunnel had been real or the fragment of a dream. I crossed the room to stand before the mantelpiece and quickly ascertained a part of my experience, at least, had been real. The mechanism that opened the entrance was readily visible. I had only to reach up and touch it to corroborate my former experience; but in the cold gloom of the morning, I walked away and headed toward the warmth of the library fire.

Dropping into one of the leather chairs as soon as I entered, I stared into the heart of the flames. They burned vibrant colors—orange, blue and red—and shimmered like dancers performing a wild tarantella. A deranged mind could easily be drawn into them. How strong, I wondered, must an illusion be before it's accepted as truth?

Realizing I was deliberately delaying my reading of the letter, I chided myself and tore open the envelope. In some ways, I wish I'd left the contents unread and committed the whole of it to the flames, for if I imagined my experiences of the last few days were unsettling, I was unprepared for what the message revealed.

My dear Rachel,

By the time you read these words I will either be dead or incapacitated. I hope the fears which plague me prove false and that we shall enjoy one another's company for many years. Nevertheless, I have made preparations in the event my premonition proves real and that my death will occur sooner rather than later.

If you are reading this note, you will know I have made you heir to my portion of the estate. My cousin, Christian de Hess, is part owner as I've told you. He is a troubled man who will test your mettle at every turn, so you must be strong if you wish to succeed with our plans.

No doubt you are wondering why I have made you my heir when there are those who have shown me years of allegiance. I refer to Amelia and Mathiam. I do love them, Rachel, just as I love you. But in death, I must be honest. They cannot be trusted. Not where Christian is concerned. They think of him as a harmless, if wayward, child. That's why I must place my faith for the future in you, though you might consider yourself a relative stranger. That's not so. For years, from afar, I've watched you grow. And I confess, I lured you to France with the intention of making you my heir. Yes, that's right. I never intended to have anything written. It was a ruse based upon your interest in history. If you had been an art student, I'd have invented some other story to bring you here.

To put things simply, my dear, I knew your father. No, let me continue to be honest. We were lovers. I was aware he had a wife, but I was young, and given the effects of war, no one counted on the future. I took my happiness where I found it, without question. I suppose, too, I was arrogant enough to believe I could hold him. But he had a child. He'd never abandon you. And so, when the time came, he left. I hated him, at first, and then as the months and years passed, and with no children of my own, I came to understand his decision. That's when I took an interest in you.

Hiring an investigator was easy enough. And then your parents died, so suddenly and so tragically, my heart went out to you. I decided to bring you here to a new life. Why not? In a way, I'd watched you grow up. You became a part of me.

As to my cousin, I have no idea what he will do when he learns of my death. You should know I have tried to buy him out on several occasions but he has always refused. I suspect he prefers to remain a thorn in my side. But I intend to have the last laugh. You shall be my thorn in his. Don't be angry with me. I have deceived you but I warned you earlier, you held too high an opinion of me. Dealing with Christian may cause you some pain. If it proves true, I am sorry. But who knows, once I'm gone, he may lose interest in the place. I've always believed his hatred of me was part of the attraction.

In any case, please believe my reason for making you my heir is pure, in part. I do want you to have some inheritance. I do it on behalf of your father whom I loved.

I hope this letter isn't too much of a shock and that in time, you will not think ill of all my deceptions.

May God send you sweet dreams my dear, dear Rachel.

Her sloping signature, which had become blurred by my tears, followed. Whether it was reasonable or not, I felt exhausted. For the past several days so much had been revealed in so short a time, and now this disclosure of Odeil's relationship with my father... I couldn't take it all in.

Outside, a crow swooped past the windows, followed by a second and a third. A tree in the middle distance, barren of leaves, swayed in the wind. Gray clouds drifted overhead. My inner world had become congruent with the outer one. I was sad and angry, as well.

What offended me most was being manipulated like a pawn in some game Odeil de Villiers had been playing. Had our friendship been a sham? And how was I to feel, learning I'd been spied upon the bulk of my life? If I'd been alone with her at that moment, I would have expressed my contempt without restraint. And what arrogance had led her to believe I would willingly take up her feud with her addicted cousin? I owed the woman nothing. She'd admitted she'd hoped to destroy my parents' marriage and deprive me of a father. Her every word from the outset of our meeting had been a ruse to embroil me in a vendetta she'd hoped to carry out from the grave. Well, I would not be used in this fashion. I had the option to walk away.

For the space of an hour, my thoughts raged unfettered; but anger has its limits. Like any force, once the energy is expended, the mind clears. After that, I was free to consider all that had happened untainted by emotions. First, I asked myself, what harm had befallen me? True, Odeil had not been honest. She had brought me to France under false pretenses; but hadn't my life changed for the better? Second, I loved living in the chateau and now fifty-one percent of it was mine. Its restoration was a responsibility, true, but also a privilege. Could I really walk away from my inheritance and from the two friends who had proved loyal to me? And where would I go? Back to San Francisco? I didn't want that. What did I want?

I went to bed early that evening even although my mind was fitful. I needed the solitude of my rooms to give air to my thoughts, especially about the absent cousin who was a total stranger. Would I face more lies with him? More games?

Despite my anxieties, I must have dropped off for I remember awaking to the sound of a bell. The moon had disappeared and no light shone in from the windows. Despite the dark, I manage to find my dressing gown and hurry to the top of the hall stairs. From my vantage point, I see in the light of a hundred blazing candles the company below. Although the walls shimmer, nothing else stirs. What I observe is a tableau of masked dancers, an androgynous group by appearance, for above their gagnas each wears a three-cornered hat and a voluminous domino of black silk that conceals any hint as to whether the dancer wears a gown or trousers beneath. These costumes, despite the light's brilliance, reduce the world to an undifferentiated palette of gray and black, an image that is as disquieting as it is stark.

Without music from an orchestra, these figures begin their stiff twirls like figures atop a music box, each pair keeping equal distance from their neighbor so that the effect is like watching a hypnotist's wheel. I begin to feel dizzy and, being unable to steady myself, I slip over the balustrade…only to be caught by the many hands reaching up for me. Once I am firmly on the ground, the dancers link arms and form a chain as they draw me across the hall.

In this fashion, we thread our way from one room to the next, to the next while doors fly open before us without noise. Unimpeded, we reach Le Salle de Persephone and, there, the entrance to the tunnel stands agape. It draws us to it like birds being sucked into a maelstrom.

Down, down, down we descend into that utter darkness, our ears assaulted by the cries of what seems a multitude. Some of what we hear is laughter, but there are screams of terror, as well. We continue to fall for several minutes with suffocating effect. At last, our speed slackens and we land, light as feathers, into what appears to be a series of dimly lit catacombs. The walls are lined with votive candles, but each tiny flame casts more shadow than light, and into these dark spaces the dancers disappear. I stand alone in that vaulted crypt.

The surrounding space is large and houses many sepulchers, some ornamented with dancing gods and goddesses. Others are scrawled with brave words meant to defy oblivion. But stone and grandeur is no defense against time's decay.

Most dramatic are the coffins with effigies modeled on their surfaces meant to depict the former likenesses of the cadavers within. Their expressions—sometimes beatific, sometimes terrified—provide a clue to the conscience of the departed. The old, their skulls peeking beneath their transparent skins, seem the most at peace, almost contented by their deaths. They'd lived their lives to the full: had known the best and worst of their fellow men, had suffered pain, had wept with happiness and had cheated the grim reaper as long as they could for the sake of their loved ones. But the faces of the young strike a different chord, one of sadness and envy. They had tasted so little of existence that their passing went largely unnoticed by the world. Yet, they'd dwelt long enough to be loved by a few and in their brief span were guilty of no sin, had neglected no duty and except by their death, they'd caused no pain to any living creature. Little wonder that being unsullied, their memories evoked the utmost tenderness.

> *Here lies Elspeth Jardan*
> *Beloved daughter of Robert and Denine.*
> *Born April 23, 1632*
> *Died April 23, 1632*
> *She opened her eyes for a moment*
> *Before closing them again.*
> *In that instant, she stole our hearts*
> *For eternity.*

As I wander among these shades, I am surprised to feel a tenderness invade me. I feel a communion with the departed. Their passions spent, all their follies and the hungers that drove them to heroic or unspeakable deeds have come to this: darkness and dissolution. As their fate is common to all, I wonder that we humans find it so hard in life to forgive what in death must be forgotten.

I thought of Odeil and Christian, each tormented by an insane hatred of the other. Could they not see, could they not anticipate how it would end—both of them staring into an abyss with eyes no longer alert, hands unable to touch, tongues without the power to ask for forgiveness?

A light, shimmering like a halo, draws me to a far corner of the catacomb. There, I come upon a stone coffin that is smooth and without ornament. The name chiseled upon it, although eroded, in part, is still legible: Rachel Farraday. Beneath it a koan is written which I recognize but have never understood.

> *Seeing forms with the whole body and mind,*
> *hearing sounds with the whole body and mind,*
> *one understands them intimately;*
> *Yet it is not like a mirror with reflections,*
> *nor like water under the moon —*
> *when one side is realized, the other side is*
> *dark.*
>
> *— Koun Ejo*

Standing in that house of the dead, surrounded by gloom and silence, the meaning of this paradox whispers to me. Words are inadequate to describe what I mean. All I can say is that for a single moment I experience the difference between hearing laughter and being laughter.

Chapter Ten

FOR TWO WEEKS AFTER THE reading of Odeil's will, I neither heard from, nor saw, Christian de Hess. According to Mrs. de Toi, when at last he did make his appearance, he arrived at midnight during an evening harried by storms. As she described it, she'd been in the kitchen lingering over a cup of tea when there was a drumming at the front door. Filled with dread, she'd hurried to answer it, fearing some new mishap had befallen—for she could think of no other reason that someone should be demanding entry at such a late hour. What she'd found on the threshold was a spectral figured, draped in a dark cloak and wearing a large hat that shadowed the face. Her inclination had been to slam the door and shut the apparition out, but it waltzed into the foyer before she could react.

"Don't you recognize me, Nana?" The prodigal had removed his hat to reveal a crown of golden curls.

Mrs. de Toi had clapped her hands, delighted to see him, and then started her gentle scolding. Where had he been all this time? Why hadn't he written or telephoned?

"Were you worried about me?" He'd twirled in place to allow her to get a good look at him. "As you see, I am in one piece."

"Yes, yes, but there's been no preparation," she'd told him. "Your old room's not ready…" As she'd stared into those cornflower blue eyes of his, she had been able to see how tired he was. "And you've not been caring for yourself. You're so thin."

"You always say that," he'd laughed. Next, he'd asked for a robe of some kind so that he could remove his wet clothes.

Mrs. de Toi had looked around. "But where is your luggage? Is it in the car?"

When he'd told her he'd walked from the train station, a journey of two miles, her hands had flown her cheeks. "Walked? On a night like this?"

She hadn't waited for an answer but had busied herself by removing his outer garments. "You could have been struck by lightning or fallen into a ditch."

With his cloak and hat left to drip on a coat rack, she'd led him to the kitchen where a fire was burning. There, she'd prepared a hot toddy for him and hurried up the stairs to make up the bed in his old room.

By the time she'd returned, he'd been looking less pale but still tired. She'd handed him an old robe of hers and, certain that what he needed most was rest, she'd bitten off her questions and bid him good night deciding there would be time enough to hear his story later.

The next morning, having been informed by Kathrine that breakfast was being served in the dining room, I entered and was surprised to discover two places had been set...one of them had a soiled napkin lying beside it. Mrs. de Toi stood ready to acquaint me with the events of the previous night and, when I'd heard everything, she added that Monsieur de Hess and Mathiam had left in the gardener's truck to retrieve the luggage that had been left behind at the train station.

In the gray light that filtered through the windows, I sat alone, consuming fresh muffins and strawberry jam, and contemplating how best to greet my new partner. Our previous encounter had left me with two minds. I was aware he thought of me as an interloper and, to some degree, I understood his feelings. Perhaps, he'd been under the illusion the property might go to Mrs. de Toi, someone over whom he would have great influence. If so, then I could understand his disappointment. But being of sound mind, Odeil was free to dispose of her property however she chose and she'd chosen me. My obligation was to carry out her wishes and if he thought otherwise, I would have to prove him wrong. But how to do so when one had a volatile temperament like his was the question.

Naturally, I had no wish to engage in a power struggle if it could be avoided and over coffee and eggs, I considered the matter, factoring in the possibility he might still be addicted. If so, that would pose a significant complication. Time, however, was the only way to make that assessment. My best course was to treat him with good will and see how he responded. In the meantime, I would set about my task of sorting through Odeil's personal effects.

As it was the weekend, Kathrine's sister, Lucille Bevard, was waiting for me in the foyer. I'd asked her to assist me in my task, wanting to spare Mrs. de Toi the heartbreak of that responsibility.

Lucille was no more than eighteen, I would guess, slim, with dishwater blonde hair and a smile that brightened her otherwise pallid complexion. To say she was excited to find herself in such luxurious surroundings was an understatement. As we walked toward the stairs, she pointed to objects of interest as if we were tourists. "Look, Mademoiselle, is that jardinière with the hand painted flowers not beautiful?" Or, "Look that at that portrait overhead. The pearls are so real. I long to paint like that."

When I inquired if she had an interest in art, she admitted she dabbled in water color.

"At school, my teacher encourages me and says I have talent. But there is no money to further my studies. I must work to help the family."

She looked so forlorn, I felt obliged to encourage her in some way. "I'd like to see your paintings, if you'd allow it."

The girl's face brightened. "Would you look at them, Mademoiselle Farraday? That would be wonderful. Perhaps you could give me some pointers."

I shook my head as I smiled at her. "No, no. I've no talent. But I admire those who do."

By now we'd entered Odeil's capacious rooms, which consisted of a sitting area, a bedroom and a dressing area. The girl's eyes sparkled as she gazed at the opulence around her.

"Oh, to live in such a place. I would die. I would absolutely die."

"That would be a waste," I laughed.

Our task that day was to begin sorting through Odeil's wardrobe to determine what should be stored in the attic and what might be given to charity. As we began our work, Lucille chattered away happily, unaware that, for me, the task was difficult.

"I like all the impressionists," she said, continuing with her interest in art. "Van Gogh is wonderful. But Monet is my favorite; his scenic gardens, his water lilies… Who do you like best, Mademoiselle?"

I admitted I, too, was fond of the impressionists but kept a place in my heart for the expressionists, as well; Edvard Munch, in particular. When I mentioned his name, the girl squealed and clasped her hands to her bosom.

"Me, also." 'The Scream.' Doesn't it send shivers down your spine?"

Not waiting for my answer, she continued to prattle about other expressionists she favored, so that holding up my end of the conversation took little effort. As we continued to work, I had the luxury of observing how different Lucille was from her sister. The younger girl was exuberant, like the fizz in champagne, while Kathrine kept herself to herself, and seemed to view the world through the narrowed eyes of a miser. That they were related at all struck me as amazing.

What caused me to laugh outright was the way Lucille would pet each garment as she lowered it into one of several boxes, treating each as if it were a furry animal.

"Oh, Mademoiselle, look at this one." She almost purred as she showed me the diaphanous gown she'd pulled from the closet.

Seeing it, my heart sank. It seemed only days ago that Odeil had waltzed into the library wearing it, twirling in full circles while the gown floated around her like gossamer wings. Her smile, her pleasure in the cloth's airy lightness, was a memory that brought a mist to my eyes.

Lucille looked stricken. "Mademoiselle, have I said something wrong?"

I shook my head, struggling to regain myself. "It is a lovely dress. Rather like a Monet painting. Why don't you keep it, Lucille? I've no use for it."

"Keep it? For myself?" The girl's eyes grew wide. "Do you mean it?"

"Of course," I said, wiping away a tear. "Madame de Villiers was taller than you but otherwise, it should fit."

"Oh, I'll make it fit," the girl promised, her eyes shining. She held the gown in front of her and executed a pirouette. "See how it floats?" She was looking down as the colors swirled around her. "Like a cloud. But are you certain, Mademoiselle? This dress would look beautiful on you."

"No. I want you to have it. Take it, please."

Lucille needed no further coaxing. She laid the garment on one of the nearby chairs where she could keep her eyes on it throughout the morning.

By noon, although we'd worked with diligence, the closet — comprised of three walls of clothing — seemed barely touched. The racks still bowed with outfits and we had yet to examine the accessories drawers or the numerous shoe boxes.

Lucille's determination to fondle each gown was one reason we made little progress, but my indecision about what to store and what to give away was another. At heart, I didn't want to see the room emptied. That would be too final.

"Why not keep some of these beautiful things for yourself, Mademoiselle? Or, at least, leave them where they are. Dresses like these should be worn, not stored in the attic where they'll grow moldy." Lucille laid two of the evening gowns across Odeil's bed — one a black velvet and the other a red satin. "You would look wonderful in these."

I knew she meant well but the suggestion brought a frown to my face. For me to wear Odeil's clothes struck me as an affront to her. These belongings were too personal. By wearing them, I'd deface her memory. I was shaking my head at Lucille's suggestion when I was aware of someone approaching the room.

"I happen to agree with the girl. You'd look wonderful in either one of those dresses."

Startled, I looked up to see Christian de Hess leaning against the open door. He didn't wait for an invitation to enter but took possession of the space with his presence. Feeling shy, Lucille excused herself to help prepare lunch in the kitchen. In her haste, she'd left the gossamer dress behind on its chair and this he tossed upon the bed in order to sit down.

"You look upset. May I be of help? I like nothing so much as to come to the aid of a beautiful damsel."

I turned my back on him and continued my sorting. "I understand you arrived last night," I said, tossing the remark over my shoulder. "If you'd have given us the least warning, we'd have made arrangements to meet you at the station. Or do you delight in making an entrance?"

A ripple of laughter came from behind. "I seem to have made a habit of that, haven't I? Perhaps, you're right. Perhaps, I do have a flare for the dramatic. And I'm guessing that you are one given to frankness. Am I right?"

"I respect honesty, if that's what you mean? I turned 'round to give him a pointed look.

Instantly, he slapped his hand across his heart. "A woman both honest and fair. What would Hamlet make of it, I wonder?"

"I assure you, I neither know nor care."

Irritated by his banter, I prepared to leave the room, but he took hold of my arm. "Don't judge me too harshly, Mademoiselle Farraday. Even a scoundrel can reform if he has the right inspiration. Will you sit for me?'

"What?"

"I wish to paint you. I heard a little of your conversation with the maid as you came up the stairs. I'm fairly good at portraits, you know. I'd like to impress you…or capture you, at least."

"I'm afraid I'm not easy to capture, Monsieur." I shrugged free of his grip and glared down at where he sat in his chair. "I'm inclined to fidget."

"Really? Then I must insist on trying. I enjoy a challenge."

"Nonetheless, I must decline."

"But why? I thought women loved to have their portraits painted."

"I don't happen to be one of them."

"Do you doubt my talent?"

"How could I? I know nothing about you."

"Then put me to the test. You'll discover I'm no fraud."

"I never said you were."

He rose, and as he peered into my eyes, his lips curved in a wicked smile. "Come, now. You said you were honest. Admit my dear cousin has left you with...how shall I put it...some impressions?"

"Odeil de Villiers had a sweet nature—"

"Yes, yes. I know." A well-manicured hand waved my remark away as if it were a pesky gnat. "But that fails to answer my question. She must have said something about me. She made you her heir, after all."

My cheeks grew warm under his intense appraisal and I felt the need to bring this man barring my way down a peg or two. "I regret to inform you, Monsieur, your cousin hardly mentioned you, at all."

"Call me Christian, please," he said as he gave me a second wicked smile. "And I shall address you as Rachel, a beautiful appellation worthy of its owner."

"Perhaps, when you get to know me better you'll think otherwise. Now, if you'll step aside, I'm needed downstairs."

"I will if you promise to keep an open mind about me. Is that possible?"

"Of course."

His cornflower blue eyes softened. "And you will pose for me. I'm certain of it."

He stepped aside and I escaped from the room, annoyed by the giddiness that had come over me.

Chapter Eleven

THE NEXT DAY WAS CLEAR so, after a breakfast where Christian badgered me to sit for him, we agreed to meet on the terrace that overlooked the rose garden. He wanted a natural light in which to begin my portrait. I was so nervous about the sitting, I ran to my room to consider what to wear and how to arrange my hair. Lucille followed and made a few suggestions, but in the end I dressed sensibly, donning tweed skirt and white, cable knit cardigan. My hair was confined to a ponytail and as to makeup, I wore little.

If the artist was disappointed by my preparations, he gave no sign of it as he led me to one of the wrought iron chairs. Next, he situated himself before his easel and asked me to strike a pose. When I looked bewildered, he made a few suggestions. One of them was that I free my hair and let it hang loosely about my shoulders.

"Much better," he asserted, when the deed was done. "Now, turn a bit to the left...no, not that much. Yes, but tilt the chin a little, as though you're looking into the distance."

A few more minutes were spent experimenting with the correct angle before he found one to his liking. After that, like the caryatids, my movement was restricted.

Becoming the object of such close scrutiny was unnerving, even though Christian set about his work in earnest and without comment. His eyes crinkled as they skipped from his canvas to his subject and back again. Sometimes he erased a line but more often, he added new ones.

His intensity was robust and allowed me the leisure to study the artist to the same degree he was studying me. As I did so, I was struck by the fragile, almost feminine aspect of his features. The delicate scale of his bone structure and the pallor of his complexion created this impression that was augmented, too, by his manner and the graceful sweep of his hands. All, and each of these aspects, hinted to a degree of vulnerability, an orphan's defenselessness, if you will, which helped me to understand Mrs. de Toi's fierce protection of him.

We'd been working for a couple of hours when the housekeeper appeared, carrying her ubiquitous tray with its mounds of pastries and steaming mugs that, on this occasion, contained cocoa. She'd been right to suppose the breeze had turned cold.

Christian seemed as eager for a break as I. He laid down his brush and rubbed his hands together as if they'd grown numb. "It's going slowly," he admitted as he examined his canvas. "But it's a good start."

I asked to see what he'd done, but he threw a cloth over the easel explaining that, as yet, he'd barely laid down the basic composition. "I confess, I'm finding you a challenge," he said as he gave me a wry smile. He handed me a mug, which I was glad to accept.

"A challenge? Is my face so strange?"

He laughed outright. "No. You have a beautiful face and you know it. I'm talking about the spirit behind that placid expression. That's what I want to capture."

"You flatter me by supposing I'm a mystery."

"Indeed, you are. I fear I may need a lifetime of sittings to explore your complexity."

"And as people can change, you might never finish."

"That's true. Of course, there's another question that might be asked: how much do you know about yourself?"

"Does anyone ever truly understand themselves?"

We were standing side-by-side, gazing out across the barren rose garden, so it was easy to let a moment of silence pass between us. When Christian spoke again, it was to offer another question. "Do you think you'll be happy here, now that Odeil's gone?"

Fearing his off-handed remark had a pointed meaning, I stiffened.

"I've no thought of leaving, if that's what you imagine. Of course, I'll miss Odeil but I think of the chateau as my home, now. There's no one waiting for me back in San Francisco."

"Not even a boyfriend?" Christian peered at me from the corner of his eye, his eyebrows lifted.

Was that what he wanted to know? Was he wondering about my ties back home? I told him no one was waiting for me, and even allowed myself to feel a little flattered by his question.

"Have you any doubts about your living here with me? I mean, I didn't make a good first impression, did I?"

"I'm not completely without understanding," I assured him. "You were in a state of shock. Anyone could see that."

The man beside me shook his head. "No, I won't allow you to absolve me with that chestnut. Let's not pretend I was grieving. If we're going to become friends, we must be honest with one another."

"I wasn't thinking of Odeil's death," I corrected him. "I was thinking how you must have felt when you learned her share of the estate had come to me. You must have thought someone else—Mrs. de Toi, perhaps—might have inherited...someone you knew, at least."

Christian's laugh conceded the point. "Yes, I was stunned; it's true. My plans were to offer Mrs. de Toi a buyout. But I underestimated my dear cousin. She was always one to surprise..."

"Not unpleasantly, in my case, I hope."

"No, of course, not."

"How do you account for the animosity between you? Was it a dramatic outburst or years of wearing one another's patience thin?"

Christian looked at me as if he couldn't believe his ears. "Good God! Isn't it obvious? She locked me away, had me declared incompetent. How would you feel if someone deprived you of freedom?"

"But if she thought it was for you own good—"

"Oh, yes." Christian laughed bitterly. "What else *could* she say? Simply admit she wanted me out of her life? And the lengths she took to do it. Have you any idea, what it's like to live under lock and key? To be unable to make even the most elemental choices: whether to sleep or eat or bathe? *Nothing* was under my control. My life was reduced to the earliest stages of infancy. If anything, she confined me to an asylum, not for my protection, but to drive me mad."

"It wasn't an asylum. It was a hospital."

"What's the difference if you aren't free?"

"Then you don't agree you needed help? What about Mrs. de Toi and Mathiam? They said–"

"Oh, yes, I know how she manipulated them. Lots of people my age experiment with drugs. That doesn't make them addicts. That doesn't justify having them locked away." Christian ran his fingers through his hair to register his frustration. Given his agitation, I should have let the matter drop, but I needed to explore the depth of his wound.

"She also said something about…poison."

He threw back his head. "My God! She painted quite a picture of me, didn't she? Well, I can't explain what happened. I was affected, too. I don't suppose she told you that."

"As a matter of fact–"

"I don't care what she said," he snarled, losing control of his temper. "Believe me, Rachel, I was not the one who was mental. If she could have seen me charged with attempted murder, she'd have done it without batting an eye. You call that sane? And failing that, she chose the sanatorium. Either way, she could be rid of me. I've no doubt she managed to convince herself, and others, she was being charitable. That's the extent of her derangement. But if you want to know what I think, I think *she* did the poisoning."

"That's ridiculous. Why would she poison herself? She wasn't the least bit suicidal."

"I didn't mean suicide. It was a set up so she could be rid of me. I promise you, she'd go to any lengths to keep the chateau under her control. By rights, she always felt it should be hers and hers alone."

"I don't believe you. She'd never be capable of such thoughts."

Seeing my opposition, Christian's words became measured. "I have no proof, of course. It's all speculation. Let's just say she was always a better chess player than I was. Somehow, she managed to keep control of the chateau and I found myself locked away in a sanatorium."

His voice broke over his words so that I had no doubt he believed what he was saying, whether it was delusion or not. Odeil, too, had spoken with similar passion of the rights and wrongs of their relationship. I had no way of knowing which of them was telling the truth.

"At least give me the benefit of the doubt, Rachel." Christian took hold of my shoulders, forcing me to look at him. "I can prove myself to you, if you'll let me. A chance, that's all I want."

Whether it was reflex or fear, I pulled away from him and saw disappointment immediately fog his eyes.

"You aren't afraid of me, are you? She hasn't twisted your thinking to that extent, has she? I've no wish to harm anyone. Ask Mrs. de Toi...or Mathiam. They'll tell you I'm not capable of violence. How long have you been here? Five months? Six? How well did you know her? Why did she hire you all the way from the United States? She had to be up to something."

"Y-you won't help your case by attacking her."

Christian sensed I *was* hiding something. "How did she get you to come here, Rachel? What did she tell you?"

"She wanted to write a history of the chateau..."

His laughter shattered my confidence. "She hired a total stranger from halfway around the globe? That's an absurd story on the face of it. Did you never question the fact? Or maybe you already knew the reason. Maybe that's why she made you her heir. There's some connection between you. What is there you aren't telling me, Rachel?"

I didn't know whether to feel guilty or furious that he would accuse me of colluding with Odeil, although in a way, it was true. I was keeping her secret and was no longer certain whether I was doing it to protect her...or me. My only recourse was to strike back.

"Don't try to pretend you've no idea why Mrs. de Toi didn't become heir to the estate. You said it yourself. She knew your nanny would be putty in your hands. Heaven knows you've embroiled the poor woman in enough of your schemes–"

"Schemes? What are you talking about?"

"Don't pretend you didn't get her to steal for you."

Christian's jaw dropped, a gesture as good as a confession. "Odeil knew that?"

"She did, but never confronted her. Apparently, your cousin cared more for your nanny's feelings than you did. She protected the woman while you used her."

Still appearing shaken, Christian allowed his gaze to leave me and wander out over the rolling hills. "Well, I won't deny it," he said, at last. "Why shouldn't I take what's mine?"

"Half yours."

"Oh, for God's sake, don't be such a purist. I needed the money. How else was I to keep my sanity in that institution?"

"You talk as if it were a prison. Apparently, you could have walked away anytime. You did so to be here for the reading of the will."

"Walk away?" His blue eyes flashed in my direction. "And do what? Return here? Odeil would have thrown me out. What's more, as my guardian she had complete control of my money. I had to steal, don't you see? How else was I to live? How else was I to make life bearable?"

"You certainly convinced Mrs. de Toi of that."

"All right, yes! Yes, I used her. You've made your point. But I was desperate–"

"For what, I wonder."

Christian tossed me another withering glance. "My God, you sound just like Odeil. She's bewitched you."

"Maybe, she has," I shrugged. "But, at least, I don't hate you. It's just that I don't trust you, either."

"Then tell me what to do. How am I to gain your trust?"

Surprised by the sincerity of his expression, I didn't know how to respond. My answer was banal. "I guess we shouldn't lie to one another."

"But I haven't lied. That's what you don't see. If you can't trust me, how can we work together? This partnership can't work without trust. We should dissolve it. Allow me to buy you out."

When I started to argue, he overrode my objections. "Listen to me for a moment. You've no ties here. With the money from the sale you could go wherever you liked. You'd be free of me and this place. It won't be difficult for me to raise the money, if that's what you think. I have friends who have offered to lend me the sum before, but Odeil wouldn't hear of it. I can understand that. She grew up here."

"But she wanted to turn the chateau into a guest house and—"

"Guest house?" Christian looked incredulous. "Good God, no! The last thing I'd want is tourists traipsing about the place."

"And where would you get the money to maintain the estate and pay back your friends' loans?"

"You needn't concern yourself with that, Rachel. Besides, why should you care? You'll be living thousands of miles away, like a queen, in San Francisco."

"I'd never go back there."

"Well then, wherever you liked. The world's your oyster."

"You do understand." As I spoke, I could hear my voice harden. "Or maybe you weren't listening during the reading of the will: to inherit, I have to live here and turn the place into a business."

My partner looked non-pulsed for a moment, then waived the objection away. "There are always loopholes, my dear. Allow my friends to consult with their attorneys. I'm sure there's a solution."

When I refused his request, he looked disappointed. "I won't allow this place to become a tourist attraction, I promise you."

"As the majority interest holder, I don't see how you can stop me."

The eyes peering down at me narrowed. A mean smile spread across his face.

"Then it seems, my dear Rachel, we are stuck with one another…for the time being."

* * *

An uneasy truce settled between us and, for the next few days, I continued to sit for Christian on the terrace. The weather was unreliable and sometimes gusts of wind came 'round the corner of the building, upending the easel and sending preliminary sketches flying so that we had to chase them. These skirmishes served to ease the tension between us and sometimes ended with laughter.

Of course, there was no further discussion about the sale of the chateau or converting it to a tourist spot. As to the latter, the weather put that project on hold. With winter in the wings, now was not the time to wrangle about such things. Now was the time for warm fires, good books and comfort food. Frankly, I looked forward to a period of enforced hibernation and hoped Christian did as well, as it might give us time to get to know one another better.

Such hopes were dashed on the fourth day of the sittings. Mrs. de Toi arrived, as usual, with our morning tea and, after she'd set the tray on the table, she paused to peer over Christian's shoulder. Stepping aside, he allowed her a full view of the painting as if eager to gauge her reaction.

"It's not finished, of course, but I think it's a good likeness," he said as he stood wiping his brush with a rag.

Whatever she saw, Mrs. de Toi appeared to be surprised...so much so that I asked if I could look, as well. Christian consented, so I joined the housekeeper. When I saw what he had done, my reaction was equally stupefied.

Certainly, the artist had an eye for color, but his combinations were untamed and almost hallucinatory. He'd applied his paint in thick wedges, more like a pallet knife rather than a brush so that the effect was not only wild but seemed to be full of anger. The features, too, appeared distorted. I doubted anyone viewing the canvas would recognize I was the model even if I was posed beside it.

"That's Odeil, that is," Mrs. de Toi said as she pointed her finger at the image's cat's eyes. "But she looks demented, doesn't she? I've never see her look that way. Never in all her life. What made you paint her like that?"

The moment he heard her, Christian bent forward to look closely at his canvas. His expression went by stages from bewilderment to rage. It was like watching an eclipse blacken the sun. At the peak of his emotion, he knocked the canvas to the ground and stomped on it with his heel, smearing the paint and breaking the frame.

Once his work was destroyed, he stormed away from the terrace without a word, his features still distorted by his anger. The moment we were alone, the housekeeper's shoulders began to quake. Taking pity on the woman, I led her to one of the wrought iron chairs and forced her to sit down. Next, I poured out a cup of tea with plenty of milk and sugar and handed it to her.

"It's not your fault, Mrs. de Toi. I saw the resemblance and would probably have said something if you hadn't. He shouldn't have bolted off in that way. You said nothing wrong."

I pulled up a chair beside her and held her hand as she started to whimper, "I meant no harm, but anyone could see the resemblance…"

"That's right. And you know Christian—by lunch time, he'll have calmed himself and come looking to apologize. You see if he doesn't."

The older woman wiped her eyes with the handkerchief from her apron. "Maybe," she answered doubtfully. "But he's been so impatient, of late. That place he's been in hasn't done him much good. If anything, he's worse. He's like a caged animal, he is. I just don't know what he's thinking anymore. The other day he said he thought Mathiam and I should go away. 'Take our well-deserved rest,' he said."

"Was he angry?"

"No, as gentle as a hare, like he was pleading with me. I just don't understand. We're not old, Mathiam and me. We've got a few good years left in us. Why would he want us to leave?"

"I don't know, but you can put that idea out of your head. You're not going anywhere. I'll talk to him."

"Oh no, Mademoiselle, don't do that." The housekeeper looked affrighted. "He'd only get worse if he thought I was talking behind his back. Maybe he'll cheer up when he has his party."

"Party? What party?"

The housekeeper looked at me wide-eyed. "Why, hasn't he told you? Next Saturday he turns twenty-five. That's when he comes into his money. He's invited a few friends for dinner to celebrate. I know he means for you to come."

"He's said nothing to me. Perhaps he's forgotten."

"Oh, I doubt that. Maybe he's waiting for the right moment. Believe it or not, he can be shy, sometimes."

When I snuffled my disbelief, Mrs. de Toi rushed to reassure me. "It's true. A beautiful girl like you...he's attracted to you. I can tell. That always complicates things, doesn't it?"

"I suspect you're match-making, Mrs. de Toi," I said, patting her hand a second time. "I get no sense of his interest in me. He offered to buy me out the other day. Does that sound like someone with an interest?"

"You didn't listen, did you?"

"No, I didn't."

The housekeep rose to her feet. "Good. Mathiam and I want you with us. Never mind what Christian says." She picked up the tray— that had hardly been touched—but before returning to the kitchen, she paused to cast me an earnest gaze.

"I think you'll be a good influence on him, Mademoiselle, if you'll have the patience. I really do."

I offered a smile in return for her good will. "I hope so, Mrs. de Toi. I'll try."

Chapter Twelve

THE NIGHT OF THE BIRTHDAY party arrived with great anticipation. By then, Christian had more than made amends for
destroying the portrait. I'd been invited to his party and he had
apologized to Mrs. de Toi and me on so many occasions that we'd
forbidden him to raise the subject again. As to the suggestion of
any future sittings, the artist remained mum and I was happy to
be free of the obligation.

In the interim, I used the time to continue my research on
the history of the chateau, although I realized that producing a
work had never been Odeil's object. Still, the project struck me as
a good one, particularly as I remained curious about the underground passages. It might be an angle to exploit, although I admit
my initial experience in them had been so unnerving I continued
to avoid the area...for the present.

About my work, I said nothing. Whether or not Christian knew
of the tunnels, I didn't know but if Mathiam had talked about
them with Odeil, it would follow he might have also said something to her cousin. Still, that had been so long ago and Christian
had been so young, he may have forgotten. Until I'd worked out
my ideas fully, I saw no reason to broach the subject. In any case,
the real point of my research was to distract me from thoughts
about Odeil and the pain of her sudden death. To be honest, I
looked forward to the party as another diversion.

At seven in the evening, I left my studies in the library and climbed the marble stairs, headed for Odeil's apartment. I'd refused Mrs. de Toi's suggestion that I move into Madame's rooms even though they were in a quiet area of the chateau. That night, however, I had a purpose for being there.

As I entered, the scent of Cabochard perfume filled my nostrils, a ghostly reminder that I was a trespasser. Not surprisingly, I was hesitant as I proceeded into the dressing area and slid back one of the glass panels that hid a voluminous wardrobe. Lucille and I had made little progress in our sorting. Most of the gowns continued to hang in their customary place like multicolored Christmas ornaments.

"Oh, are they not beautiful?" The maid came up behind me and I jumped. Even though I'd arranged for her to help me select an outfit for the evening's formal occasion, her sudden presence still surprised me.

"Mademoiselle is as nervous as a kitten," she said as she pulled back another of the mirrored panels of the closet and removed three gowns from their hangers. She spread them across the bed for me to consider.

The blue sapphire crepe and the black velvet dresses had always been her favorites whenever we went through Odell's wardrobe; but this time she added a red, satin gown, a floor length empire, with a square neck and long sleeves.

"The black gown is very chic," she said, her fingers tracing the shape of the plunging neckline. "And the crepe clings to the body like a glove. But for tonight, the red seems the most elegant, and the color will compliment your hair and dark eyes." That said, she lifted the black gown from the bed and held it in front of her as if reconsidering. "Ah, but you would look so fetching in this."

Lucille, I feared, was going to be of little help. She loved every gown she saw. Still, I agreed with her selections, so when she headed to the closet to forage for more, I told her I'd settle on one of the three she'd already laid out. In the end, I chose the red satin so like the color of the dying sun.

Lucille clapped her hands with approval as I stood before a mirror surveying myself with the gown held up against me.

Finally, I slipped it on, and was gratified to discover it was a perfect fit, as though it had been tailored for me. Truth to tell, I felt wonderful in it.

Lucille walked a circle around me, looking for defects. Finding none, she considered next how I should wear my hair. "You have such a lovely, swan-like neck. I suggest a chignon to set it off." She lifted my hair from behind, and I had to agree with her suggestion.

When the foyer clock finally struck nine, I descended the stairs, feeling a little like Cinderella, nervous and excited, as I prepared to join the company gathered in the dining room. Approaching the double oak doors, I could hear the voices of our guests. Who I would find behind them remained a mystery. Still, there was no mistaking the sounds of camaraderie.

Drawing a deep breath, I entered.

"Ah, here she is at last." Christian, looking both relieved and impatient, leapt up from his seat and hurried to my side. "Gentlemen," he announced in a voice that rose above the others, "I have the honor to present my new friend and partner, Mademoiselle Rachel Farraday."

Everyone in the room rose at once and stood at attention, time enough for me to count a gathering of seven men...all of whom were wearing black masks resembling the visors of bandits. By now, Christian had taken me by the hand and was leading me toward the remaining empty chair to the left of his place at the head of the table. "You must excuse this unusual dress convention, my dear. Some of my colleagues are, how shall I say it...here unofficially? Their presence would be of great interest to certain people so their identities must be protected. But I'll say no more of that. Tonight we celebrate my freedom."

"Hear, hear." A number of voices shouted as wine glasses were lifted.

I confess to feeling ill at ease. How else can I describe being the only woman in a room of masked men, a few, at least, who were fugitives of some kind? As he helped me into my chair, Christian whispered that he hoped I would do or say nothing to embarrass his guests. I thought the remark uncalled for, if not ironic. I was not someone who needed to hide *my* identity.

"They are an odd crew," he said as he sat down beside me. "But they have a certain loyalty to me."

I made no reply but placed my napkin across my lap and prayed the evening would hold no further surprises. Certainly, it began conventionally enough with a number of toasts being made in honor of the host on the advent of his birthday. The accolades were as plentiful as was the amount of wine being imbibed. On this evening, Mathiam was nowhere in sight. The two attendants, also in masks, were unknown to me. Perhaps they'd come up from the village for the evening, I didn't know. I did hope I could rely upon Mrs. de Toi being in the kitchen.

When the first course appeared, a leek soup, served with butter rolls, I took heart. The food looked edible but I soon observed the service was flawed. In fact, the waiters seemed to have little acquaintance with their duties. Not only was their presentation uneven, serving right to left or left to right as they chose, but they spilled so much liquid on the table that in a matter of minutes the white linen was covered in blotches. Worse, one server tossed a dinner roll on my plate with his bare hands having dropped and retrieved it from the floor.

Christian looked amused, but I was not. These mishaps were too egregious to be explained as amateur bungling. Clearly, the scene was staged tomfoolery, but for whose benefit—Christian's or mine? I can only admit that reticence, rather that courtesy, prompted me to endure and make the best of it.

Turning to make polite conversation with the guest to my left, a humpbacked man who'd spent a good part of the meal smacking his lips as if it were a form of applause, I was met by a stare that was alarmingly vacant.

"Have you known Christian long?" I began.

The man answered nothing. Christian was the one to speak for him.

"Chanson has no tongue, Rachel. It was cut out after the war by his brother and a few of his compatriots. You see, my friend, here, was accused of spying for the Germans. They had no proof, of course; but they thought punishment was due. Naturally, Chanson took umbrage with their decision and, after they'd done their worst, he hunted them down and strangled each man with his bare hands. Isn't that so, my good fellow?"

The man who was stuffing a dinner roll into his mouth managed a snicker. The memory of his murders seemed to fill him with delight.

Upon hearing the story, I let out a shudder. Whether this was a game or not, I'd had enough and would have risen had not Christian anticipated my action and taken hold of my arm.

"I hope you're not planning on running away so early, dear Rachel. The evening is young and we've not yet had our entertainment." He smiled at the humpback beside me. "Chanson, a preview, if you please."

At this suggestion, the other guests broke into applause and I was obliged to remain in my chair while the humpback bent down to retrieve a bow and a battered violin from beneath the table. Next, he rose and placed the instrument under his chin. The others in the room seemed to wait breathlessly, so I dared to hope the evening might take a turn for the better. Perhaps this loathsome man was the maestro to his instrument, a savant who, despite his apparent madness, had within him a touch of the divine?

I waited with anticipation as he began to draw his bow across the strings, but what little hope I'd nurtured soon died. What I heard was not music but something akin to the groans and screams that might escape from an abattoir, frightening to say the least. The cacophony persisted for several minutes and was followed by an outburst of applause and calls of, "Encore! Encore!"

Hearing them, the little man took up his tortured instrument a second time, but instead of drawing the bow across the strings, he plucked them to produce discordant sounds which left me wishing I was deaf. When he had finished, the applause was again thunderous but, mercifully, the performer returned to his seat and resumed slurping his soup, a sound far more pleasing than those he'd made on his musical instrument.

If I thought the time was ripe to make my escape, however, I was mistaken, for a troop of clowns rushed in after the violin performance. They were dressed in various forms of motley and their sole purpose, as far as I could see, was to insult the guests with every obscene gesture known to man. There was much scratching of private parts, lewd gestures and contortions which left no doubt as to their lascivious nature. When one of the performers attempted to stick his tongue in my ear, I'd had enough. Christian's attempt to detain me was useless against my anger. I broke free and stormed from the room.

As I slammed the double doors behind me, laughter, and a quantity of shoes—or bread rolls—thumped helplessly at my back. My humiliation was complete. I ran up the stairs to my rooms and threw myself across the bed. The purpose of the party had been made all too clear. Christian had fired his first salvo across my bow. If I would not sell him the chateau, he would use every means at his disposal to drive me away.

I dissolved into tears, realizing that if I chose to fight, the next move was mine.

Much of the night I spent tossing and turning. I admit the impulse to pack my bags and run away was overwhelming. How was I to carry on under these conditions? I had no authority to evict him, although he obviously had devised a cunning plan to evict me. Should I report what had happened to the police? If so, what was his crime? Spilled soup? Rude guests? Appealing to the authorities was not a solution. An alternative was to rail at him at breakfast. But what would that accomplish except to assure him he'd rattled me? Perhaps I should behave as although nothing untoward had happened and let him stew over what my next move would be?

But I had no next move. All I had was my anger.

In my present mood, Odeil came in for hard thoughts, as well. I understood now why she wanted to keep the chateau out of Christian's hands. He was not in his right mind. But she should never have plunged me into this struggle without my consent. Under the circumstance, I owed her no loyalty. It had never been my intention to make France my home. Why should I fight? Why shouldn't I seek some loophole and escape?

As to that, I had no answer for it was never a real consideration. A hardness was growing within me. Whether it was a protective response to defend me, or Mrs. de Toi and Mathiam, I didn't know, but I was determined that Christian would never have his way. Never!

I arose the next morning to the mantle clock chiming eight and in the same state of confusion as when I'd retired the previous night. I slipped on my dressing gown and, pulling a curtain aside, saw it was a fine day. The sun was everywhere in evidence. Hearing a rap at my door, I turned to see Lucille enter my rooms, bringing tea and a sweet roll. She set her tray on a table beside the hearth and lit the fire that had already been prepared. We both stood watching the flames grow with a steady energy.

"That must have been quite an affair last night, Mademoiselle Rachel. Mrs. de Toi said not to wake you, but I brought your tea, anyway. She's so busy with Kathrine downstairs. They found the dining room in a terrible state this morning. She blames herself for allowing Monsieur de Hess to send her off to the pictures with Mathiam last night. Now, she's paying for it. Down on her hands and knees, she is, scrubbing the floor and vowing never to leave the master in charge again. I've never seen her in such a temper. Still, if you had a good time…"

She drifted from the room with a cat-like smile, no doubt assuming I'd been a willing participant in the debacle.

Having eaten little the previous night, I was grateful for the tray Lucille had provided. I ate the roll and drank the tea pot dry. After that, I had no idea how to fill the rest of the day. I needed to be engaged in some activity to keep the memories of the birthday celebration at bay.

As it was Sunday, I decided to dress and walk to the church in Sainte Enimie. I wasn't looking for spiritual guidance, but I had heard the choir was superb and, in that tranquil setting, I hoped to be allowed to arrange my thoughts.

The winding path that led to the village was a distance of a mile and a half. On a pleasant morning such as this, I had no need to hurry. I would reach my destination in good time with enough leisure to spare, so I could enjoy the rural scenery along the way.

I made certain no one saw me leave and my walk, as I'd anticipated, was tranquil. The road meandered across cow fields and orchards. The trees were bare but arranged in rows like chess pieces so that one derived comfort from the sanity of imposed order. Overhead, the clouds were innocent white puffs without the menace of either snow or rain. Several times, I paused to enjoy the view but, eventually, I was near enough to the village to hear the church bell strike the hour.

St. Jude was a gray stone structure with a tower and narrow rows of leaded windows on either side. When I arrived, some of the villagers were milling on the lawn in front of the entrance, a few puffing their cigarettes before the service began. Others seemed to be engaged in friendly gossip, a bucolic scene worthy of a Gainsborough painting.

I threaded my way through the crowd with little recognition from anyone, and it was true—there were few in number whom I could count among my acquaintances. That's why I was surprised to hear my name called out.

The voice came from the vestibule. I drew closer and looked inside. Christian rose from the shadows to greet me.

Seeing him, I backed away, intending to retrace my steps all the way back to the chateau, if necessary; but he came down the stairs after me and took hold of my arm...although not roughly as he'd done the night before. This morning, he was gentle.

"Our place is at the front," he whispered, and guided me in the direction of the church. "I didn't expect to find you here, but I'm glad I did. After the service, we must talk." His tone was confidential, as if he were carrying a message across enemy lines.

As all eyes seemed to be fixed upon us, I followed his lead and sat in the pew where he directed. Sinking down beside me, his eyes focused upon the pulpit with all the insouciance of a choirboy. After that, the priest entered, attended by two altar boys.

Once the service began, I struggled to take no further notice of the man beside me, though, if I'm to be honest, my thoughts never left him.

What followed was a traditional mass where there was much liturgy and much kneeling, and sitting, and kneeling again. The choir, however, was all that I'd hoped for and, despite Christian's hypocritical taking of communion, I exited from the building feeling much improved; calm enough, in fact, to listen to whatever explanation might pour forth from my partner's perfidious lips.

Unfortunately, any apologies or explanation he planned to make had to be delayed by the numerous greetings he received from those around him. Even the priest seemed overjoyed to see him. The prodigal had returned...especially to the delight of several marriageable young ladies who fanned him with their fluttering lashes. I wondered how keen they would have been if they had suffered as I had the previous night.

Despite my cynicism, I found it difficult to discount the welcome he received among young and old. And he, in return, seemed pleased to see them. His eyes shone with delight and his smile appeared genuine.

Here was a person so different in aspect from the one I'd grown to dread that I could almost have convinced myself that the variance could only be explained by the existence of twins—one good and the other evil. This Jekyll and Hyde behavior was so marked that I wracked my brain to understand the cause. Was it drugs? An illness? Or did he simply delight in toying with people?

Eventually, Christian broke from his admirers and sauntered toward me, looking a bit sheepish. "Sorry about that."

"It's not your fault if you're popular with the locals."

"You seem surprised." When I said nothing, he hurried on, "Yes, of course, you would be after last night. I owe you an explanation—"

"Yes, you do. You must have known I would be offended, so what was your purpose? And who are Chanson and those other men, really? And why the masks?"

"I thought I'd explained that."

"You mean, they really are fugitives? From where? And why would you want to harbor them?"

Christian's gaze bounced around him—at the sky, the far horizon, even his shoes—but never into my eyes. "I can't explain here. Not properly. For the moment, just accept that I didn't mean for things to get so far out of hand. I suppose it was the drink."

"Oh no, you won't get off with that excuse. You weren't drunk. You were in complete charge of the evening." My voice must have risen because a few stragglers looked back in our direction.

"Let's talk about it in the car," Christian pleaded. He pointed to a red Karmann Ghia located in the church parking lot. Following him, I allowed myself to be bundled into the vehicle and remained silent while he backed it into the cobblestone street.

After that, he drove fast, covering the distance from the village to the chateau in so few minutes we had no time for conversation. As we pulled into the gravel driveway, Mrs. de Toi came out to greet us. She descended the steps hurriedly and pointed to a black sedan parked several feet ahead of us.

"You have a visitor," she informed Christian. "I put him in the solarium as he insisted upon waiting for you."

Christian was helping me emerge from the car when he heard her. "Did he give his name?"

"Yes. He said he was Abbas Afreet. Dr. Abbas Afreet."

Christian slammed the car door behind me. "How long has he been here?"

"A quarter of an hour, I'd say. He wouldn't tell me his business, only that he'd wait for you. I gave him a cup of tea and left him to amuse himself in the solarium where he'd be out of the way. There's so much cleaning up to do…"

"Yes, I've said I was sorry about that. I hope I don't have to spend the rest of the afternoon apologizing."

Mrs. de Toi's cheeks reddened but Christian didn't notice. His eyes were fixed on a bank of windows, but with the sun bouncing off the glass, it was impossible to see inside. As if forgetting the housekeeper and I were with him, he rushed up the front steps and entered the foyer.

I was not far behind and found him near the entrance, peering past the solarium door, which had been left ajar. The room faced the east corner of the chateau where it could catch the morning sun yet escape the afternoon heat. It was an airy space that accommodated a variety of horticultural species, including miniature fruit trees and delicate gardenias. A few ferns hung from the ceiling and one or two tall plants were scattered in pots along the floor, but for the most part, the vegetation had to be hardy as the staff was too busy to provide anything more than water and occasional nourishment.

From my vantage point, I had a good view of the man pacing inside, his hands locked behind his back. I'd guess he was in his early fifties; his dark hair and beard were flecked with gray, and he had an ample girth not entirely out of keeping with his short, stocky frame.

"Damn!" Christian muttered. Then he excused himself and left me to hurry in to his visitor. He was shaking the man's hand as he kicked the solarium door shut behind him.

Turning to Mrs. de Toi, I'd hoped for more enlightenment, but she shrugged helplessly. "I am ignorant, Mademoiselle. His name isn't one I've heard before. Yet, he made himself at home at once, examining the place as if he owned it. I do not think I like him much." She went to the hall table where the man had left his card. "See," she said, bringing it to me. "It says 'MD and PhD.' He's something more than a medical doctor."

I examined the card she'd placed in my hand. "He's a psychiatrist, by the look of it."

"Yes, but why is he here?" Mrs. de Toi blustered, staring at me with her eyebrows lifted.

"I've no idea." I handed the card back to her.

She took it gingerly, as if were a thistle that might sting, and returned it to where it had been left before she disappeared to the kitchen.

I was on the upstairs landing, on the way to my rooms, when I heard voices below. They were shouts, really, coming from the two men in the solarium. I paused, wondering what, if anything, I should do; but before I'd come to a decision, Christian shot from the room into the foyer and burst through the front door, which he left open. Next, the Karmann Ghia's engine sprang to life and the car peeled out of the driveway. My gaze returned to the solarium. Dr. Afreet stood in the open door, looking up at me.

He gave his shoulders a shrug. "I've made him angry. But what can I do, except my duty?"

I was too stunned to reply and he took advantage of the moment to step forward and introduce himself. "Please forgive me, Mademoiselle. I am Dr. Afreet...from the sanatorium...in Mende. You've heard of it? Place de la Déconvenue. Christian de Hess is my patient."

"Is he?" I couldn't help registering further surprise. "I assumed he'd been released."

"To my care," he corrected.

The man watched as I descended the stairs and came forward to introduce myself and shake his hand. I noticed he was shorter than I by about two inches and, like many men lacking in height, he carried himself like a rooster with his chest thrust forward. The confidence he exuded filled the room and I disliked him at once.

"Yes, you see, he is still under treatment but well enough to return to a normal setting. We were supposed to arrive together, but I am afraid he became impatient with the release procedures and, as his cousin had died, well..." Here the doctor raised his hands with palms toward the ceiling. "He simply stole away. Very like him. But I suppose you've noticed he is moody. Yes? Not taking his medications, I would suspect. I will soon put that right. Now, as it's been a long journey, I'm wondering, Mademoiselle Farraday, if you'd be so good as to show me to my room? And perhaps someone could see to my luggage. It's in the car."

His voice was assuming, which rankled me, so I made a point of appearing surprised. "You plan to stay with us, Monsieur? No one informed me. I regret no accommodation has been made."

"Then if you'd be so kind as to see to it now, if you please?"

"But—"

"I'm afraid I must insist, Mademoiselle. Otherwise, my patient and I must return to the sanatorium at once."

"That sounds very much like a threat, Dr. Afreet."

"No, not at all. A simple fact, only. If Christian is not taking his medication, well…" The doctor shrugged to suggest that he would not be responsible for what might happen.

"Are you insinuating he could become dangerous?"

"No, no, no. Mademoiselle has a vivid imagination. Would he have been considered for release if he were dangerous?"

"Then, what's the problem? I think I have a right to know as we are partners."

The man opposite me withdrew a gold watch from his suit pocket and looked at it. "Your claim is strong, Mademoiselle; but not strong enough to break the doctor-client privilege, I'm afraid. About his illness, I can say nothing except that I am needed here. Now, if you would make some accommodation for me, I would be most grateful."

He started to climb the stairs without invitation which forced me to respond. "Our staff is small this late in the season. If you'll return to the solarium, I'll see to your accommodations."

Dr. Afreet wrinkled his nose with displeasure. "That room is too cold. Perhaps some other room?"

"There's a fire in the library…"

The doctor stretched out an arm, inviting me to go ahead of him. "If you would be so kind as to lead the way?"

We were crossing the La Salle de Persephone when the man altered his steps to examine the caryatids which seemed to fascinate him. He stood before them for a minute or two, stroking his beard, appearing to admire the workmanship; or perhaps he was carried away by their ethereal siren song. Whatever possessed him, a distant look came into his eyes and, for a moment, he seemed to have forgotten I was in the room.

"The library is straight ahead, if you'd care to go there."

Hearing me, he swung 'round as if surprised by my voice. "Yes, yes. A fire would be most welcome. Please, lead on."

After I'd made him comfortable and was about to leave, he made yet another demand. "My room is to be near Christian's, Mademoiselle. I'd be grateful if you would see to it."

"As it happens, there is an adjoining suite next to his, but it's been shuttered for some time. Without a proper airing, it's likely to be a bit musty."

"Nevertheless, I insist. Those are the rooms I must have." The man's smile was affable but his manner made it clear he would tolerate no contradiction.

I found Kathrine crossing the foyer and informed her that a guest would be staying in the Blue rooms opposite mine and asked her to see to the linens immediately. For once, she didn't appear out of sorts when asked to extend herself. She even remarked, "Even though the Blue rooms overlook the garage, they have a lovely view of the hills and will be a restful place for the visitor."

Mrs. de Toi's response when she heard Dr. Afreet would be with us for an extended stay was different. "Who is this man, Mademoiselle? What has he to do with the master? Not something good, I think, otherwise Christian wouldn't have bounded off the way he did. Why was the poor boy so angry?"

As I had no answer to any of her questions, I advised her to be patient and to hope things would go well so that the doctor would not be with us long.

Hearing me, she sniffed and marched toward the kitchen leaving a trail of objections behind as if they were bread crumbs meant to lead me out of the forest. "He's up to no good, that one," was her last volley.

I was inclined to agree with her and had begun to regret I'd left him in the library where my research lay in an open folder on the desk. No doubt, the new arrival was making good use of his solitude and probably knew as much about my project as I did.

He did not disappoint. When I returned to announce his rooms would soon be ready, I found him pouring over my notes. He looked up without the least sign of embarrassment and told me I'd made a few math errors in my cost estimates. He advised me to get several bids before drawing any conclusions about expenses.

Annoyed, I tossed the folder into a desk drawer without comment. He saw my mood but mistook the reason. "If I could be of any help in these matters," he persisted, "I have had some experience."

"Thank you, no. I'm not very far along in my thinking." I pointed to one of the leather chairs. "Would you care to sit by the fire while you wait?"

For once, he did as I suggested.

"So, you have no idea how long you will be with us?" I said, taking the vacant one opposite him.

If my remark continued to sound rude, the man took no notice. He brushed a speck of lint from his suit and repeated his length of stay depended upon the progress of his patient.

"But surely, you have some idea how long that might be. He's been with us a number of days without mishap. If it's a matter of monitoring any medications, Mrs. de Toi can see to that. She used to be his nanny, you see."

Again, I was met with a condescending smile. "He needs more than prescriptions, Mademoiselle, but beyond that I am not at liberty to say."

"Am I to gather he still needs psychiatric supervision? If his condition is serious, I think I should know."

"Perhaps, Mademoiselle...in time. At the moment, I wish merely to assess his moods. You must not be alarmed by that. We all have moods, even I. The same is true for you, is it not?"

"I wouldn't equate a passing mood with aberrant behavior, especially if one needs the constant attention of a psychiatrist."

"You mean, you've never suffered a depression? Never even taken Valium?"

Although I thought it was none of his business, I answered truthfully. "When my parents died, I was given a prescription to help me sleep."

"That was not so long ago, I gather. You seem tense remembering. See how your hands clutch at the arms of your chair, Mademoiselle. A bird held in those hands would be crushed."

The truth of his observation caught me by surprise. I dropped the offending appendages into my lap, interlocking my fingers.

The doctor leaned forward to touch my hand. "Have I upset you? I do apologize. How recent was your loss, may I ask?"

"Two years ago. And I'm not upset."

"No? But the pain seems intense."

"You forget that a dear friend has died recently."

"Ah, yes. Madame de Villiers. I had forgotten…"

"Forgotten, Monsieur? That single event is the reason why you are here now."

"I mean, I did not stop to consider you might be close to her. But, of course, you were. She made you her heir. Why do you think she did that, Mademoiselle? You have been here how long? Six months?"

"I wasn't aware you were acquainted with the terms of her will. Did Christian tell you?"

"I believe he did say something in a letter. The bequest must be a curious one, even to you."

"It is. That's why I'm unable to satisfy your curiosity. If you require an answer, I'm afraid you'll have to cross the river Styx to find it. I can't help."

I had crossed my legs and was swinging my free foot with impatience. The doctor took notice. "You must forgive my curiosity. When faced with a puzzle, my inclination is to make every effort to solve it."

"As I said, I can't help you there."

"Ah, well," he sighed, hearing the finality in my voice. "Perhaps in the future, all will become clear."

He rose as if intending to stretch, and then held his hands behind his back as he perused a row of books nearby. From his expression, I could tell he found the selection wanting, but as the collection wasn't mine—well, only technically—I didn't care. What concerned me most was how soon this little tête-à-tête might end. I considered one of a dozen excuses I might make to steal away but chose none of them. To be honest, a part of me was fascinated by the man…not in a complimentary way, but the way a mouse might fix its eyes on those of a snake. One was made to feel that a wrong move might be ruinous.

"You mentioned the River Styx. Do you believe in another life?"

"Do you?"

He smiled. "A question answered with a question? You do not wish to reveal yourself. Very well, I will speak first. Yes. I'm a man of science but I have room for faith. I believe there are mysteries beyond my comprehension."

"Mark Twain said that faith 'is believing what you know ain't so.'"

My retort provoked bellicose laughter. "Yes, yes. I've read your countryman. An amusing fellow and not without insights. Still, I think he is wrong about faith; though I prefer to call it 'mystery.'"

"Solved by death?"

"Perhaps."

"Then you have something in common with Odeil de Villiers. She had faith."

Paused before the row of books, he appeared to be trying to conjure up an image. "I regret we never met. I understand she was very beautiful. One needs beauty in this world."

"Why worry about this world when one expects to travel to the next?"

"You mock me, Mademoiselle," said the doctor without rancor. "And you mistake me, too. When I referred to another life, I wasn't thinking of pink clouds and angel's wings. I was considering how the mind processes our perceptions of the world and hence creates what we believe is true. We rely on our perceptions, do we not? But if the brain were structured differently, even to the slightest degree, then the world, too, would be some other, I think."

"Planet X, perhaps?"

My flippant remark was ignored. "Consider the dog, if you will. Do you suppose it lives in the same world as ours? No. How could it? The dog doesn't perceive color. It hears sounds to which we are oblivious; and of course, it is sensitive to a greater number of scents. Given the enormous differences in capacities to see, think and feel, can it be said that a dog and a human exist in the same world?"

"As far as I know they both answer to gravity and the laws of nature. I've never seen a dog walk through a brick wall."

My opponent chuckled. "Ah, but what if a dog did exactly that? What would you think then?"

"I'd think it was a trick or that I'd gone mad."

"Precisely!" The doctor's eyes gleamed as if I'd fallen through a trap door. "You'd think it was a trick or a sign of insanity. And why? Because your mind rejects what you've decided is impossible. And why does the mind accept some experiences as real and not others? I'll tell you why. Because of our beliefs. Isn't that a wonderful irony? We educate ourselves to expand our minds, but in truth, the mind teaches us limits and makes us blind to the infinite."

I was intrigued by his argument, but I didn't take him seriously. My impression of the doctor was that he used debate to probe character, looking for chinks in one's armor.

"I'll try to remember your point the next time a dog walks through a wall," I answered him coolly.

My indifference seemed to excite him. "But do you not see? Neither the dog nor the wall matter. Your mind will rationalize the experience. You will think it a trick, or that you'd been dreaming, or that you'd gone mad. You've said so, haven't you?"

"Yes." I laughed in spite of myself. "That's exactly what I would do."

"Which raises the question: what is madness? Perhaps it is living without prejudice. Perhaps it is a mind open to every possibility."

"That would be the world of chaos, wouldn't it? We'd live in a primordial soup like a new born infant."

"And what's wrong with seeing through the eyes of a child? Is that not what the English poet Wordsworth would have us do? Does he not urge us to awake our 'primal sympathy'?"

"Poetry is nice to read on a pleasant summer day or even by a winter fire, doctor. But as one philosopher observed, what's important is how one exits a room. I doubt it will be through the wall."

At that moment, Lucille entered with a knock to announce lunch was served. As I could have predicted, Dr. Afreet followed me...not through the wall, but through the door.

Entering the dining room, we found Christian was seated at one end of the table. His manner was subdued and his eyes barely met mine as I sat down beside him. Our guest took a place opposite me and looked at his patient. "You are feeling better, I hope? Or would you like a powder?"

The younger man shook his head and began spooning his soup. Dr. Afreet did the same, but after taking one sip of it, he fell back in his chair, his face aglow with pleasure.

"Ah, potato soup. So appropriate on a cold day such as this. And the rolls, they are freshly baked?"

Lucille, who was serving, nodded, as pleased by the compliment as if it had been meant for her. "Your room is ready, Monsieur," she added. "And the gardener has carried your luggage upstairs to the Blue room."

Christian looked up from his plate with displeasure, but the doctor took no notice. He was too busy slathering butter on his bread and devouring it in large bites.

By the time he'd eaten his third roll, Lucille had returned with a pear and walnut salad. When he saw it, he rubbed his hands together. "Excellent. Excellent."

"Is your wife a good cook, Dr. Afreet?" I couldn't help noticing his robust interest in food. "Or are you the cook in the family?"

Christian stabbed at his lettuce without looking up, showing no interest in the answer.

The doctor returned my gaze. "Alas, I have no wife. Most of the time I am subjected to institutional food which, as you can imagine, offers no delights. Christian would agree, I'm sure."

The man addressed gave no reply.

"No wife? I'm surprised."

"You flatter me, Mademoiselle." Dr. Afreet patted his belly. "I'm afraid, I'm no catch. Besides, my work keeps me too busy to go courting."

"You live at the sanatorium, then?"

"Happily, no." He sat for a moment brushing away the crumbs on his suit. "I take lodgings in Mende. That's where I met Kathrine, who attends you now. She worked in the boarding house where I stayed."

"Did she? I didn't realize you and she were acquainted. What a small world. I understand the proprietors let her go because it was the end of the tourist season. That's how she came to us."

Dr. Afreet waved away the remark. "Of that I have no knowledge."

"Do they get a lot of tourists in Mende? It seems an out of the way place."

"I presume so, Mademoiselle. I see a few Arabs, like myself, in the summer, but generally, I'm too busy to pay attention."

Christian reached for his glass as if desperate for wine and, finding it empty, called for Lucille. "Where is that girl? She should have left the decanter on the table."

"Do you think another glass is wise?" The doctor touched his lips with his napkin. "If you are thirsty, there is water."

"I'm not thirsty. I want more wine. Is that a crime?"

Christian's murderous glare was met with a condescending smile.

"Did you say where you're from, doctor?" I intervened, fearing an argument might ensue. "You speak French without a trace of accent."

"I'm from Algiers, Mademoiselle. But I came to France to pursue my medical education as a young man."

"And you've never gone back?"

"Not to stay, no. And under the present circumstance, travel would be difficult."

"Yes, the war makes things hard on everyone, doesn't it? Especially, if you have family there, which, I presume, you do."

The doctor threw me a look as if to say he doubted the innocence of my question. "I assure you, Mademoiselle, I think of myself as a Frenchman."

"Here, here! I'll drink to that." Christian lifted his water glass in a mock salute.

I hurried on. "I hadn't meant my question to offend in any way, I assure you. I've met others with similar ties. Our gardener has roots in Algiers. He fought for France during the war and is a decorated hero. But when it comes to this quarrel over independence, our cook tells me he has strong opinions."

"His sympathies lay with Algeria?"

"To some degree, if Mrs. de Toi is to be believed. He and I have never talked about the war. I simply assumed that as his mother was from Algiers…"

"And where do your sympathies lay, Mademoiselle? Your country fought for its independence, did it not?"

Christian interposed before I could answer. "Why ask her? She's an American. They pay little attention to international politics. I doubt she could find Algeria on a map."

Dr. Afreet smiled to suggest he was in agreement with his patient. Seeing it, I felt my feathers ruffle.

"I know my geography well enough. But to form an opinion, I'd need more facts."

Dr. Afreet laid his fork across his bread plate and seemed about to give a lecture. "But the papers write of the war every day. What more facts do you need?"

"They tell the French side, of course…"

"True, but the question is one of independence, isn't it? You should know how you feel about that. Isn't that the reason your country fought against England?"

"I thought you were loyal to France?"

"I am. But you asked for the facts and the facts are simple. Algerians wish to be free."

Lucille reappeared to collect our salad plates, an interruption that gave me time to organize my thoughts.

"You're right, of course," I said once the maid had left us. "I can't be indifferent to people's desire for independence. But I can't subscribe to terrorist tactics either. Why kill innocent people? It flies in the face of the Geneva Conventions."

Dr. Afreet reached for the decanter that had been placed at the center of the table. He filled my glass, then Christian's before adding more of the crystal liquid to his own. "A lovely Chenin Blanc, perfect for the soufflé which is to follow, if my nose tells me correctly. Such rich food may prove injurious to my health. But" —he shrugged— "one cannot live forever."

"Allow me be the first to wish you a happy death," Christian said, and he raised his glass in the manner of making a toast.

The doctor chuckled but eyed his patient thoughtfully before returning his attention to me. "About these Geneva Conventions, I'm afraid I must say 'Ha!' to them. In a time of war there is only one imperative and that is to win. Rules are written by the victors after the struggle is over."

"You don't really believe that, do you?"

"I do, my dear. War is a rebellion against a social order, just as disease is an outbreak against health. Does one talk of rules when fighting a disease? No, one instinctively knows that is folly."

"Oh, for God's sake!" Christian threw his napkin on the table and stood. "Can't either of you talk of something else? War, war, war. Where does one go to get a little peace?"

He was trembling so violently, Dr. Afreet looked alarmed. He rose also and took hold of his patient by his shoulders. "Calm yourself, dear boy. We are having a conversation, nothing more. Breathe deeply as I've shown you. Yes, that's it. Here, take a sip of water."

Under the doctor's direction, Christian did regain himself and the rest of the meal was conducted in relative silence, a circumstance that allowed me to observe how pale the younger man looked. As to his outburst, I could make nothing of it except to suppose our conversation—the doctor's and mine—had triggered some childhood memory of his parents who had died in the resistance. Knowing the pain of such a loss, I could see the benefit of having the doctor in residence.

Chapter Thirteen

NEITHER THE DOCTOR, NOR CHRISTIAN, appeared at dinner. Trays were taken upstairs, and when I questioned Kathrine about the men's absence, she informed me the master had taken a turn for the worse. Dr. Afreet had chosen to dine with Christian in the patient's rooms.

When I pressed her for details, she cut me off.

"I'm not the one to ask, Mademoiselle. I'm just a servant here."

I was surprised by her off-handed manner but blamed myself for it. As the mistress of the chateau, I had many shortcomings. Handling the staff was one of them. Mrs. de Toi needed no directing, of course. I relied upon her to teach me. Unfortunately, Kathrine exhibited the personality of a porcupine without its industrious habits. Perhaps, she'd been offended that I'd given Odeil's diaphanous dress to her sister but had offered nothing to her. If so, the omission could be remedied. My former employer had a closet full of garments that needed to be cleared. I would make Kathrine a gift of one of them. I had my doubts, however, that any gesture of mine would amend her character.

When I finished my solitary meal, I headed for the library, my place of refuge, and settled myself with a book before a blazing fire. Unconscious of the time, I was made aware that three hours had passed when I heard a knock on the door. Dr. Afreet entered the room carrying two steaming mugs of cocoa.

"The patient is asleep. I thought perhaps you might care to join me. I make of habit of taking cocoa before retiring."

"That's very thoughtful," I said, accepting the mug he handed me before he settled into the empty chair opposite mine.

"More a prescription," he corrected. "It will help you sleep and, with your slight figure, cocoa is an indulgence you can afford."

I thanked him for his compliment and then settled back to enjoy my drink, which was not only hot but laced with brandy. As I stared into the fire, I considered how kind the doctor had been with his patient that afternoon, behavior I had not expected. He'd taken no offense at Christian's taunts and had sat by his side throughout the evening like a guardian angel. Perhaps, I'd been wrong to jump to a conclusion about the need for his presence. True, Christian made it clear he had no love for the practitioner, but who in authority did he embrace? Certainly not Odeil and certainly not me who had replaced her as the controlling partner of the estate. Thinking of the younger man's behavior—past and present—I decided to give the doctor a second chance. Perhaps, I had been too hurried in my judgment.

"I hope you'll call me Rachel," I said, in an effort to be cordial. "'Mademoiselle Farraday' sounds much too formal."

Dr. Afreet's eyes crinkled with what I took for pleasure. "Ah, yes, first names...an American informality. Not like in Europe. We are far too stuffy. I shall be honored to do so. Thank you, Mademoiselle."

"Rachel," I corrected.

"Yes. Rachel, a lovely name." As the doctor sprawled, relaxed, before the fire, I noted he made no reciprocal request that I call him 'Abbas.' His failure to do so suggested this was a man jealous of his title and professional status. Inwardly, I smiled, having observed how he'd let his mask slip a little.

Perhaps, the brandy had loosened my tongue that evening—for I cannot say I, as yet, trusted the man—but by the time I'd drained my cup, I had described the events at Christian's birthday party in detail, curious as to how he might react to the story.

His response was one of concern which I felt justified my telling him. "I'm glad you have confided in me, dear Rachel," he said, nodding sympathetically. "What a trial for you. He must have upset you greatly. But such wild behavior does not surprise me. I can testify that his coming of age has been his obsession. At the sanatorium, there was a large calendar in his room on which he marked off the days. They couldn't pass fast enough. When he became agitated, I would remind him he was wishing away his life. But he brushed aside my observation. Living in an institution isn't a life, he'd say.

"Of course, I understand how he might feel. The truth is, despite his mood swings, he can be very likeable at times...like that children's rhyme about the girl with the curl in the middle of her forehead. When he is good, he is very, very good, but when—"

"He is bad, he's horrid," I finished for him. We smiled at one another, having come to an understanding.

The doctor's eyes were soft as he continued to look at me. "Above all, you mustn't blame yourself for what happened. I cannot account for it, myself. But in the short time I have been here, I have noticed his attraction to you. Perhaps his conduct was no more than the infatuation of a mischievous school boy who longs for your attention."

"Forgive me, Doctor, but I don't think the answer is as simple or as flattering as that. The trouble arose after he'd offered to buy me out and I refused. I think his game is to drive me away."

My companion looked surprised. "You refused his offer?"

"Not refused, exactly." I outlined the terms of my inheritance so that he could see that selling was impossible.

"But surely, putting up with a sick man is no option. There must be some way—"

"There isn't. If I don't live here, I lose everything."

"What then? Christian inherits?"

"No. The fortune goes elsewhere. She was clear Christian should never get his hands on the controlling half of the estate."

The doctor let out a whistle. "*Mon dieu*, there must have been great enmity between them. How sad to see a family so divided. But as you say, Madame de Villiers has left you with little choice."

"Exactly. But I have no wish to sell, in any case. The Chateau l'Ombre is my home, now. I've no desire to return to the States."

Dr. Afreet shook his head. "After what you've told me tonight, you might not feel that way in a few months. I'll do what I can to moderate Christian's behavior, of course, but were I in your position, I'd talk with those Paris attorneys. There may be another option. If not, this chateau could well become your prison instead of your home."

* * *

Dr. Afreet's characterization of my inheritance troubled me, as it reinforced my view that I had been made a pawn in Odeil's game to thwart her cousin. Again, I wondered how much loyalty she was owed, or if I would be wise to consider other options.

I confess, my feelings tugged in opposition to reason. I wanted to stay even though, at the moment, I was tied to a man whose mental and physical stability I questioned. There was always the hope that with proper treatment, he might regain himself. I must allow the psychiatrist to complete his work. For me to retreat any sooner would be ill-considered and, perhaps, foolish. Life might right itself, after all. At least, that's what I told myself.

At breakfast, Dr. Afreet arrived in the dining room alone and rubbing his hands together in anticipation of a hot meal. That morning he enjoyed a plate piled high with eggs and sausages. Whether it was the food or the accord he and I had achieved the previous night that brightened his mood, I do not know. But he remained in good spirits even as he announced that Christian had slept fitfully and required a powder to calm him.

"I've taken possession of his car keys," he added as an aside. "In his condition, it would be unwise to allow him to storm off as he did yesterday. You agree?"

Flattered that he would seek my opinion, I concurred, although inwardly an alarm bell went off in my head. Christian wasn't a child, despite his outbursts, and I didn't like to see him being treated like one. Still, the decision wasn't really mine so I let the matter drop.

The doctor poured himself a cup of coffee, and advised me that he wished to consult a local physician for a second opinion on Christian's condition. "Being a specialist of the mind," he explained, "I have no wish to overlook a physical cause for his current behavior."

When I gave him the name of the local doctor, he shook his head. "He wasn't available so I called someone else."

As I knew of no other in the village, I was puzzled...but not for long. A moment later, Kathrine appeared to announce that a Dr. Cartouche had arrived.

"Ah, good man. Good man." Dr. Afreet rose and wiped his chin with his napkin as he waved the stranger into the room. "Perhaps you'd care for something to eat or for some coffee, at least?"

The smaller man entered slowly, giving me time to note his pinched features and bushy mane of silver hair. I judged him to be in his mid-sixties and, like the psychiatrist, he was impeccably dressed in a gray suit, his black medical bag clutched in his right hand.

"Coffee would do nicely," he said in answer to Afreet's offer.

"Wonderful, wonderful." My houseguest pulled out a chair for the new arrival and then handed him his beverage of choice.

Having set down his bag on the sideboard, the older man accepted the cup and saucer with both hands and sniffed at the contents appreciatively.

"These days, I'm so often served with instant coffee. It's not the same as brewed, is it? Not the same, at all."

Dr. Afreet pushed the pastry dish in his direction but the man shook his head. "Thank you, no. Coffee is sufficient. I'd like to hear about the patient, before I examine him, if I may. Would you mind telling me again about his symptoms?"

Before the two men got too far into their medical assessment, I felt obliged to introduce myself and give my own account of Christian's condition.

The new arrival stared at me over the rim of his cup before setting it down. "Forgive me, Mademoiselle Farraday. I, too, should introduce myself. I am Dr. Abdul Cartouche. I have only recently established myself in the area and was surprised to get the call."

"Yes, I wondered about that. Dr. Chalmers is the local here. But apparently, he was unavailable?"

"I have no idea. I have yet to have the pleasure of meeting the gentleman."

"Dr. Chalmers was on another call, Rachel, as I've told you," Dr. Afreet interjected. "Fortunately, Kathrine knew of Dr. Cartouche and although he and I have never met, I took the liberty of sending for him." He turned toward the new arrival. "It was good of you to come, Monsieur."

"Not, at all. I'm meant to be retired, but it's good to keep a hand in."

The formalities concluded, the two men began their medical consultation. By their demeanor, I was made to feel unimportant, like a napkin that had fallen unnoticed to the floor. Eventually, I excused myself and I asked the doctor to see me after he'd had time to examine Christian. "You'll find me in the library when you've finished."

Half an hour passed before Dr. Cartouche discovered me among my books. He had a quick eye and, as he glanced about the room, one could see that age had neither dimmed his sight nor his curiosity. He picked up a statuette of a glass horse by Limoges and seeing the signature, he sighed.

"Lovely. Quite lovely." He sighed appreciatively once more as he set it down again.

Next, he drifted to my desk and peered over my shoulder. "You are interested in architecture, Mademoiselle Farraday?"

I told him that I was, then closed the book and invited him to join me by the fire. "Would you care for some tea or another coffee?"

The doctor declined. "Thank you, no. I need to get back to my unpacking."

"Then I won't keep you long. What can you tell me about Christian? Is anything seriously wrong?"

The gray-haired man shrugged. "I'm happy to share what little I can, but I was hoping to learn more from you. Have you known the patient long?"

"Only a few weeks. Why?"

"I thought perhaps you might be able to tell me about his habits."

"I'm not sure what you mean. He doesn't smoke. I know that. He drinks a bit more than he should, but that's simply my opinion."

"Yes, we must try to curb that. With all his medications…"

"Are there many?"

The doctor paused before answering. "As to his treatment, Mademoiselle, you must ask Dr. Afreet. All I can tell you is that it would be wise if you left the wine carafe off the table in future."

"That might be a problem. He objected strongly the last time it was missing. But I suppose we can weather another storm if it's in his best interest. I'll inform our housekeeper, Mrs. de Toi."

"Ah, yes. She was his nanny, was she not? Or at least that's what Dr. Afreet thought. If so, she might have influence over him. With your permission, I'd like to speak to her on my way out."

"Of course, but you've said nothing about Christian's health. Have you no opinion?"

"If it will relieve your mind," the doctor said as he rose from his chair, "I suspect nothing serious. I'll come again in a few days. Naturally, if there's a turn for the worse, send for me. Dr. Afreet knows my number but I'll give it to you, as well." He took out a pen from his gray suit pocket and wrote his telephone number on the back of his card. His former address somewhere in Paris was on the front but crossed out.

"What made you decide to retire in Sainte Enimie?" I asked, as he handed it to me. "Do you have friends or relatives in the area?"

"No, no." The doctor shook his head. "A matter of happenstance, I assure you. I was passing through and liked the place."

He seemed anxious to depart so I walked with him to the door, where he paused long enough to impress his view upon me that Dr. Afreet was a skilled physician whose judgment I could rely upon.

* * *

Three days later, Dr. Cartouche was called for a second time. Christian's condition had worsened.

Earlier, I'd managed to slip into his rooms while Dr. Afreet was downstairs, a feat that would have been impossible had our house guest not begun to make frequent trips to the kitchen to consult with Mrs. de Toi about Christian's meals and to make special requests for himself. She'd already complained once about his interference, and I'd promised to speak to the doctor as soon as the patient was feeling better. My assurance had left her unsatisfied and she continued to grumble.

"He's everywhere, Mademoiselle Rachel, poking and prying into things that don't concern him. Mathiam found him in his tool shed the other day. Now tell me what business he had being there? He said he was out for a bit of air. I ask you, who takes air in a tool shed?"

Her suspicions had been uppermost in my mind as I'd opened the door to Christian's room to make my visit. His quarters were hot; a fire burned angrily in the hearth as if gasoline had been poured on it. Normally, I'm grateful for a fire, as winter that year had brought with it a bone-chilling dampness. In fact, I was wearing a wool skirt over which I'd layered a long-sleeved sweater and a pullover, but regardless of my attire, the room was far too hot.

I found Christian in his bed, his hair matted with sweat. He seemed to be asleep but when I placed my hand on his forehead, his eyes snapped open and, seeing me, he shot up from his pillow as though he'd been activated by a spring.

"Thank God, you've come. I prayed you would." His eyes, deep pools of endless blue, drifted toward the water carafe on the table beside him. Pouring a glass, I helped him drink. When he had finished, he laid back again, his eyes scanning the room. "Where's Afreet?"

"I'm not sure. I haven't seen him this morning."

Christian took hold of my hand and squeezed hard. "We haven't much time, so you must listen carefully. I know I've done nothing to earn your trust, but I've had my reasons for behaving as I did."

Here, he paused as if to regain his breath. His reedy voice frightened me, as did his pallor. I started to rise to get help but he clung to me, forcing me to sit down again.

"Listen to me, Rachel. You must leave this place, now—or tomorrow, at the latest. Promise me you'll go. Promise me." By now, he was squeezing my fingers so hard, I cried out in pain.

He released me immediately. "I'm sorry. I've made such a mess of things."

Despite the heat, he began to shiver as if he might go into convulsions. Pouring water into my handkerchief, I laid it across his brow to cool him and, at that moment, Dr. Afreet entered the room.

His eyes widened in surprise when he spied his patient's condition and he hurried to a nearby table where he'd left his medical bag. Rifling through it, he found an envelope that contained white powder. This he dissolved in the glass of water and forced his patient to drink. The effect seemed almost immediate. Christian relaxed and closed his eyes, as if preparing for sleep.

"He's getting worse." I lashed out at the doctor. "What's wrong with him? Why haven't you been able to help him?"

Hearing me, the voice of the accused crackled with indignation. "I? It is you, Mademoiselle, who have sent him into this paroxysm. I have warned against these visits, have I not? And now you see the consequences. So again, I ask… No, I must insist you do not enter these rooms without my permission. Otherwise, I cannot answer for his condition."

Afreet looked so intimidating with his chin jutting forward like an angry mastiff that my impulse was to back away and leave the room. But Christian's words prevented me. Whether or not his warning was the effect of his fever or something more sinister, I couldn't be sure, but rather than apologize, I stood my ground. I did lower my voice, however.

"Come now, Doctor. You don't expect me to believe my presence has endangered Christian in anyway? His condition has been deteriorating over a matter of days. These powders you've been giving him may make him sleep, but I don't see that they've improved his condition. Dr. Cartouche should pay another visit and I intend to call him, now."

The face opposite mine broke out into a thin smile. "That won't be necessary, Mademoiselle," he hissed. "The gentleman has already been summoned."

Chapter Fourteen

NOT 'TIL LATER THAT MORNING did the paths of Dr. Afreet and I cross again.

The rain had continued to fall and the lawn, already saturated, was unable to absorb the excess. Pools formed at low points on the ground, reflecting the clouds as if they were fallen pearls. I was standing at the library window looking out when the doctor entered. His colleague, looking worried, shuffled in behind him.

Seeing the older man, I rushed forward to greet him. "Thank you for coming on such short notice. I take it you have seen Christian?"

Dr. Cartouche stood with his dark overcoat slung over his left arm and his medical bag held in the opposite hand. "May, I sit down?"

"Of course." I motioned for him to take one of the leather chairs beside the hearth and, while I took the other, Dr. Afreet pulled out the captain's chair from behind my desk and sat down between us.

"May I offer you coffee?"

"No, thank you, Mademoiselle. I'm afraid what I have to tell you cannot wait." His eyes shifted to his colleague as if he sought approval before he began.

His caution was unnecessary. His colleague spoke for him. "We've only a suspicion, mind you. But to be on the safe side, Dr. Cartouche has taken some samples."

"Samples? What are you talking about? What kind of samples?"

"Some hair and nail clippings," Dr. Cartouche explained, his brown eyes blinking at me kindly. "You mustn't worry. As Dr. Afreet has said, it's only a precaution."

"A precaution for what? You haven't told me what you're looking for."

The older man again sought Dr. Afreet's direction, but this time, I interposed, wanting my answer to come from Dr. Cartouche's lips.

"Please don't try to shelter me. I've a right to know." My words sounded brave but already a premonition was taking hold of me as it had on the day I'd learned of my parents' deaths. I had been standing at my dormitory window at Mills when I'd noticed two policemen crossing the lawn. Somehow, I had known they were looking for me.

"Dr. Cartouche is correct," Afreet continued, even though my remark had not been directed at him. "It's too early for you to become alarmed; nonetheless, it is possible Christian may have ingested poison, somehow."

"That can't be true! I don't believe it. No one would ..."

Without realizing it, I had leapt to my feet, behavior which brought Afreet to his, as well.

"Calm yourself, Rachel. It won't help to become hysterical."

"I'm not hysterical. I'm shocked. Who wouldn't be?"

Dr. Cartouche was the one to encourage me to sit down again. "Of course, you're shocked. But there's no need to speculate until the tests are done. We must be patient. It could be nothing more than a severe case of flu."

"But you don't believe that, obviously."

Dr. Cartouche took hold of my hand and gave it a pat. "I believe your friend is in good hands. We came to suggest a change in the way the patient's food is prepared–"

"But Dr. Afreet consults with Mrs. de Toi on a daily basis–"

"Yes, but I don't actually cook the meals, do I?" Afreet broke in.

"I had no idea you had any pretensions of being a chef," I answered coldly. "But if you're suggesting Mrs. de Toi has something to do with Christian's illness, the idea is stupid beyond words."

"Now, now, now. There's no need to get upset. I only want to suggest…"

"What, Dr. Cartouche? That I sack Mrs. de Toi?"

"Please, my dear girl. No one is suggesting anything so drastic. And there's no need. No, Dr. Afreet and I simply feel that, for the moment, the patient requires plainer food—not all those creamy sauces your good cook likes to make. What he needs is a little clear broth, some scrambled eggs, nothing that would demand expert hands."

"Mrs. de Toi can accommodate. She's raised Christian since he was a toddler. I assure you, she's capable of preparing clear broth and scrambled eggs."

"Yes, but we thought we'd relieve her of that. She has so many other tasks being housekeeper as well as cook. Why burden her with this need to prepare a special diet? We thought it might be better if the other girl—Kathrine, is it? We thought she might accommodate—"

"Kathrine?" I stared at Dr. Cartouche in disbelief. "She's not a cook and I'm certain Mrs. de Toi wouldn't allow the girl to fuss about in her kitchen."

"Forgive me, Rachel," Dr. Afreet interrupted. "But I thought you were the mistress of this house."

"I-I am, but—"

"Then you shall tell Mrs. de Toi I've made Kathrine my assistant in all matters regarding my patient, including the preparation of his meals. Frankly, I suspect she'll welcome the change as she makes no effort to conceal her hostility towards me."

"I'm afraid you don't know her as I do. I promise you, there will be hell to pay."

* * *

If there is a God in Heaven, then I imagine He must have looked down on me with pity that afternoon for when I sought to inform Mrs. de Toi of the new arrangements, she'd apparently developed flu-like symptoms, too, and had taken to her bed. I'd never known her to be ill before. She was robust and had enjoyed good health all the months I'd been with her. Still, under the circumstances it was natural that Kathrine should assume her duties, a transition so seamless one might have imagined it was wrought by divine will.

Although it annoyed me to admit it, the younger woman proved to be able at her duties. Her menus were simple but well prepared and beautifully seasoned. As for the remaining responsibilities, the household hummed along without complaint. What's more, as if an ad had been placed in the Heavenly Gazette, a new girl arrived looking for work. She had few references, but who was I to sneer at Providence? Winter was the lean season for obtaining help. With the tourists gone and the shops that catered to them closed, most of the young workers had migrated to the larger towns. And so, Claudine Trainard was hired.

During the interview, she asked to be domiciled in the servants' quarters as she had no family or contacts in Sainte Enimie. She explained she'd been wandering through the town in search of work when someone suggested the chateau.

Lucille was delighted with the additional help. Add to that, Claudine was near her age, although she lacked the former's vivacity. After a few days in the new girl's presence, I came to the conclusion she was a bit slow. Even the simplest instructions needed repeating and it was not unusual to find her wandering in the halls looking lost. Nonetheless, she seemed eager to please and that was to her credit.

I realized, of course, that the momentary peace which had descended upon the house would be upended as soon as Mrs. de Toi regained her strength, and I hope I may be forgiven for having mixed feelings about that, even though I did my best to aid in her recovery.

For three days I visited my friend in her room, and for three days she apologized for her condition. When I assured her an apology was unnecessary and that the household was running smoothly, I was accused of putting on a brave face. With Kathrine at the helm, Mrs. de Toi insisted that what I'd told her couldn't be true. Nonetheless, I encouraged the woman to take as long a rest as was needed. "After all," I argued. "We can't risk having you suffer a relapse."

How long I would enjoy my peaceful hiatus—two days more, perhaps, or maybe three—I didn't know. But I confess to feeling blessed each day Mrs. de Toi remained in her bed suffering with red eyes and a stuffy nose. I was almost humming after my latest visit until Kathrine came looking for me.

I was descending from the servant's quarters when I met her at the bottom of the stairs. She announced two policemen were waiting in the library. Doctors Afreet and Cartouche were there, as well. She offered no other explanation as to their presence but her expression was grim enough to set off alarm bells. Hurrying to the library, I found it populated with the people I'd been warned to expect.

The moment I entered and saw the gathering of serious faces, I knew the tests on Christian's hair and nails had confirmed poison.

Dr. Cartouche rose at once to offer me his leather chair. "I am so sorry, my dear. But you understand I had to make my report."

Numbness crept over me as I nodded and sat down under the glare of the two policemen, both of whom eyed me as if I were a swab in a Petrie dish.

The older of the two officers, a man I'd guess to be in his forties, introduced himself. "I am Inspector Tromperie, Mademoiselle, and this is my associate, Detective Boueur."

The man to his right offered me a brief smile. He was painfully young and, by his shy demeanor, seemed new to his position. Certainly, his uniform showed little wear.

Doctors Afreet and Cartouche arranged themselves in the remaining chairs while the two police officers continued to stand.

"A few questions, Mademoiselle," Inspector Tromperie began. "I understand you are an American."

"Yes, that's right. I checked in at your station when I first arrived. You must have a record of my papers."

The Inspector smiled. "We are not local, Mademoiselle. We are a special branch from Vichy."

"Vichy? But why?"

"There is no need to be alarmed. We have only a few questions."

"Yes, of course. But what's the matter? What's happened?"

My request for information was ignored.

"You have been living at the chateau for six or seven months, I understand."

"That's true," I nodded.

"And how well did you know your former employer, Madame de Villiers? Were you acquaintances before you arrived or complete strangers?"

"I learned about the job opportunity from the Dean of my college and I came here soon after I graduated. Madame de Villiers and I had never met."

"How strange for her to hire someone from the United States, someone she didn't know. Surely, she'd heard something about you before offering employment."

"Well, no...I mean, yes." Uncertain about how much of our prior connection to reveal, I continued to stammer while the inspector stood frowning.

"Which is it?" he interrupted. "As you can guess, I am here on a serious matter. You must be entirely honest with me."

"She was acquainted with my father during the war," I confessed, deciding the truth could do no harm. "I didn't know of their connection when I took the job. Is Christian going to be all right? Exactly what has happened?"

The Inspector waved my query away. "The gentleman will recover. A matter of poisoning, however–"

"*Poisoning?* I don't believe it. It can't be true."

"But it is, Mademoiselle, I assure you. That's why you must answer my questions with complete honesty. Now, let me go back. Am I to understand that your father and Madame de Villiers were lovers? Is that what you're saying?"

"You are very direct, Monsieur."

"I must have the facts, as I've said. Am I right to suppose you may be...*related* to her in some way?"

"I'm not a love child, if that's what you think. My father was already married to my mother when he and Odeil met. I was a toddler, at the time. There is no blood connection."

The younger detective, who'd been silent until now, was unable to contain his surprise. "*Mon Dieu!* And now you own all of this?

That is good fortune, certainly?"

Seeing the frown of his superior he fell silent again.

"Let me understand you, Mademoiselle. You ask me to believe your employer chose to leave her possessions to—the child of a former lover, a man who had obviously abandoned her after the war. Is that right?"

"He didn't abandon her," I snapped. "He returned home to his wife and child. She understood that."

The inspector's eyes became owlish. "Did she indeed? Then she was a woman of a most generous spirit. But she had a cousin, did she not? Why not leave the estate to him, as she'd never clapped eyes on you until a few months ago?"

"I don't believe they got on well, but if you wish to know more, you must speak to her solicitors. They might be able to satisfy your curiosity."

"Curiosity? I assure you, Mademoiselle, I am not indulging in curiosity. Someone in this household wishes to see Monsieur de Hess dead and I intend to discover who that person is."

Outraged at the bald accusation, I leapt to my feet. "Why assume someone is trying to kill him? It could have been an accident. I understand it has happened before—"

"We are aware of the former incident. And we are also aware of the complaint Madame entered against her cousin—"

"If you know that, then you know why she didn't make him her heir."

"What I know or do not know is of no concern of yours. I will ask you simply to answer the questions." The inspector's eyes contracted to the size of buckshot. "What I wish to ask *now* is who inherits in the event of Monsieur de Hess's death? Perhaps, you benefit in some way?"

Dr. Cartouche rose to stand beside me, his lips quivering with indignation. "What are you implying, Inspector? This line of questioning strikes me as completely uncalled for."

"Sit down, my good fellow. Sit down." Afreet, who'd been watching the proceedings with what appeared to be a degree of amusement, became animated. "Let the inspector do his job. We must not interfere."

"Thank you, Doctor." The man in charge of the interrogation gave a nod in Afreet's direction before returning his attention to me. "Now if you will answer–"

"What's going on here? Why are these men here?"

Ten pair of eyes swung round to see who had spoken. To everyone's surprise, Christian stood clinging to the door in a near state of collapse. Seeing him, both doctors rushed to his side.

"My dear boy!" Cartouche had taken his patient by one arm to lead him to his vacant chair. "You must sit down. Here, take this chair by the fire. What on earth possessed you to leave your sick bed? That was a foolish thing to do. You could have lost your balance and tumbled down the stairs."

He went on scolding until Christian was safely ensconced before the fire with an afghan thrown over his lap. I had taken it from the settee where it was usually draped.

Once we were settled for a second time—Dr. Cartouche in the captain's chair and Dr. Afreet perched on the edge of the desk—the inspector took charge of the room once more.

"You are feeling well enough to leave your bed, Monsieur de Hess? I am glad to see it. A tragedy has been averted, thanks to these doctors." He was staring down at the patient with his arms crossed in front of him.

"What tragedy?" Christian's voice, although weak, had an edge to it. "Kathrine told me you were here. Why? Who sent for you?"

"Now, now, dear boy." Dr. Cartouche smiled. "You mustn't worry about the presence of these men. This is Inspector Tromperie and his assistant...what was your name again?"

"Boueur. Detective Boueur." The younger man bowed a little as he answered.

Despite Cartouche's effort to be gracious, Dr. Afreet broke in with a display of urgency. Whether he was anxious for his patient or for some other reason, I didn't know, but the agitation was real as he urged Tromperie to continue.

"Choose your words carefully. He knows nothing."

"I see. I thought…"

Christian, who'd been staring hard at both men, spoke in a sudden outburst, "I want to speak to Rachael. I want to speak to her *now*, and the rest of you should leave."

Everyone stared at him, failing to understand his sudden pique. In ordinary times when the master of the house spoke in such manner, even if his voice was weak as watery tea, people would retreat in haste. But on that day, no one moved…except Dr. Afreet, who rose and, after approaching his patient, laid a firm hand on his shoulder.

"Not now, Christian. The police have business here. I suggest you listen."

The young man cowered a little but maintained his petulant resistance. "I mean to speak to her. You can't stop me. If you try, I won't answer for what I'll do."

"Yes, yes," Afreet conceded. "No one will stop you. You can speak to her, later. But for now, be quiet."

"This is a farce and you know it," Christian grumbled.

This time Inspector Tromperie was the one to reply. "Monsieur de Hess is apparently unaware that traces of arsenic have been found in his hair and nail samples. No wonder he is surprised to find the police here. I understand. So, it is my duty to inform you, Monsieur, that as of this moment, I am in the midst of a criminal investigation."

Christian's gaze flew from one doctor to the other in search of an explanation.

"We didn't want to alarm you, dear boy." Afreet was tight lipped as he spoke and he continued to keep his grip on his patient. "Dr. Cartouche took samples while you were asleep and had them analyzed. Given what they showed, we were obligated to call the police. Now that you know what's happened, perhaps it would be best if you returned to your rooms. You look tired."

"But that's rubbish. You said—"

Afreet ignored Christian's objection and made a firm effort to lift the younger man to his feet. The latter, however, clung to the arms of his chair. "*No.* I want to stay. I've a right to know what's going on."

Afreet backed away rather than engage in a tussle.

"As you wish. But your role here is as an observer. Do not interfere with the inspector's interrogation."

The strain Christian was undergoing became apparent for he suddenly he fell forward with his head dropping into his hands. No one was sure whether he was resting or had fainted.

"I-is he going to be all right?" Tromperie gasped.

"Yes," Dr. Afreet hissed. "If you'll be quick about it."

The physician rolled Christian back into his chair. From that position everyone could see he was still conscious. Cartouche rose to take his pulse as a precaution, while Tromperie looked on with a glazed expression.

"Get on with it!" Afreet prodded a second time.

"Yes, yes. Now, where was I? To be honest, I've forgotten..."

Detective Boueur, who'd been standing in the background, offered his assistance. "You were suggesting Mademoiselle had a motive for murder..."

"That's right. Now, I remember." Renewed of purpose, the inspector turned his pale eyes in my direction yet again, although throughout the ensuing interrogation, he stole glances at the collapsed man.

"So, Mademoiselle, your employer was a stranger to you when you arrived in this country. What a brave thing to do: traveling thousands of miles to a foreign land to work for a woman who was something of a mystery."

"I didn't consider it brave, at all," I answered him. "My parents had died in an accident two years previously, and, having no family, I looked forward to the change."

"You have my condolences, Mademoiselle. To lose both parents is a tragedy. No doubt you grieved and suffered a depression, perhaps?"

"For God's sake! What has that to do with anything?" Christian objected.

Inspector Tromperie straightened himself and looked offended by the remark. "I'd advise you to heed your doctor's warning, Monsieur de Hess. These repeated interruptions only prolong matters."

Christian fell back in his chair to indicate he would remain quiet.

"I repeat my question, Mademoiselle. Did you suffer a breakdown after your parents died?"

"Not a breakdown, exactly."

"Then what, exactly?"

"I underwent therapy for a while."

"Were you prescribed medications?"

"Yes, but I'm not taking any now. I don't see the relevance of these questions."

"Perhaps the therapy was incomplete," Dr. Afreet offered. "Such wounds are not quickly healed."

"This is getting ridiculous," I objected. "There's nothing wrong with me. I'm fine...fine, fine, fine!"

"Methinks the lady doth protest too much," Afreet muttered loud enough for me to hear.

I answered him nothing but sat glaring in his direction, too angry to speak. Since my last therapy sessions in San Francisco with Dr. Justin Devane, a course of several months after my parents had died, I'd developed an aversion to mind healers. The appointment had ended on a sour note. I'd told the psychologist I wanted to stop seeing him as I felt our sessions weren't helping. He had opposed the idea and had accused me of not only refusing to confront my feelings of alienation but of insisting upon seeing myself as a victim. He'd warned that if I kept my parents the centerpiece of my life, I would remain isolated. Infuriated, I'd stormed from the office and never returned.

"I-I'm sorry, Inspector," I said, looking up at the man who'd been scrutinizing me. "Your news has given me a shock. I'm not feeling well, suddenly. Do you suppose we could continue these questions some other time?"

"You do look pale, my dear," Dr. Cartouche agreed. "I'd advise you to get some rest. Would you like a sedative to help you sleep?"

"Thank you, no. I don't have trouble sleeping. Kathrine provides me with cocoa in the evenings. I find that helps."

"My prescription." Dr. Afreet leered.

The inspector stood with his hand touching his chin, gazing down at me. "Very well, Mademoiselle. We will conclude for today. As you say, our conversation can be continued another other time."

As I left the library, I could feel Christian's eyes at my back. He was trying to warn me of something, as he had done during our brief meeting in his room, but what he was attempting to convey escaped me. Worse, I had no idea when we might arrange to be alone together. Both doctors seemed to be making a concerted effort to keep us apart.

When I reached my *boudoir*, I collapsed on my bed and tried to read, although my mind was racing. Eventually, however, even a tightly wound clock will run down and, without my meaning to, I fell asleep. In my dream, I saw Odeil in the land of the twin suns. She was standing in the poppy field dressed in white and looking more beautiful than was possible in life. Her skin, her eyes, glowed with an ethereal light.

Strange...even in the dream I realized she was dead, but it made no difference. I was happy and I linked arms with her. Together, we walked a great distance in perfect silence.

I would have liked to remain in that place forever—safe from a reality that was becoming more and more troubling. But the choice of either dreaming or waking was not mine. A knock on my bedroom door recalled me to my cream-and-gold-striped rooms. Dr. Afreet was standing on the threshold.

"May I come in?"

The ormolu clock was chiming four as he entered, but already the outside landscape was dark enough to illuminate the falling snow. The tiny flakes tapped like fingernails against the windows. Winter had arrived in all its blue-white, arctic glory, a rare phenomenon in that part of the world.

Seeing my comforter had fallen to the floor, the doctor approached and laid it across me once more. Then he drew up a ladderbacked chair to sit beside me.

"I wanted to see how you were doing." His dark eyes seemed to express genuine concern. "I've taken the liberty of ordering light refreshment." As he spoke, he turned to look back at the open door where Kathrine was standing with a tray. He motioned for her to enter, which she did, and she placed her burden on the night table beside me before leaving. Afreet poured the hot tea into one of the cups and handed it to me. I didn't object, but drank greedily, realizing, at that moment, how thirsty I was.

The beverage restored my tranquility. When I was satisfied, I sat up against my pillows and stared for a moment at the snow silting the windows.

Afreet was the first to speak. He apologized for the scene below and for his part in it. He'd been obliged to call in the police but had become carried away by the seriousness of the matter. Even so, he'd been wrong to mock me.

I accepted his apology and, by degrees, our conversation became less strained. For a time, we talked of nothing important, both of us reticent to say what was on our minds, I suppose. We might have gone on endlessly talking of cabbages and kings, but I grew weary of these evasions and decided to put some candor between us.

"Have you formulated any conclusions, yet?"

"Any conclusions?"

"Am I neurotic, do you think? Or do you subscribe to Freud's opinion that all women are hysterical?"

"My dear girl!" The doctor threw up his hands. "I assure you this visit isn't about my concern for your mental state. I wanted to see how you were, that's all. And as for Freud, you needn't be so defensive for your gender. He accuses us all of being beasts under the skin. That is why I prefer Jung."

"Why him?"

"Because he sees the angel in us. Compassion, he argued, unites us all and is the universal that makes us one. Individuality is a grand illusion."

"Meaning?"

"Meaning the world we inhabit is a mind game where division is false and wholeness is true."

"Ah, yes. I think I hear a dog barking somewhere."

He shook his finger at me in a mock gesture of reproach. "You are a wicked young woman to tease me. If I had the time, I'm certain I could make a convert of you."

"We have the time now, don't we?"

"What, are you serious?" The doctor looked at me with his eyebrows lifted. "You'd be interested in hearing my theories?"

"Why not? At least, they aren't boring."

The doctor chuckled lightly. "That's an odd invitation, indeed. But why not? What I have to say is not complicated but amazingly simple. My reference to Jung was to point out that, like him, I believe truth lies not only in what we see but in psychic phenomena—the world of the mind—though it is not subject to the laws of proof which science requires. But to believe in one set of truths without the other is like seeing with one eye. The vision lacks depth. The truth is there is no differentiation between the external and the internal world. It's all one."

"You think science alone distorts our view?"

"Exactly!" Afreet looked down at his hands as if gathering his thoughts. "Let's use language as an example. We talk of French as if it were composed of many parts: subject, predicate, nouns, and verbs to name a few. But what, in fact, have these parts to do with conversation? A child learns to speak before it knows anything of the rules of grammar, true or false?"

"True, of course."

"That's right. Grammar is a dissection having nothing to do with meaning. If we spend all our time dismembering the language, we distract ourselves from the essence of communication. Likewise, if we separate the mind from the body or the external from the internal world, we fail to understand the whole. You, me, Dr. Cartouche...this chair I'm sitting on, we are like parts of grammar. We are an illusion."

"But how are we to live in a world without our illusions? Should I no longer rest in this bed since I am the bed? Shall I instruct Kathrine to cancel tonight's pot roast as a bed does not eat?"

The doctor, who loved his pot roast, chuckled again, full of good nature. "My dear Rachel, it is cruel to use a man's weakness against him. If I do not surrender to your logic, am I apt to lose a good dinner?"

As he spoke, the ormolu clock struck five. Dr. Afreet pulled out his pocket watch for confirmation. "My goodness, is that the hour? I must look in on Christian. It's time for his medication. Forgive me, my dear girl. We must defer our conversation to some later time. For now, you must get your rest. We will cross swords again, I promise you."

Chapter Fifteen

B<small>Y THE TIME THE DOCTOR</small> left me, the weather had turned to rain but patches of snow remained so that the light shining from the house left the grounds gleaming like crystal. I opened a window to embrace the evening air and was met by an icy blast. About to shut it tight again, I spied Mathiam walking below. His face was hidden beneath his plaid cap, but I knew that stoop and that trudge. I shouted to him and he waved back.

"Is everything all right, Mademoiselle?" He'd been outside for some time, apparently, as his nose and cheeks were rosy.

"What are you doing?"

He answered he was checking the shrubbery for storm damage. So far he'd found little.

"Can I join you?" I'd called down in a burst of enthusiasm that surprised me. He looked surprised too.

"It's cold out, Mademoiselle. You'd need to dress warmly."

Ten minutes later, I found him bending over a shrub in the rose garden. "I don't like to prune these shrubs until later in the season, but this one's suffered a bad break. Can't ignore it." He gave the branch a snip with his secateurs then righted himself to greet me. "You're looking bright-eyed and bushy-tailed, if I may say so. I heard you was ill. Don't look like it, now." Mathiam scratched his head through his cap as he looked at me. "Is somethin' on your mind, Mademoiselle?"

As a matter of fact, there was, but I didn't want to blurt it out at once, so I ignored the question and peered 'round. "Everything looks so beautiful. I envy your work in all this fresh air."

"Oh, it's fresh, all right." The gardener grinned. "Like to freeze your lungs, it will." He paused a moment, then asked a question that was apparently on his mind. "Everyone all right at the house?"

"If you mean Mrs. de Toi, I think she's on the mend. And Christian made his way downstairs this morning."

"That's good." Mathiam turned to scan another row of roses.

Finding nothing wrong, we began to walk.

"Be glad to see Amelia up and about," he offered. "That girl Kathrine's been takin' on airs. Told me to wipe my shoes and laid out papers like I was a dog when I came in for tea. Amelia never did that. She just made me come in with stocking feet. I don't mind troddin' on papers, mind; but I don't like the way that snippet of a girl's been talkin' to me these last few days. She's got no sense of seniority, she hasn't."

"I'll speak to her, if you like."

"No, no. Don't do that. Amelia will set things right when she's herself again."

We continued to walk while a light wind arose from the east. Its direction meant the temperature was likely to drop a few degrees later in the evening. Despite my warm clothing, I was beginning to feel the cold.

"Mathiam, I've been meaning to ask about the time you found me, unconscious."

He'd bent forward to prune another broken branch "Yes, I remember. What do you want to know?"

"Well, I may be confused, but before I collapsed I'm pretty sure I was in a tunnel. Mrs. de Toi said you used to talk about a tunnel under the chateau and about a black monk who was supposed to be buried there. She said she stopped you because she was afraid the children might become frightened."

He righted himself to squint at me. "Now why'd she be telling you about that? It was a long time ago."

"But there is a tunnel?" I asked tentatively, not wanting to let the conversation wander.

"Tunnels," he corrected. "There's a nest of 'em."

"Really? Then you've been in them?"

"A few times. Odeil's papa thought of hidin' some of his art works down there. That was before I went off to the war...when he suspected the Germans might invade. But he never did."

"Why not?"

"Too damp. The important pieces he hid on the grounds. Buried some of 'em. When the fighting was over, me and a few men dug 'em up as per his written instructions."

"Monsieur de Villiers knew he could rely on your loyalty."

"I did my duty." He paused to draw a red bandana from his coat pocket and wiped his nose.

"And what about the black monk—is that story true?"

"Naw, it's one I made up. Young'uns love a ghost story, they do. Of course, all that was after I was sent back because of my injury."

"I heard you were decorated."

"Weren't nothin'. Any fool can get hisself shot."

"That's not what Mrs. de Toi tells me."

"Oh, you can't listen to Amelia. She exaggerates."

"You're being too modest." I paused wondering if my next question might put him off. "How well do you know the tunnels? Are they safe enough to explore?"

He squinted at me again...harder this time. "Now, I'll tell you the same thing I told the young'uns. Don't go getting any ideas about them tunnels. Them passageways are old. They could collapse on you, or you could get lost. You shouldn't be down there."

"But I already was. At least, that's how I remember it. So, I wondered if that's where you found me."

"Me? I know better'n to go wanderin' around those nasty spaces. I found you in the grove, just like I said. Don't know why you'd think otherwise. Must have been the fever or that bump on the head."

Mathiam looked upset, like he might be hiding information.

"You're telling me the truth, aren't you? You're not just trying to protect me from something…?"

The gardener waved his secateurs in the air as if to cut me off. "Now, why would I be lyin'? If you think you was in a tunnel, how do I know you weren't? I didn't find you in one, but you was near an exit."

"Was I?" This new piece of information felt like a shard of ice sliding down my back. "Where? Can you show me?"

He pointed in the general direction of the trees. "Over there, near what I call the old graveyard. Leastwise, that's what I think it was. The stones are so ancient, the names coulda worn away but they's too many of 'em to be ordinary stones."

"Really? I've walked along there and never noticed anything."

"Most people don't. You'd have to be lookin' sharp. Most of them stones is buried part way. Odeil used to walk there. She said the place was peaceful. I guess it would be if it was a graveyard."

"And you say the exit to one of the tunnels is nearby? Can you show me?"

"What? Right now?"

"No time like the present."

Chapter Sixteen

WHEN I ENTERED THE DINING room later that evening, I was disappointed to find the table laid for two and not three. Dr. Afreet was already seated. Christian, he explained, was resting in his rooms but in one or two days he might be well enough to join us. The doctor seemed in an affable mood, in marked contrast to Kathrine, who stood at the sideboard with her eyes burning like hot coals. He sent her off for the wine decanter which she had neglected to place on the table.

"I'm afraid Kathrine is a trifle miffed," he said once we were alone. "But you'll soon put it right, I'm sure."

"Me? What have I done to offend her?"

"Nothing. It's Mrs. de Toi we have to contend with."

"What's she accused of now? The poor woman's sick."

"Sick or not, she wandered into the kitchen about an hour ago and there was a terrible row. You didn't hear it?"

"No, I was out for a walk. What were they arguing about? Wait. Don't tell me. I can guess."

"A matter of territory." Dr. Afreet smiled. "When two women share a kitchen, tiffs are inevitable."

"But I looked in on Mrs. de Toi this morning and she was the picture of misery. What was she doing downstairs?"

"A misplaced sense of duty, perhaps. Admirable but foolish. Anyway, when she saw how Kathrine had rearranged her kitchen...

well, you can imagine what happened. I tried to mediate in your absence and had a pot thrown at me for my pains. Fortunately, your cook was too weak to hurl it far."

"Where is she now?"

"In her room. Her exertion brought on a coughing fit and I practically had to carry her up the stairs. I gave her a sedative. She'll sleep through the night; but there's no telling what we will be up against come morning. I was hoping you would have a word with her."

"I'll try, but I'm pretty certain she won't stand for Kathrine's rearrangement, much less allow her to go on preparing Christian's meals once she's well again. I'm glad to hear he's feeling better, by the way."

The doctor shrugged as he took a sip of wine. "His exertion of this morning has left him weak. But overall, he is recovering."

"You mean, he's getting better now that Mrs. de Toi has no opportunity to put arsenic in his soup."

"You needn't take the matter personally, Rachel. As I said at the outset, using Kathrine is simply a precaution."

"A temporary one," I reminded him. "In the meantime, I'm left to negotiate peace between the combatants. Not a very easy task, and a pointless one, I might add. Mrs. de Toi would do nothing to hurt Christian. If she's guilty of anything, it's that she dotes on him too much."

"So, it would appear. But for the moment, as I've said, we must continue to be cautious."

"That's easy for you to say. You don't have to keep the staff happy."

The doctor shrugged. "There is always the possibility of bringing on a new cook."

"What? I'd never fire Mrs. de Toi. If that's your idea, you can forget it."

Dr. Afreet smiled as he helped himself to a dinner roll. "You mistake my proposal, Rachel. I know you are fond of her. I'd never suggest dismissing her. No. But acting as cook and housekeeper can't be easy for a woman of her years. It isn't as if you can't afford the extra help. Madame de Villiers, despite her penurious habits was, I believe, a wealthy woman."

"Penurious? Why do you say that?"

"Do not misunderstand me," the doctor corrected himself. "I offer no criticism of the lady. I admire her austerity. It shows an indifference to the material world. But she could have afforded more servants. Am I not right in this conclusion?"

He was right. Once I'd been made privy to Odeil's accounts, I'd had the same thought. The woman had lived as though she were a pauper when the truth was quite the opposite. Perhaps, she'd acquired frugal habits as a result of the war. Or perhaps, she feared hard times might come again. Whatever the reason, it was true her habits went beyond frugality. The one exception was her wardrobe. There, she allowed herself to binge like a dieter restricted to water but with a secret stash of chocolate.

"No, I do not accuse her of being miserly." The doctor's words penetrated my thoughts. "Even Christian, who has no love for his cousin, admits she was generous with others. I'm told she made several sizeable bequests to her favorite charities. But where the chateau was concerned, she was not a good steward. Perhaps she didn't know how. You, my dear Rachel, are in a position to make better choices. And so I ask, is it fair to expect Mrs. de Toi to cook and clean seven days a week…?"

"She has Sundays off."

"Surely, that isn't enough."

"You talk as if she had no help. There are other servants."

I could feel myself growing defensive, but Afreet was right again. I could make other choices and felt guilty that I hadn't. Even so, I wasn't ready to admit my neglect. "You don't understand. Obtaining help in winter is difficult. I doubt you could find someone to work in the kitchen even if Mrs. de Toi would consent."

The doctor looked up from his plate of pot roast, his face painted with a smug expression. "Would you allow me to try?"

Somewhere in the distance, I imagined I heard a trap door falling.

"I'll think about it."

* * *

By the next morning, after sleepless hours, I hit upon a compromise that would address the presumption Mrs. de Toi could have poisoned Christian. I'd eliminate the opportunity for her to do so. In future, meals would be served family style rather than as individual servings. If believing she wished to kill Christian was crazy, it was crazier still to think she'd kill us all to accomplish it. With opportunity eliminated, so, too, was the need to keep Kathrine in the kitchen except to serve the meals. My solution struck me as so satisfying that I remember heading for breakfast with a light step, aware that the day was clear and that sunlight washed the landscape with a golden glow.

Dr. Afreet sat holding forth in conversation as I entered the dining room.

"I assure you, it's true. The ancient manuals of Yoga science described the internal structure of human physiology even though the Yogis never dissected a single cadaver." He was addressing his remarks to Dr. Cartouche who was seated opposite. The older man shook his head to indicate he doubted such an achievement was possible; but when he saw me, he rose from his chair.

"Ah, there you are, Rachel," Dr. Afreet said as he also rose to pull out my chair. "We wondered if we should wake you. And now you've come, looking lovely and refreshed."

As I sat down, I inquired about the purpose of Dr. Cartouche's visit. Had Christian taken a turn for the worse, I wondered.

Both men chuckled as they retook their seats but, as usual, Afreet was the one to answer. "No, my dear. After this morning's consultation, my colleague and I have agreed our patient is much improved. In fact, he will join us this afternoon. I hope that makes you happy."

"It does. We have financial affairs to discuss as well as staffing matters." I threw Afreet a thin smile.

To my surprise, he shook his head. "I wouldn't expose him to too much detail, as yet. He still needs his rest. But if you have monetary concerns, perhaps I could be of help. I'm good with figures."

"Thank you, no. The decisions can wait until he's ready, though I have made one on my own already."

"Really, my dear? And what is that?" Afreet stuffed a morsel of bacon into his mouth as he smiled at me.

I told them about the new serving arrangements but instead of seeing relief on their faces, or acquiescence, at least, I noted that Afreet's eyes drifted to those of Dr. Cartouche, and that the latter gave a slight shrug, looking nonplused.

My houseguest pressed his lips with his napkin, as if giving himself time to consider what his next words should be.

"Service family style is one possible solution," he replied at last. "But it fails to provide Mrs. de Toi with the much needed assistance, she requires. I thought we agreed—"

"Mrs. de Toi has yet to complain of her duties, doctor. Why don't we put the matter to her?"

The man confronted poured coffee into my cup without looking at me. "It goes without saying that you know her better than I, my dear. And you are the mistress here. But Christian will have an opinion, I should think."

His subtle challenge left me speechless. A stranger seated at the table would have been hard pressed to determine who was in charge of the chateau. By all appearances, the doctor was. In the short while since he'd arrived, he'd not only gained control over the life of his patient but had also rearranged much of the workings of the household. Now, he proposed to gain another concession by using his patient against me. This battle of wills was one I dared not risk, not only because I'd no wish to sap Christian's his strength but also because I doubted his capacity to act independently of his doctor.

I left the challenge unanswered and, in the absence of further distraction, the doctors returned to their debate about the mystical powers of the Yogis. After coffee and a sweet roll, I left them.

Just before lunch, Lucille entered the library where I was at work. "The police are here again, Mademoiselle. They wish to speak to you." She looked rueful as she made the announcement, her dark eyes round with empathy.

"I don't suppose they told you why?" The maid shook her head, no. "Then you'd better show them in."

Moments later, Inspector Tromperie and Detective Boueur appeared. I offered them chairs but, as before, they chose to stand. The younger man looked uncomfortable but his superior stood with his chest thrust forward as if it were stuffed with pillows.

He was not long in getting down to business. "I understand the patient has improved. That is a good thing. Unfortunately, we've been unable to find a cause for the incident, so the danger remains."

"You refuse to consider the possibility of an accident?"

"We continue to look for a suspect, yes. But we have uncovered carelessness on the part of your gardener which should be corrected."

"You suspect Mathiam, now?"

"I'm advising you that he should keep his chemicals under lock and key. Anyone can access his shed, even a passerby."

"You think Christian's been poisoned by a passerby?"

The Inspector's cheeks grew rosy at my impudence. "We are not suggesting a stranger has poisoned Monsieur de Hess. You misunderstand me, entirely. I'm saying that under the current arrangements, some very dangerous poisons are available to anyone. You must take precautions...unless you have some motive for failing to do so?"

"Am I still a suspect, then?"

The detective shook his head while the inspector shrugged before answering. "We have determined you do not benefit in the event of Monsieur de Hess's death." He looked disappointed as he made his admission.

"Then, I'm not a suspect?"

"*Everyone* is a suspect, Mademoiselle, until we discover what occurred."

"And when do you think you'll know?"

Trumperie's cheeks turned scarlet. "I'm sure Mademoiselle is aware that what she asks is absurd. We will know when we know. That's when we will know."

"Thank you, Inspector." I smiled demurely. "You've made yourself perfectly clear. And I will speak to Mathiam about locking up his chemicals. I thought he'd already taken that precaution but, apparently, he needs reminding."

Lucille entered the room to announce lunch was served. Her eyes drifted to the two men who were standing as if to ask if they would be staying. As a courtesy, I extended an invitation.

Inspector Tromperie glanced at his watch and nodded. "You are most kind."

Without further comment, I led my guests to the dining room and was surprised to find both doctors and their patient already seated. Christian looked frail but better than the last time I'd seen him. What had not changed was the air of hopelessness that hung about him. Throughout much of the meal, his eyes seldom met mine or anyone else's. The body might be recovering but the mind was proving a laggard. Seeing him so despondent upset me, although I admit there were times in the past when I might have gladly poisoned him, myself...metaphorically, of course. But that afternoon, seeing him almost quaking in his chair, I felt nothing but compassion.

Having two policemen seated at the table seemed to inspire Dr. Afreet. Instead of his normal discourse on mysticism, he began a conversation about good and evil, insisting that one was little different from the other. To my surprise, Christian took immediate exception and with more vehemence than I would have thought possible.

"That's absurd. You put murder and mayhem on the same plane as charity and sacrifice? God could not be so perverse."

"You think so?" Afreet laid his fork across his plate to make his response. "Yet, He created Lucifer, did He not, at least, according to your Christian beliefs?"

"Yes, so we could choose between good and evil. He gave us free will."

"And that is a good thing, is it not, this 'free will?'"

"You know, it is," Christian hissed, his fist clenched.

The doctor leaned back in his chair, a rare moment when his food was forgotten. "I know nothing of the kind, dear boy. Freedom—true freedom—is not a choice at all. It is the highest form of comprehension. To understand is to recognize that good and evil are the end points of a single line. Milton knew this. Otherwise, he could not have fallen in love as he did with his villain."

"Do you hear that, Inspector Tromperie?" I interposed. "Crime is an aspect of good and therefore it should not be punished. It appears we have been wasting your time."

If I'd expected the policeman to take a commonsense view of the world, I was wrong. He looked up from his plate with an earnest expression. "I understand what the doctor is saying. God is the creator. Whatever one does in His service is good no matter the harm done."

The gleam in Afreet's eye as he looked at me was insufferable. "The French have a saying, I believe: 'To understand everything is to forgive everything.' Do you not agree, Rachel?"

"No, I do not," I told him. "Some people are simply evil. Terrorists who blow up the innocent are among those."

"And yet, in Algeria, such men acting in the service of their country would be hailed as heroes." Dr. Afreet returned to his meal and the room fell silent.

* * *

Christian remained confined to his rooms for the next two days. Perhaps Dr. Afreet felt his outburst at lunch was a sign of an impending relapse. I suspected, however, it was part of his determination to keep his patient secluded…especially from me. But why? I needed to get to the bottom of it.

When I sought formal permission to see Christian, however, the answer was always the same: "inadvisable." Finally, I'd had enough and after twice being rejected, I was about to give argument when there came an outburst from the kitchen.

Mrs. de Toi, it seems, had risen from her bed like the great white whale and was wreaking havoc among the pots and pans. When I entered, she was upbraiding Claudine for neglecting to put fresh towels in the rooms and Kathrine was taking the girl's side. The chorus rising from three high-pitched voices could have awakened the spirits in Mathiam's imaginary graveyard. Probably fifteen minutes or more elapsed before order was restored and the combatants sent to their separate corners, so to speak. After that, I retreated to the library but was not long at my reading when Mrs. de Toi burst into the room with eyes aflame, her hair coiling under her cap like errant snakes.

"Either that new girl goes or I do," she glared at me.

If we had been alone, I might have easily consoled her, but Kathrine had quick marched in behind her, intent upon telling Claudine's side of the story, again. Pandemonium broke out a second time as the two women shouted and shook their fists at one another. It took me a minute or two before my voice could be heard above theirs and I was able to separate them. I sent Kathrine from the room with the promise I would talk to her later. In the meantime, Mrs. de Toi stayed behind, having hurled herself into one of the leather chairs.

"I'm sorry, Mademoiselle, but this new girl...she dropped the salad on the floor, picked it up with her hands and put in back into the bowl. Can you believe it? What's more, I continually have to remind her to wash her hands. The rest of her could use a good wash, as well." The housekeeper looked up for consolation and, by my glance, she got it. "Who is this girl?" she went on. "Where did she come from? She's never been in service, I can tell you that. Kathrine always takes her side. And what's this about Kathrine being in charge of Monsieur de Hess's meals? Am I incapable of making a little soup?"

"Of course not, Mrs. de Toi. As you were ill, naturally Kathrine was put in charge. But if you're feeling better, things shall be as they were. Christian is feeling better anyway and will not require a special menu. So, you see? There's no need to fret."

Gazing down at my friend, I could see how tired she looked. Whether it was the aftermath of her illness or the fact that Afreet had observed rightly that she was feeling her age, I didn't know, but it was apparent to me additional staff would be desirable. I only hoped when I broached the subject, Mrs. de Toi wouldn't interpret my suggestion as an affront.

Drawing the captain's chair next to hers, I took hold of her hands. "As for Claudine, I ask you to be patient. We can't throw her out in the dead of winter. Besides, if she wants to be in service, who better to train her than you? Why don't we give her a try? Three months, if you like. If you haven't made a silk purse out of that sow's ear by then, I'll eat one of Odeil's hats."

Pleased with my compliment, the housekeeper gave me a half smile. "I suppose there's something in what you say. It is winter and the girl seems willing enough, but she's so backward. I can't imagine where's she's been all her life. Giving her instruction is like speaking to a child raised among wolves. But as you ask, Mademoiselle, I will try. Kathrine, however, is to stay out of my kitchen, except to carry the dishes to and fro."

"I'll speak to her after you've gone," I promised. "By the way, I'd like to suggest a change in the way we serve the meals." I told her of my idea about family style with trepidation but, to my relief, Mrs. de Toi agreed.

"Lord knows, we have enough bowls and platters. It wouldn't hurt to use some of that fine china. When it was just Madame de Villiers, it didn't make sense to be formal but with all the traffic about these days, family service is a good idea."

Still basking in the glow of my success with the housekeeper, I spoke to Kathrine next. Unfortunately, I had little success in placating her. Her chin wobbled on the point of tears as she flounced from the room having been shorn of her cooking duties.

For a full hour, the library was quiet again. I was becoming drowsy, listening to the mantle clock ticking, when Mathiam appeared with his plaid cap in hand.

"I put a new lock on them chemicals like I was told, Mademoiselle. I didn't realize the old one was broken... I wondered if you wanted one of the keys or should I give the spare to Amelia to keep with her lot?"

My answer that I should keep the key came too swiftly and the gardener noted it. After he handed it to me, he remained standing, shifting from one foot to the other.

"What is it, Mathiam? What's the matter?"

"Well, I was wondern'... I mean, why are those policemen still pokin' about? They don't suspect Amelia, do they?"

"Who told you they suspect her?" My eyes were focused entirely on him as he stood twisting his cap in his hands.

"That younger one, the little detective, he hangs around Claudine a lot. I heard him sayin' he thought Amelia would be goin' away soon. They're not thinkin' of arrestin' her, are they?"

"Arresting her? That's ridiculous. No, I assure you, the police haven't a clue about what happened and probably never will. Whatever made Monsieur de Hess ill, there's no evidence it was anything but an accident. Locking up the pesticides is just a precaution."

Mathiam looked apologetic. "I promise I'll be more careful in future. It wouldn't be fair if my carelessness brought Amelia under suspicion, especially when she's so particular. She's always after me about washin' up and changin' my overalls before I come into the kitchen. But I forget. So, if anyone's to blame, it's me. That sweet woman would never hurt a fly."

"No, she wouldn't," I agreed. "She's one of the dearest people, I've ever met."

"That's right, she is," Mathiam snuffled.

"Maybe, you should tell her that," I said by way of encouragement. "It wouldn't do any harm and she could use a few kind words, couldn't she?"

The gardener let a grizzled smile cross his lips. "Maybe, I will."

Chapter Seventeen

As Afreet had promised, Christian appeared for his meals after a two-day absence. The rest of his time the invalid spent resting or strolling in the garden when the weather wasn't too bleak; but he was never alone and so there seemed to be no occasion for us to be alone together, although I didn't stop trying.

In the meanwhile, I enjoyed the relative peace that had descended. Mrs. de Toi, having reclaimed her kitchen, was content; Kathrine sulked, but that was normal; and Claudine showed a marked improvement in her habits. What's more, the police had not carted anyone off to the Bastille.

I allowed myself to relax, unaware Afreet had another trick up his sleeve. Being the innocent, I studied, took long walks, also, if the weather permitted and dreamed of sending Afreet packing. All that tranquility shattered on a day that was washed in beautiful sunlight.

I recall I was crossing the foyer on my way to the library, when I noticed the door to the solarium had been left ajar. Thinking Claudine had been watering the plants and had neglected to close it, I retraced my steps but stopped on the threshold when I discovered Christian seated alone in a lawn chair.

He was turned in profile, staring out the windows, and failed to notice me, at first. In that moment, I was struck by his beauty — those patrician features and that cloud of blond curls. It seemed a shame to disturb him as he looked so tranquil. I might have withdrawn, except his gaze turned in my direction. In those sapphire eyes, I saw a mixture of pleasure and dismay.

He didn't get up to welcome me but pointed to an empty wooden chair near him and asked me to join him. This I did and, for a time, we let the silence fall between us as we admired the sun speckled foliage. When I inquired about his health, he replied he'd felt well enough to manage the stairs on his own.

"You mean, Dr. Afreet allowed it?" I regretted my snide tone, but Christian smiled with understanding.

"He doesn't know. He left for the village a while ago."

"But it's Sunday." I frowned. "What could he possibly be doing in Sainte Enimie today? Not church, surely. He's not a Christian, is he? I never thought about his religion before."

"You mustn't ask me about such things. I'm just a patient."

The sigh which followed was one that spoke volumes. I could imagine the strain of living under constant supervision. I would have liked to free him but, as yet, I'd devised no scheme that would succeed in sending the doctor packing.

"You'll get better and soon will have no need of a physician," I said by way of encouragement.

The voice that answered was flat and without hope.

"That decision isn't mine, I'm afraid."

"I don't really see why he's here," I continued. "Mrs. de Toi and I can look after you."

"I can't just show him the door, Rachel." Christian turned his head to look at me, his eyes full of despair. "I thought you knew. He has the power to recommit me to Mende, if he likes. I couldn't go back there. I don't think I could survive."

"But you're of age, now. He has no authority over you any longer, does he?"

"You don't understand. When I signed into the sanatorium I was examined and, after a time, Afreet recommended my status be changed from voluntary to involuntary commitment. He wrote Odeil as my guardian and she agreed. I'm sure she must have danced with glee when she read his report."

"Surely, it's not possible to commit someone without a hearing, is it?"

"You forget, I was a minor at the time."

"Even so…"

"Don't ask me to go into the details, Rachel. It happened. That's all I know. I've seen the papers."

"I'm sorry. I-I suppose Odeil thought it was for the best…"

"Yes, by all means, go on defending her. You've seen what's happened to my life, but don't allow that to alter your opinion. My cousin was an angel."

The bitterness in his voice, I knew, was meant for me, as well as, for Odeil and I was stung by it, although I refused to leave him without hope.

"But you're twenty-five, now. Surely, you can appeal…"

He behaved as if he hadn't heard me and continued to stare out the window. "I can't believe how she's charmed you. Yet, why should I be surprised? She charmed me, too. Once I thought she was my sun. No more. No more."

When I started to rise, thinking I could do nothing to console him, Christian took hold of my hand. "Don't go. I shouldn't have spoken as I did just now. I know your feelings for her and I should respect them. Besides, we have to talk and there isn't much time. I suppose I should begin with another apology for the birthday party. I haven't been able to do that 'til now. I can't deny I was trying to drive you away. As you'd taken Odeil's place, you became another impediment to my freedom. Naturally, I wanted to hurt you. My life has been one of constraints, and you became another one. Can you understand how I felt?"

"Yes, I think I can."

"But you wouldn't fight back. Instead, you were kind. All that gentleness made me feel worse. When a person becomes ashamed, he grows even more resentful. That's what happened to me. Not now, of course. When I realized your concern was genuine and that you weren't playing games, I was grateful. God knows, I needed a little compassion in my life." Christian stared down at his hands. "I suppose you think I'm a fool wallowing in self-pity and maybe you're right. I'm lost, Rachel, and I don't know how to help myself."

His voice broke and, instinctively, I put my arm around his shoulder. "It'll be all right. We'll work things out, somehow."

"Will we?" He turned to look at me. "Don't you understand? You're a pawn in my cousin's game as much as I am."

"Of course, we're not. If she thought we'd become enemies, she was wrong. We're free to sort out our lives for ourselves. She has no control over us. She's dead, Christian. She's dead. You and I can be friends, can't we?"

Suddenly, the man at my side let his head fall into his hands. "Oh God, if only I'd known you as I do now. If only…" He began to shiver as if the cold from outside had invaded the room. "Rachel, I'm so sorry. I'm so very, very sorry."

Wrapping my arms about him, I clung to him as if I feared he might drown. "I promise you, Christian, we've already won. Don't you see that? Look at me. Can't you see I care?"

When he refused to respond, I let go of him and slipped to the floor on my knees so I could look up into his face. His eyes were flooded with tears. As I brushed away a lock of his hair that had fallen across his forehead, I could feel his breath mingling with mine. Our lips were so close, they were almost touching.

"Ah, what do you think, Fripon? Waterhouse's 'La Belle Dame sans Merci?' A case of life imitating art, surely."

Startled, Christian and I swung to face the door of the solarium, which I had left open. Dr. Afreet stood on the threshold with a strange man beside him; a tall fellow, possibly six feet, with a pale mustache and a bald head. From his thin lips hung a lighted cigarette, its plume of smoke rising into his gray eyes so that he was forced to squint. He appeared to be Afreet's age, in his mid-fifties, although thin and wiry while the doctor was stocky. A difference, too, extended to their clothing. Afreet was meticulous in his appearance. The stranger's garments were old and shabby, a neglect that spoke to his slovenly habits. All-in-all, his was a surly and unwholesome appearance.

I rose from my crouched position in time to be introduced to the stranger, noting his look of disapproval of me…similar to mine for him. Our hands barely touched in greeting. His eyes looked over my head and were fixed upon Christian, who ignored him, having turned his gaze to the far horizon.

Dr. Afreet ignored his patient's behavior and addressed his remarks to me. "Fripon has had a long journey, Rachel. He could do with a rest before assuming his duties. If you would be so kind as to have Kathrine show him to his room?"

"His room? What do you mean?" My frown didn't seem to disturb the doctor in the least.

"Why, hasn't Christian told you? I left him with the understanding... Well, never mind." He gave me a cunning smile and went to the heart of the matter. "I've done as you asked, my dear. I've found you a new cook, or should I say, *sous chef?*"

When I heard him, I confess I was angry, almost too angry to speak. I had to force my words from me. "B-but I don't need a new cook. I thought I made that clear. What's more I gave you no authority to—"

"Your partner approved of the idea," the doctor interrupted. "And you needn't be concerned about the man's salary. Christian will pay for it. So, you see, you've no need to worry. All is well."

"It is *not* well." I spun 'round to glare at the man whom I had almost kissed. "You knew about this? We sat together for half an hour and you said nothing? How could you make such a decision without consulting me? And what about Mrs. de Toi? Have you given any thought to how she will feel?"

As usual, the doctor interceded on behalf of his patient. "Frankly, Rachel, the poor boy has only done what you should have done long ago. This place is understaffed. What would be more natural for him than to wish to lighten his nanny's burdens? Fripon has been hired as a *sous chef* to assist in the kitchen, not to replace your precious Mrs. de Toi. Try him for a time before you make a judgment. No one is challenging your authority. For the life of me, I cannot fathom why you should be upset."

"Can't you, Doctor?" My voice was shaking. "Then we exist in different worlds."

* * *

The rest of the morning I spent hiding in the library, making a pretense of my research. A book was open on my desk and my notepad lay beside it, together with some pencils and a pen; but none of these tools was put to use. My thoughts churned like the ingredients of a stew, roiling in a heat that made them rise and fall and rise again, never allowing me to rest.

I supposed the scene in the solarium was staged, worked out between the doctor and his patient. Afreet almost suggested as much. But, besides making me angry, what had Christian to gain? Or the doctor?

I decided to take a page from Afreet's book of philosophy. Perhaps, it was time for me to examine what I thought was real. Christian was who he said he was. Mrs. de Toi and Mathiam had testified to that. But what about the doctor? Was he a doctor? Did he have control over Christian's life or were the unfolding events merely scenes from a play designed to end with me fleeing from the chateau?

That I could harbor such thoughts caught me by surprise. When, I wondered, had I become a cynic? I usually took appearances at face value. Yet, unaccustomed as I now was to deception, I could not allay my suspicion. The more I considered, the more I began to suspect that this doctor might be no doctor at all, but some actor Christian had hired to perpetrate a hoax. Odeil had warned me of her cousin's devious nature. And hadn't he admitted the birthday party was designed to drive me away?

A call to the sanatorium in Mende might put my mind at rest. I decided to place one that night, when no one was about.

Having made my decision, I was flooded with relief. I even managed to doze off in one of the leather chairs.

The mantle clock was chiming the hour of noon when shouts awoke me. They were approaching from La Salle de Persephone. I had barely time to adjust my clothing when the library door flew open as if subjected to a meteoric blast. Mrs. de Toi stood in its wake.

"Mademoiselle Rachel, this person, this c-r-re-a-ture" — she extended the word as she gestured at the man behind her— "has commandeered my kitchen. He insists he is the new *sous chef*. Absurd! I do not need a *sous chef*. And look at his nails! Surely, this is some lunatic who has wandered into my kitchen. You must tell him to go away, and if he will not, you must call the police!"

The woman with flour on her face and hands didn't wait for my answer but continued her rant. "First Kathrine and now him. How much am I to endure? I have means, Mademoiselle, as you know. I'll not stay and be humiliated."

I hurried forward to offer her a hanky in case she might be on the brink of tears. She was too angry for that. Her face was red, not from the heat of the kitchen, but perhaps from a pending bout of apoplexy. With a shooing gesture I made it clear to Fripon I wanted him to leave. He threw me an insolent glance but did as I required, although with a slow pace to indicate his displeasure. When he was gone, I shut the door with a sigh.

Once we were alone, I seated Mrs. de Toi in a leather chairs and took the one opposite. My first task was to assure her no one wanted her to leave. I had to say it several times and loud enough to override her bursts of temper. Finally, she calmed down and listened while I explained the hiring was Christian's idea because of his concern for her. He wanted to ease her burden, but I assured her the arrangement was a trial. If the man didn't work out, he'd be asked to leave. The decision would be hers.

The cook's eyes grew large. "I-is that true, Mademoiselle? Christian was thinking of me?"

"But, of course, it is. He knows that Kathrine and Claudine need supervision, and as Lucille will be going to away to school soon..."

"Yes, that was wonderful of you to pay for her tuition. She talks of nothing but art since she's been accepted at college. You've been very kind to her."

"The point is," I persisted, "with her gone, you're going to need more help."

"But a cook..."

"A *sous chef*," I corrected. "He's not in charge of the kitchen. You are. And look on the bright side. With him here, Kathrine will be kept in her place. That should please you, shouldn't it?"

"Oh, that one!" Mrs. de Toi leaned forward with a burst of zeal, "She could never be a cook. She uses too many dishes and never cleans up properly. I'd sooner teach a stone to dance."

"And now, you won't have to. Fripon can find his way around a kitchen. That's a plus, I should think."

"Only if he does as he is told and cleans under his nails." Mrs. de Toi looked at me with an expression that suggested she was unsure whether or not she might not be leaping from the frying pan into the fire. "Who is this Fripon, Mademoiselle? What are his qualifications? Did he bring references?"

Not knowing the answer to her questions, I evaded them. "I'm sure Christian has seen his papers and that the man comes highly recommended. But remember, if he's not satisfactory, you must have a word in Christian's ear."

"The poor boy looks so poorly," Mrs. de Toi mused. "One hates to bother him. But I'll do as you say, Mademoiselle. I'll give this new man a try."

She left me like a woman threading her way through a minefield. Still, I congratulated myself for having averted another crisis.

* * *

I did not see Christian or Dr. Afreet until dinner. At the table, my partner did his best to avoid looking at me, but Dr. Afreet was in a flamboyant, almost theatrical, humor. I tried to ignore him, at first, but unchecked, his assertions became more and more outrageous. Finally, I heard myself saying, "That's an exaggeration don't you think?"

The doctor peered at me over his wine glass. "But I assure you, Rachel, I do not exaggerate. The mind seeks patterns to use as landmarks in our quest for understanding. These are patterns which magic and science share. There is little difference between the two disciplines."

"You'll forgive me, Doctor, but I think the two are nothing alike. Science confirms our view of reality while magic mystifies it."

The doctor snorted at my statement. "You are succumbing to prejudice, Rachel, preferring one set of outcomes above another. But consider the folly of that."

Dr. Afreet paused in his discourse long enough to savor another bite of Mrs. de Toi's pot pie. Crumbs from the pastry cascaded down his beard and these he wiped away with his napkin. "Superb," he muttered, before continuing. Then he waved his empty fork in the air. "To prove my point, let us consider Occam's razor, the scientific dictum that says we must connect evidence in the simplest fashion."

"I'm aware of it."

"Good, because this same dictum applies equally in magic. If a magician closes his left hand slowly over a coin held between the thumb and forefinger of his right, and then he separates the two to reveal the coin has disappeared, your eyes lead you to assume the object has been transferred to his left hand, does it not?"

"Well, yes, but—"

"And why do you make this assumption? Because experience and Occam's razor have taught you to do so. You accept the simplest explanation for where the coin has gone. But where is the truth now, dear girl? Where is it? You have been tricked. You have drawn your conclusion based on one set of beliefs when another should apply. No, no, Rachel. I must insist science is no hook upon which to hang our notion of reality. All we can say of this world is that we should take nothing for granted."

That said, the doctor attacked his meal with renewed energy, satisfied he had delivered some sort of coup-de-grace. Given what I knew of him—or rather didn't know—I was inclined to sympathize with his conclusion about taking things for granted. Certainly, had I been able to draw upon magic's power, I'd have had him gone in a poof. Perhaps, tonight, after my call to Mende, that would be possible. At least, I hoped so.

* * *

The foyer clock was striking ten when I made my way down the staircase toward the phone. Through the vertical windows on either side of the door, silver bars of moonlight spilled across the marble. The space was bright enough for me to find my way without a torch.

I dialed the number I'd acquired earlier for the sanatorium but did it slowly, hoping to muffle the sound. I was barely breathing as I listened to the call go through.

By the seventh ring, a voice came on the line, that of a young woman. She seemed unsure of herself, wary, perhaps, of an incoming call that late at night. When I told her I was a relative attempting to reach Dr. Afreet, she sounded relieved.

"The doctor is not at this number, at the moment," she answered crisply. "He's on leave for several months."

She offered no further information, so I persisted. "The doctor's aunt is gravely ill and wishes to see him. Is there another number where he could be found?"

When the voice at the other end of the line remained silent, I went on. "Aunty Em hasn't long to live. I need to contact him as soon as possible. The man I'm looking for is in his mid-fifties. That's him, isn't it?"

"I-I've only worked here three months and didn't see much of him but, yes, our Dr. Afreet is about that age."

"Does he have a beard, by any chance? I remember how he used to tickle my cheeks with his beard when I was a child."

"Oh, yes." The receptionist seemed to be smiling as she spoke. Perhaps she'd known a relative who'd done much the same when she was young. "He takes great pride in his appearance. I noticed that."

"Short men try to make the most of their other assets, I suppose."

"Y-yes. That's probably true." The voice at the other end of line sounded uncertain, as if she feared going too far with her confidences. "Anyway, he's not here. If you leave a message, I'll see it's forwarded. We're not supposed to give out personal information, you understand."

"Well, I was hoping for an exception under the circumstances." I allowed my voice to sound as if it were choked with tears. "Aunty Em was like a mother to all of us. Now there isn't much time…"

"I'm awfully sorry. I wish I could help."

"Just think how he's going to feel when he learns the family tried to reach him before…before… If I could have an address or a phone number?"

I heard a sigh, which gave me hope. "Oh, very well. Hold on. I'll see what I can find."

The line went silent a minute or two before the young woman came back. She hadn't found a phone number but she could supply an address. Mail should be sent in care of Dr. Abdul Cartouche, 14 Rue de le Chat, Sainte Enimie.

"Dr. Cartouche? A-are you certain?"

"Oh, yes. The handwriting is very clear."

"Is this man also employed at the sanatorium?"

"Not that I know of. At least, there's been no one working here by that name for the last three months."

Stunned, I thanked the receptionist for her help and carefully placed the receiver back on its cradle. The room seemed unusually cold—icy, in fact— and I could feel my body begin to shiver. Here was a conundrum. Why had Afreet allowed me to believe he and Dr. Cartouche had only recently met? What sort of charade was being played and how deep did it go? Certainly, what I had just learned left me in grave doubt that anything the doctors had told me so far was true.

I admit my head was swimming in confusion, so much so that, dreading to lose my equilibrium, I propped myself with both hands against the hall table to steady myself. Was there anyone in these environs I could trust?

"Are you all right?"

I spun 'round to discover Christian peering down at me. "You looked unsteady. Who on earth would be calling at this hour?"

"It's still early in the States, if you remember. I was calling a friend." The lie which sprang to my lips came with such alacrity, it occurred to me then, I'd been in the company of charlatans too long.

"Yes. Yes, of course. I should have realized…"

"What are you doing up at this hour? Does your keeper know you've escaped?"

My remark provoked a nervous twitch that passed for a smile. "Actually, I was looking for you and then I saw you here in the foyer."

"Looking for me? Why?"

Christian shook his head, not understanding. "Surely, after all that's happened… I thought you'd be furious about Fripon. I know

Nana wasn't happy. She came to me after she'd talked to you. Thank you for covering for me."

"You're welcome. But why hire the man in the first place? You knew it would hurt her. What's more, I should have been consulted, shouldn't I?"

"I never meant to hurt her, or you. It's…complicated…"

I stood with my arms crossed looking up at the man whose blue velvet robe matched the color of his eyes. "I'm listening."

"I'm afraid I can't explain, at the moment. Look, I know I don't have a leg to stand on but I must ask you to trust me. I came looking for you because there may be some rough times ahead. I want to urge you again to leave this place, at least, for a little while… and as soon as possible."

When I started to object, he tapped my lips gently with a finger to silence me. "I repeat, just for a little while."

"How long?"

"I can't say for certain. But the longer you remain here… Please, Rachel, do as I ask."

I looked at him blankly. "That's it? After all your evasions and lies, you want me to trust you without any explanation? Sorry. You'll have to do better than that."

I tried to get past him but he took hold of my wrists. "This isn't a game I'm playing. I'm telling you, you must leave."

The desperation in his eyes only made me angry. "Why? So you can sell the chateau out from under me? Is that your plan?"

"That's absurd and you know it."

"Do I? I suspect I know very little. Why didn't you tell me there was a connection between Dr. Cartouche and Afreet? Why are they pretending they barely know one another when, in fact, they're colleagues?"

Christian's grip on me tightened. "Who told you that? No one knows–"

"You do, apparently."

Defeated, he let go of me and allowed his eyes to drift toward the ceiling as if words might be found there to satisfy me. "God, oh, God, either way I go I meet disaster."

His sigh was so sorrowful, I forgot I was the one offended. "What's going on, Christian? If you're in some kind of trouble, tell me. If I've got to trust you, then you should trust me."

I brushed his cheek with my hand in an effort to draw his attention to me. He looked down at once and what I saw in the dark pools of his eyes was a desperate longing.

"Doubt everything, Rachel" he whispered hoarsely, "except that I care…very much." Then he kissed me with an urgency that left me feeling weak.

What might have passed between us, I don't know, but we broke apart at the sound of hands clapping overhead. Afreet stood at the upstairs landing looking down at us.

"What is it this time? Gustav Klimt's 'The Kiss,' I think. Very apt."

Neither Christian nor I answered. We hadn't recovered from the shock of being found together.

Ignoring our silence, the doctor continued to speak as he descended the stairs, his face appearing hardened in the moonlight. "How long have these little trysts been going on, I wonder?"

"Believe it or not, Afreet, there are some things that don't concern you." Christian had found his voice and it was defiant.

"Not so, dear boy. I am interested in all aspects of your life. Besides, if there is anything between you and Rachel, you have no need to be discreet. You are among friends."

"You're reading too much into what you think you saw–"

"Am I? Yet, from where I was standing, you and she appear to be on the best of terms."

"But as you say," I interjected, "one cannot always trust one's senses."

The doctor, who by now had reached the foyer, emitted a light chuckle. "How right you are, dear Rachel. How right you are. I'm having some influence on you, after all. But I confess, I am a trifle disappointed to hear your denial. Young love is so exciting. It makes one's pulse race, does it not?"

When I refused to parry his remark, he sighed. "Ah, well, life goes on. And plans go forward, isn't that so, Christian?"

His patient didn't answer but glared at the doctor with undisguised fury. His lips tight, he pushed past the medical man and hurried up the stairs. I watched him go, not knowing what to think. Was it cowardice or a fear of doing his doctor an injury that drove him away? At the moment, I knew nothing, only that I had been abandoned.

Unruffled, Afreet headed for the kitchen. "Care for some cocoa, Rachel?"

Chapter Eighteen

THAT NIGHT I SLEPT SOUNDLY, although I remember several times trying to rouse myself from a dream. The details of the scene from which I was attempting to escape are sketchy, but I remember the colors and sounds were unfamiliar, almost as if I'd left the earth and had been transported to another world. The garden where I walked was shadowy, empty of flowers or trees or birds of any kind. Rather, the panorama was comprised of sharp-edged crystals that gleamed as though from the light of multiple suns, except that the atmosphere was grey and cold. Here was a place hostile to all life forms.

I awoke the next morning as though in a drunken stupor. Worse, my skin felt clammy and my throat was parched. An empty cup of cocoa stood on my night stand, but the water tumbler was empty. I rang for Lucille and was surprised when Claudine appeared. I'd forgotten Kathrine's sister had left some time ago for her first term at school, the Ecole Superieur Beaux-Arts de Marseille, or ESBAM, for short. I recalled how excited she'd been when she'd gotten her letter of acceptance, and how we'd picked through Odeil's closet looking for clothes that would be suitable for a student's life. There weren't many skirts she could wear, and the shoes were too small, but there were plenty of warm sweaters. These she carted off in large paper bags with the energy of a stevedore.

On her last day in Sainte Enimie, I went to see her off at the train station. Her entire family had been there, except Kathrine—her mother, her father, a grandmother and three brothers, the youngest being around seven. I knew my money had been well spent when I saw tears in her parents' eyes, a mixture of sadness and pride. Afterwards, Madame and Monsieur Bevard had insisted that I return to their cottage for a meal, which I did. I found it a happy place, with a cat and a dog lying undisturbed by the hearth while the boys broke into a playful tussle. It ended when the rapscallions were sent to wash their hands before sitting down to the table.

Once seated together, all of us enjoyed a meal of potato soup, bread and cheese. As I ate, I listened to the various members of the family tell stories about one another. There was so much laughter on that afternoon that, as I walked home later, I couldn't help wondering where Kathrine got her dour nature.

But, as I say, on the morning after my call to Mende, Lucille was gone and Claudine was in attendance. I asked her to refill the carafe with ice water and, for a moment, she looked confused. I repeated my request and still wasn't sure she understood, when she hurried away.

For a time, I sat on the edge of my bed waiting for her return. When she did not, I decided to fend for myself. I stumbled into the bathroom to drink water from the tap, which in my grogginess sent water splashing over the counter and onto my nightgown.

Disgruntled, I got dressed, which proved more difficult than I had anticipated. My arms and limbs felt heavy, as though I was attempting to move through mud. With great effort I managed to button my sweater, but arranging my hair into a chignon proved impossible. I settled for a ponytail, instead. By the time I entered the dining room, I was as exhausted as if I had moved a dozen packing crates.

Dr. Afreet was alone at the table. He came forward the moment he saw me.

"My dear girl, you look as if you've walked through a hail storm. Sit down." He pulled out my chair and, in a gesture of sympathy, laid my napkin across my lap.

"Do you have a fever? I could call Dr. Cartouche, if you wish."

I shook my head. "No need to call your friend," I assured him.

He seemed to take no notice of my use of the word friend and returned to his ham and eggs. Now and again, however, he paused and glanced in my direction as if attempting to read my thoughts.

Mrs. de Toi entered the dining room from the kitchen, apparently to make her own assessment of my condition. Claudine must have reported I looked ill and, as a precaution, the housekeeper had brought with her a spoon and a large bottle of cod liver oil.

"Take this," she said, after she'd looked me over. "The taste is awful, but it'll do you good. I've never seen you looking so tired. Today, you shall rest. No work. All that can wait."

She was speaking in what I imagined was her nanny voice and seemed to be enjoying it. Nor did I mind being fussed over. I felt cosseted, the way I had been as a child. In those early days, when I'd needed to convalesce, my mother would sit on my bed and, together, we'd cut out paper dolls. Sometimes she'd bring me graham crackers and juice. Best of all, I liked her to read to me. My imagination had thrived on fairytales.

After I had swallowed Mrs. de Toi's remedy, with difficulty, I was allowed a bowl of porridge and a scone, which my new nanny admitted Fripon had made. "It is passable," she said.

I wasn't interested in food but, as if the recommendation had been addressed to him, Dr. Afreet reached into the bread basket and retrieved one of the golden pastries. He was buttering a crust when Christian entered. His gaze fell with undisguised distaste upon his doctor's gluttony.

To be fair, however, Christian was seldom in good humor when he awoke. First and foremost, he expected the day to be in readiness for him. Rooms had to be warm, coffee brewed and people standing by to meet his every need. With such expectations, I often wondered how he'd fared at the sanatorium. Life there had to have been more regimented and less accommodating than at the chateau. Still, his period of confinement seemed to have done little to alter his expectations. Habits formed in childhood, I supposed, have resilience.

As I'd grown accustomed to being treated as if I was invisible most mornings, I was surprised to find his cornflower blue eyes fixed in my direction.

"Rachel has had a difficult night," the doctor stated, seeming to read the thoughts of his patient. "I've suggested Dr. Cartouche be called but she refuses. Nonetheless, I'll have no argument when it comes to her getting some rest." He waved his butter knife at me as he spoke.

"It isn't that I didn't sleep," I answered. "It's more like I was drugged. I thought I heard voices during the night, but I couldn't wake up. I was trapped in a dream."

"No doubt it was all a dream," the doctor grunted. "As for me, I slept like an innocent. If I could further your research in the library while you rest, I'd be delighted. You have only to ask."

Doubtful of his intentions, I told him there was little to do at this stage. "Perhaps later," I smiled.

Afreet shrugged with indifference. "Well, then, perhaps I shall go for a walk. I have a pair of boots I have yet to wear. Perhaps, today, I shall break them in." His eyes drifted to his patient. "What about you Christian? Would you care to join me?"

The latter shook his head, keeping his eyes fixed upon his boiled egg.

"There's a point where too much lying about can have a debilitating effect," the doctor persisted. Seeing the younger man's face turn sour, however, he dropped the matter and returned his attention to me. "My remark is not meant for you, dear girl. You must return to bed as soon as you've finished breakfast. Shall I send Claudine to assist you?"

"Thank you, no. I don't need a nurse."

As if he'd failed to hear me, he rose and headed for the kitchen. "I think it best that someone be in attendance. You shouldn't be disturbed...by anyone." He tossed Christian a hard glance before he left.

We had only a few moments alone together if we wished to exchange any confidences, but after our kiss the previous night, I was unsure of how to begin. Christian seemed to overcome his reticence more quickly and had leaned forward, about to say something, when Kathrine appeared with a fresh pot of coffee.

"Damn," I heard him mutter. During the interval that passed, neither of us looked at one another but when, at last, the maid left us, Christian leaned across the table a second time.

"Rachel, about last night... We need to talk–"

"I know. I wanted to say–"

Before either of us could finish our sentence, Mrs. de Toi burst into the room, her cheeks scarlet. Seeing us together, she broke into a tirade. Fripon was not only making a mess of the kitchen, but he'd had the cheek to criticize the way she was making her vegetable soup, a recipe upon which she prided herself. "The situation is intolerable," she wailed. "What's more, the man won't stop smoking–"

Exasperated, Christian threw his napkin down on the table, tipping over his chair as he rose.

"Why can't you accept my decision?" he railed. "I thought you'd be happy. I thought you would see I was trying to make your life easier. But no! It seems nothing I do is right."

In a fit of anger, he charged out of the room while Mrs. de Toi stood with her eyes at his back, her complaints transformed into burbling apologies that he refused to hear. He slammed one of the oak doors behind him, leaving me to pick up his fallen chair and force Mrs. de Toi to sit down in it. I poured her a cup of coffee and attempted to soothe her wounded pride. I began by reminding her Christian was never at his best in the morning.

The housekeeper nodded and, as usual, took the blame upon herself. "I shouldn't be such a stubborn old woman. I know you both mean well..."

"You're not stubborn. Please don't blame yourself. Christian and I should have consulted with you before making such an important decision. We're both new at this business of running a household. I hope you can forgive us."

"But it's true," the housekeeper sniffed. "I could use a bit of help. It's just that man... I'm sorry, but I can't bring myself to like him. I've tried, I promise you. But he's rude and never takes that cigarette out of his mouth. I keep telling him, he's likely to drop ashes in the food."

"Yes, smoking is a filthy habit, isn't it? Maybe Christian could say something…"

Mrs. de Toi looked up at me. "Oh, I'd be ever so grateful if he would. It could make all the difference, coming from the master. That man never listens to me, even if I am head cook. And when it comes to making a mess, he's worse than Kathrine. He never puts anything away or if he does, it's always in the wrong place… sometimes halfway across the room."

"Have you considered working at different times? Maybe Fripon could do his preparations in the evening. That way, you wouldn't see much of him."

"Oh, I couldn't allow that. Who'd keep an eye on him? I might never see my rolling pin again."

Feeling helpless, I asked if she had any suggestions.

"The only thing I can think to do is send him packing." She took a sip of her coffee and waited for my reaction.

"Perhaps, we could wait until after the holidays," I advised. "Surely we can hit upon some compromise, 'til then. It doesn't seem charitable to chuck him out after he's just arrived. Anyway, we need to let things settle before we tackle Christian on the subject, don't you think?"

Mrs. de Toi reached into her pocket and wiped her eyes with her handkerchief. "I suppose that makes sense, Mademoiselle. But I tell you honestly, if things go on as they are, it may come to a choice between that man or me."

"Oh, don't say that," I cried, throwing my arms around her. "Christian and I couldn't do without you. Nor could Mathiam. No, you mustn't talk of leaving. Give me a little time. I'll hit upon something."

Mrs. de Toi sniffled again but looked reconciled. "I'll leave it to you then," she said, putting her handkerchief back in her pocket. "I don't know why we've had such bad luck with the help, of late. Kathrine's not a patch on Analeese. It's a mystery to me how those two girls could ever be friends. 'Course, with her new baby boy, I don't suppose Analeese will come back to us. I miss her." The cook stared into the distance as if remembering happier times.

I gave her back a commiserating pat which seemed to give her the courage to say what was in her heart.

"There's been so much change, of late, Mademoiselle, and little of it good, I'm afraid. Claudine's not quite right in the head and, to tell the truth, I don't care much for our houseguest. He's all nose, he is. Even Mathiam's taken a dislike to him. Says the doctor told him he should plant a poppy field over by the grove. I ask you, what good would it do to plant poppies over there? Still, the doctor thought well enough of the idea to mention it to Christian. The master just shrugged, fortunately. He doesn't care a fig about gardening. Never did. That was Odeil's interest. As a child, he was always tearing through the garden with his toy trucks…ran over more than one petunia, I can tell you."

Mrs. de Toi leaned in closer so that our shoulders were touching. "I think the doctor's got some hold over him. I'm not sure what it could be, but he does. That boy's never been one to let people order him about. No, there's something fishy between them."

I agreed with her assessment but thought it best to say nothing. The last thing I wanted to do was throw more fuel onto her fire. Nonetheless, after she left me, I retreated to my rooms to think about what she'd said.

Of greatest concern was her revelation about the poppy field. Both the flower and the location so approximated the circumstances of my dreams, I almost wondered if Afreet had the power to invade them. The notion was absurd, I knew. Still, it took some arguing with myself to dispel the notion.

How long I'd been lying atop my bed in an effort to sort out my thoughts, I don't recall, but it was approaching afternoon when Christian popped his head into my room and then entered. He continued to appear agitated, as if no time had passed since his outburst of the morning. If anything, he looked more harried than before.

I sat up. "What is it? What's happened?"

"I've sent Claudine on an errand. She's been keeping guard outside, all morning. She'll be back soon so, we haven't much time." He craned his neck in an attempt to peer into the farther room. I assured him no one was present but us. He looked relieved, but his eyes narrowed again as he spied the empty cocoa cup.

"Afreet?"

"Yes, he brought it to me last night to help me sleep."

I'd barely finished my sentence before he'd knocked the china to the floor, his face seething with anger. "The next time he brings cocoa, pour it out the window or down the drain. Whatever you do, don't drink it."

Bewildered, I rose to retrieve the cup that had landed safely on the carpet. "Why? Did he put something in it?"

He took it from me and sniffed at the dried contents before replacing it on the night stand. "I suspect he drugged you last night. That's why you were so unsteady this morning."

"*Drugged* me?" I sat up and threw my legs over the side of the bed to look at him. "Why? Why would he do that?"

Christian took a seat beside me. "I've no proof of anything" — he shrugged— "but you know you weren't yourself this morning. I sense danger. Afreet's not a man to be trusted, Rachel. That's why I want you out of here."

"But he's your doctor. What do you mean?"

"Oh, he's competent enough, all right. That's not what I'm suggesting."

"What, then? I need you to tell me." As I sat peering into his eyes, I wanted to believe his concern was genuine. I thought about last night's kiss and was almost able to convince myself he did care. But given his history of betrayal, I couldn't be certain. His hand reached for mine and the moment our fingers intermingled, I was flooded with unexpected warmth for him. "Please tell me what's going on. You know something. I know you do. Why won't you tell me?"

He looked away, shaking his head. "Listen to me, Rachel. I'm trying to protect you. If I tell you more, you'll only be in greater danger. You must leave this place."

"You're beginning to frighten me. Is that what you want?"

His eyes met mine again. "If it will get you out of here, then, yes, I want to frighten you."

"I admit, you're succeeding. But how can I be sure this isn't another one of your games?"

His fingers tightened over mine with a force that betrayed his anger. "Listen, you little fool, this isn't a ruse. For the first time in my life, I'm trying to do something right...something decent..."

I shut my eyes to escape his violent expression. His hot breath poured over my face, my lips, and I knew I should cry out; but before I could react, the force of his kiss stopped me. The moment his lips fell upon mine, my passion ignited without my volition. I returned his passion with a ferocity of my own. Locked in an embrace, our hearts pounded with a tumult that should have drowned out the thin voice that suddenly wedged itself between us.

"Are you worse, Mademoiselle? Shall I fetch Dr. Afreet?"

Christian heard Claudine before I did. He leapt to his feet and made a show of helping me to lie down on the bed. "She's feeling dizzy," he answered in a husky voice. "I'm trying to help."

The maid came to his assistance, but by her smile, she appeared not so dim-witted, after all.

"That's all right, Monsieur. You needn't concern yourself any longer. I'll see to Mademoiselle's comfort."

Having no recourse, he backed away but not before tossing me a last sweet smile as he left.

That evening, I took my meal in my room. I had no doubt my behavior had been reported to Afreet who would wish to cross-examine me. I had hoped my absence would foil his attempt but I was wrong. At half past nine, he made his appearance, bringing with him a cup of hot cocoa. We talked briefly and I assured him I was better. The moment he left me, I poured the drink down the drain.

Chapter Nineteen

Two days after Christian had visited my rooms—a day that was clear with no clouds overhead—I was packed and ready to drive to Paris in Odeil's Fiat Multipla, a yellow and blue van with plenty of space for my luggage. I'd planned to be gone a few days but had kept that itinerary to myself. Having never left Sainte Enimie since I'd arrived, I told everyone I wanted to do a little sightseeing. My real purpose was to confer with Michael Allaire about the situation at the chateau.

Although she approved of my desire to visit Paris, Mrs. de Toi was unhappy to see me go. Christian, of course, welcomed the news and promised he'd look after affairs with the housekeeper's help. Only Dr. Afreet regarded my departure with a curiosity that bordered on paranoia. He kept pressing for my itinerary and asking when I planned to return, questions I rebuffed. "The wind has no schedule," I answered him. He'd looked anything but pleased and was not present to wish me a pleasant journey on the morning of my departure. Only Mathiam and Mrs. de Toi stood in the driveway to wave me off.

As I started the engine, I smiled to see them in my rearview mirror, a pair of salt and pepper shakers, different, yet meant to be together. Had I known it would be the last time I would see them, I would have viewed my departure with great sadness…if I'd have left at all. But, as I had no idea what the future held, my feelings were light-hearted. I was happy to leave the squabbles and intrigues behind.

The drive was uneventful but my thoughts were in turmoil. Christian's fear for me seemed so genuine, that I felt relieved as the distance increased between me and Sainte Enimie. But why should I believe him? He'd been guilty of tricks before. Still, I wanted to trust him, particularly as he had so greatly changed after Afreet's arrival. The doctor had brought with him an atmosphere that seemed to affect everyone. I, for one, felt I had to be perpetually on my guard. But against what? Of that I was uncertain. Even so the feeling left me wondering if was wise for me to continue to serve as Odeil's pawn in her intrigue against her cousin or whether I would be better served making my escape.

Still, each time I thought of leaving, my heart protested against it. I had made a home in France, and, small though it be, discovered a family, people I cared about and who I believed cared for me. True, my feelings for Christian remained ambivalent, but since Afreet's arrival, I experienced a growing empathy for this young man who seemed powerless in the doctor's presence. Either I must find a way to free all of us from the physician's dark presence or I must consider saving myself, leaving the chateau, and taking with me what assets I was allowed.

To learn what those assets might be, whether I could claim the money in Odeil's various bank accounts and that of her stock portfolio remained a question. I also needed to know if I could maintain my share of the property without living there year round. For answers to these questions, I presumed my attorney, Michael Allaire, would be of assistance. That's why I was driving with all speed to Paris. He had been kind to me when we first met and there had been the occasional letter that was more personal than strictly business. I felt his advice could be trusted so I looked forward to meeting my attorney this evening.

The hotel where Michael Allaire had arranged for me to stay was modest but well appointed. From my window I had a wonderful view of the Avenue des Champs-Élysées and as I looked out upon the hurly burly of a great city, a sizzle of excitement ran through my veins.

I'd checked in just before eight in the evening, which gave me just enough time to peek out my window, unpack, comb my hair and add a dash of lipstick before taking the birdcage elevator to the lobby below.

Michael was entering the hotel from the opposite end of the blue and white foyer as I stepped from the lift. He smiled when he saw me and I responded with the warmth reserved for a treasured friend. We hadn't known each other long but a rapport had established itself since our first meeting.

He looked boyish without his business suit, his brown hair falling across his forehead. The dark coat he wore that evening was unbuttoned to reveal brown corduroy pants and a navy blue sweater. I, too, was dressed casually in a skirt and sweater, my feet shod in flat heels to accommodate walking. We stood for a moment, each one taking in a view of the other, hardly believing we were together in Paris, at last.

Hurrying forward, he gave me a hug. "I've been inventing excuses to bring you here for so long; I can't believe it's really happened."

"It's me, all right." Once we'd separated, I stared down at my patent leather shoes, feeling a bit shy. "And I must admit I'm very, very hungry."

"The Cheese House is close by. They make wonderful soufflés and homemade soups. I've already made reservations."

"You remembered my fondness for soufflés?" I couldn't stifle my pleasure.

"Of course, I remember every detail about you." As he spoke, Michael took hold of my arm and pulled me toward the street, making nothing of my obvious blush.

Once outside, we were hit by the wind's icy blast. I found the sensation exhilarating and he must have felt the same for we laughed together like children as we walked, arm-in-arm, toward our destination, anticipating a superb meal and a quantity of wine.

The evening was crammed with good conversation and it seemed Michael was intent that we should get to know each other better. Our talk was about art and music, topics for which we both shared a passion. We even talked a little of the war in Algiers, which was everywhere in the news.

"Tomorrow, we go to Montmartre," he said pouring my second glass of wine, a Chardonnay that was fruity and yet dry. "We'll stroll through the street art, critiquing as we go. Then I'll take you to a gallery where the owner is a friend of mine. He specializes in up-and-coming talent and I've been eyeing a piece of Pop Art by an artist, whom my friend says has a bright future. It's a 'very in your face' style. I'd like your opinion."

"Me?" I asked, pointing to myself. "I've never heard of…what did you call it? 'Pop Art'? Is it made from Coca Cola bottles?"

Michael laughed. "Could be, but not the one I'm interested in. I'll say no more about it tonight because I want your unschooled reaction."

"I can give you that, all right. But what I think shouldn't matter. Do you love it?"

Michael raised his glass as he smiled at me. "Actually, I was thinking of it more as an investment. Let's just say, I can live with it while it grows in value."

"Spoken more like a stock broker than a lawyer," I teased, as we clinked glasses. "If only one's other goals in life could be so simple."

He sensed I was thinking of the chateau. "We can talk about the will, if you like," he said, leaning toward me.

Dessert arrived with more wine. The relaxed the atmosphere and the alcohol loosened my tongue, I recounted the recent turn of events at the chateau and of Dr. Afreet in particular.

Michael frowned the entire time I spoke to him, expressing his concern by touching my hand several times. Next I asked him about my options. When I finished, he leaned back in his chair, his eyes perusing mine with intensity.

"I shall have to review Odeil's will and my notes before giving you an answer to your questions. I'm afraid she made the last minute changes concerning you in such haste that I'm not sure I have any definitive answers. But I'll dig into it and in the meantime why don't you allow me to show you something of Paris? This is your first visit, is it not?"

I nodded that it was, a response that brought a smile to Michael's lips. "Good, then I will take great pleasure in being your guide. You need to relax before making any important decisions."

From the Cheese House, we'd ambled to a cabaret called the Scheherazade, where the walls and ceiling were swathed in silks and the floor was covered in Persian carpets—the way I might have imagined a maharaja's desert accommodations. Turkish coffee flowed like tap water as we sat listening to musicians playing exotic music and watching slim-waisted girls, all of them beauties with dark eyes and hip length hair, perform graceful dances. Along with the coffee we had our choice of pastries and dried fruits, which I nibbled upon with restraint.

Michael returned me to the hotel at half past two in the morning. We caught the desk clerk dozing when we entered. He snapped to his feet with eyes blinking when I asked for my key and I was sorry to have disturbed him. As for myself, I could have wished for the night to go on forever.

I climbed the stairs to my room in the wee hours of the morning and realized I was happy.

For the next two days, Michael was the perfect host. "It's so easy to fall in love with Paris," I thought. Everywhere I looked, the following morning, the crisp November sky was scattering a diffuse light, an atmosphere reminiscent of works by John Constable. One could understand why walking through the streets of Montmartre was a dreamlike experience and I could have lost myself in this Plein Air landscape, allowing time to pass unnoticed.

When we reached the gallery run by Michael's friend, the proprietor came forward, his face swathed in a smile, the crown of his head sporting a shock of red hair that looked like a coxcomb. We shook hands and, during the introduction, as Michael and I had just come in from the outside, it took a few moments for my eyes to adjust to the surrounding exhibit—large canvasses slashed with emotive colors, some of them looking as if paint had been thrown across them by an enraged artist. Though disturbing, the paintings were also mesmerizing. Even so, I doubt I would have wanted to live with one, no matter how great the possibility that it would grow in value. When Michael said the work he was considering wasn't among these, I felt relieved.

Roget, the proprietor, a stocky man somewhere in his fifties, led us to the back of his establishment where he stored the work of his other artists. To be honest, when I saw the piece my friend was considering, I experienced another wave of disappointment. Nothing in that framed canvas would have caught my interest. It seemed to be a section from a comic book blown up in size. The subject, a woman with purple hair, stared out through a window, a tear dropping from one eye. The entire surface was awash in printer's dots just as if it were a real comic book page. My eye wandered to the price tag and, I must admit, I thought both the artist and the gallery owner were being optimistic.

The best way for me to react when asked for my opinion was to say the piece was interesting. The moment he heard me, Michael's face fell.

"Interesting? That's how people talk when they hate something."

Embarrassed, I rephrased my answer. "Maybe original would be a better word. I promise you, I don't hate it."

Fearing the loss of a sale, Roget jumped into the conversation. "Is Mademoiselle familiar with this genre? It's much admired in Britain and the United States. The artist is your countryman, in fact, well known in New York. You've heard of him, yes?"

He told me the man's name but I remained unenlightened. "America's a big place. I don't follow the trends, I'm afraid."

Though careful to control his tone, a sneer crept across the proprietor's unguarded expression. "I can assure you, Mademoiselle, the man's a genius. Anyone who follows art is aware of his talent. In another year, this piece might triple in value."

Michael could see he'd put me in an uncomfortable position and intervened. He told his friend he wasn't prepared to make a decision, at that moment, but asked to be given first right of refusal on the painting. The proprietor agreed, though his look of disappointment was unmistakable. He followed us to the door. The two men shook hands; then Michael and I stepped out into the crisp sunshine.

"I hope I didn't offend Roget," I said, tucking my hand under Michael's arm. We began to walk. "But it's no good pretending to understand something when I don't. Frankly, I'm more aligned with these street artists who are braving the chill air, hoping to make a sale."

"In that case, you must choose a painting from one of them." Michael smiled. "I'd like to buy you a keepsake of your visit."

I refused his offer at first, but when he insisted, I accepted. We ambled past the many artists who had laid their wares along the pavement and, eventually, my eye fell upon one which made me smile. The painting was scarcely larger than a paperback book and depicted a flower vender as she stood in her white apron beneath a blue and white striped awning. Around her were buckets and buckets of flowers, tulips, daisies and lilies. The array of color was designed to gladden the eye.

Seeing my fascination, Michael reached into his wallet and, without haggling, handed the scrawny artist the amount requested. The young man looked cold despite his pea jacket and jeans, but also elated. He couldn't stop talking about the flower shop's location and the day he'd painted the scene but eventually, we were allowed to escape. We walked away from him, a brown paper parcel tied with string tucked under Michael's arm.

We jostled amid the crowds and it seemed to me that many of the couples we encountered were lovers. They were holding hands and looking dreamily into one another's eyes. I was happy for them, just as I was happy for me, for I, too, was with a charming man who seemed to enjoy my company as much as I enjoyed his.

We stepped into a little café for lunch. I ordered coffee and a croissant with an assortment of cheeses. Michael was hungry enough for an omelet.

"I think I'm going to buy that painting," he said, once we'd been served.

I looked up at him, unable to hide my surprise.

"You think I'm mad, don't you? But what can I say? I'm always been a fool for a damsel in distress."

"Every woman needs a Galahad." I smiled back at him, remembering the tear stained face of the painting.

Perhaps, I'd sounded wistful for Michael reached across the table to place one hand over mine. "You know, if you need me, I'll always be there for you."

Without understanding why, his promise made me feel misty. We were enjoying a wonderful day in Paris; I'd been given a delightful painting and St. Enimie was miles and miles away. Yet, when Michael spoke in such an earnest tone, I realized he'd sensed the shadows I'd brought with me.

What a wonderful, sensitive man, I thought, as I wiped a tear from the corner of my eye.

My companion pretended not to notice. He signaled for the check. "We're going sightseeing," he announced. "First stop is The Musée du Louvre. But don't worry; we won't attempt to take it all in. I want you to see three exhibits...just three."

Outside, he hailed a taxi, and within minutes we stood at the entrance of one of the most famous museums in the world. The first object we sought was the Winged Victory of Samothrace. She seemed to be waiting for us at the top of a set of stairs ready to descend with her greeting. There was no doubting the artistry of the piece, the way stone had been transformed to mimic the liquidity of movement. Looking at it, I was almost convinced that statue could move.

Tugging at my arm, Michael led me to our next destination: the Mona Lisa.

Like everyone else, I'd seen countless reproductions of it and thought I knew what to expect; but I couldn't have been more deluded. The vibrancy of color was as remarkable as that famous face. But to my eye, the painting's mystical background gave the work its greatest fascination. The landscape, shrouded in a mist, had a dreamlike shimmer, creating the illusion or whisper, if you will, that one had only to look deeply into its distance to discover a second world beneath the first. That haunted feeling was difficult to shake.

Our last stop brought me back to reality. The Rubens room provided landscapes of a different nature—mountains of female flesh depicted with so many serpentine curves and ripples that Michael and I broke into gales of laughter. The aesthetes around us were not amused, so we abandoned the corpulent maidens with their attendant cherubims and hailed a taxi once we were outside.

Our final destination was the Cathedral of Notre Dame. There I was sobered by breathtaking architectural beauty—aware that here was the work of artisans over several ages…a work that seemed to defy time. But as we wandered in its shadows, staring at the various graves of the once powerful and famous—Henry II and Louis Pasteur among them—it occurred to me, these monuments meant nothing to the dead. They were reminders to the living that life is fleeting.

We spent two wonderful days together playing tourist in one of the world's most beautiful cities and every evening Michael fed me lavishly. I fell into my bed each night exhausted but feeling more alive than I had in weeks. Like a child in candy land, I wished my visit would never end, but of course, it had to.

On the third day, as agreed, I met Michael at his office. We were obliged to attend to the business that had brought me to Paris, but I was late. I'd overslept and was full of apologies when I arrived. He'd been waiting for me and came around from behind his desk as I entered.

"That outfit is stunning," he said, admiring the plum colored suit I was wearing. He motioned for me to sit down and then returned to his desk which was strewn with papers. As soon as we were seated, he flashed me a look of apology. "As to Odeil's personal effects," he began once I was seated, "there is no specific mention. As I've said, her last visit was in great haste. I was barely able to make the changes she requested in time for her to sign before she was off."

"So you are telling me her personal possession and her bank accounts are tied to residency?"

"It's implied, but to be certain we would have to seek resolution through the courts."

"I see. And to the matter of residency…?

"So far I haven't found any loopholes in the terms of Odeil's will. Residency is a requirement…"

"Of course, but can you tell me, at least, what 'residency' means? Must I stay a week, two weeks, or ten months of the year?"

Michael sighed and looked even more apologetic. "That, too, is unspecified. The amount of time you are required to occupy the premises is unclear. But the news is not all bad." he went on cheerily, seeing my dour expression. "As to management decisions, you have the controlling interest."

"So what am I supposed to do if Christian refuses to go along with Odeil's plans for renovation?"

Michael leaned back in his chair and appeared satisfied he could answer this question, at least. "As controlling owner of the property, you are entitled to make the decisions. Christian is a beneficiary of any income derived from the property. I don't see why he would object to your making improvements from which he would benefit."

"But he does object." I sat forward, my voice dripping with frustration. "Is that all you can tell me?"

"For the moment, yes," Michael nodded regretfully. "Anything more will require a search for legal precedent."

"How long would that take?"

"Oh," he shrugged, knowing his reply would be met unfavorably. "A few weeks, perhaps."

"But I don't have a few weeks. I plan on leaving in the morning."

"I know. I know." His phone rang and he looked at his watch. He put the caller on hold then rose and led me to the door. "Look, have breakfast with me tomorrow. Perhaps I'll come up with a new angle. In any case, you needn't worry. I won't rest until I find some satisfactory answers for you."

I started to speak, but there was really nothing more to say. Feeling rattled, I left but agreed to have breakfast with him the next morning.

The sky was dank with cloudbursts as I prepared to leave the city. Like the heavens, I, too, wanted to weep, for I had fallen in love with Paris and hated to go back to the squabbles waiting for me.

Michael and I had breakfast together at my hotel. Over coffee and rolls, he promised to consult with his partners about my questions and vowed to stay in touch. "Perhaps I will appear in person with my news," he smiled at me. "I would use it as an excuse to get a good look at this Dr. Afreet who was so troubling to you."

He continued to reassure me as he walked me to my car and stowed my bag together with his gift of the little painting. "You have more strength than you know, Rachel. You've handled a good deal in the short amount of time I've known you. Here you are a stranger in a strange land. Give yourself credit."

I stood with a lump forming in my throat as I looked up at Michael, my car keys dangling in my hand. *What a lovely man,* I thought. *He is kind and comforting, someone who would be easy to love.*

As if reading my thoughts, he suddenly pulled me to him and kissed me hard upon the lips.

"Safe journey," he murmured. Then he unfurled his umbrella and strode away in the softly falling rain.

Chapter Twenty

THE DRIVE TO SAINTE ENIMIE was uneventful. I confess to seeing little of the landscape as my thoughts occupied me. My time with Michael had awakened a longing to share my life with someone. Paris had been wonderful. I'd enjoyed the sightseeing, the wine and foods, but being with him had made me feel less alone than I had for some time.

Perhaps, the fault was mine. I thought too much like a victim, as Dr. Devane had once suggested. Perhaps I was more than shy and my habit of protecting myself from being hurt had gone too far. Certainly, Odeil's death had driven me further into myself, particularly as I was unsure about whom to trust. Even now, as I sped toward the chateau, the mysteries it posed—the tunnels, the caryatids, the struggle between Christian and Afreet, between Afreet and me, between me and Christian—left a part of me wanting to run away. But Michael had assured me of my rights where my inheritance was concerned. What's more he had expressed his faith in me. I needed to do the same for myself. This cast of characters that had descended upon the scene, I should have sent them packing long ago. When I got back to the chateau, I would resolve to do better. So much was at stake. For once in my life I needed to show a little backbone.

Naturally, my feelings were in turmoil late that night, as I drove through St. Enimie and followed the winding driveway that led to the chateau. I'd told no one I was returning so I didn't expect to be met. Parking the car in the garage, I carried my belongings with me, entering by way of the kitchen. The hour was approaching midnight, but I'd hoped Mrs. de Toi and Mathiam might be up, having a nightcap as they sometimes did.

I found the kitchen was in darkness. Switching on the lights, I was greeted by a sight I'd never thought possible. The area was in disarray. Pots had been left to soak in the sink, dishes remained unwashed and the floor was sandy with crumbs. What's more, the large ashtray on the table was filled to overflowing so that the room reeked of cigarettes. As I looked at the chaos, I could imagine scenes of passionate arguments, invectives and tears that had gone on in my absence.

For a moment, I was tempted to climb back into my car and return to Paris without announcing my arrival to anyone. The hour was late, however, and I was tired. What I needed was a good night's rest before putting my new resolve to the test. I scribbled a note and left it on the table for Mrs. de Toi to find in the morning. After that, I mounted the stairs.

As there had been no fire in the hearth for several days, my room was icy. I washed and undressed quickly, then dove beneath my comforter with my teeth chattering. Closing my eyes, I easily drifted off. Tomorrow, I would deal with the staff.

Claudine brought tea the next morning. As she drew back the curtains, the light entering through the windows was so strong, I was obliged to shield my eyes. My head felt stuffed and a sore throat made it difficult for me to speak. My fatigue, I feared, had made it possible for the fever I'd suffered earlier to return.

Sitting up, I croaked that Mrs. de Toi should come to my room as soon as possible. When she heard me, Claudine looked as though I'd spoken in ancient Aramaic.

"Are you unwell, Mademoiselle? Shall I fetch Dr. Afreet?"

I told her no but I would be grateful if she started a fire. This she understood and performed the task with alacrity. In a short while, logs had begun to crackle in the hearth, sending welcome warmth throughout the room. Having achieved this much, I made my request to see Mrs. de Toi a second time. I spoke slowly so there could be no mistaking my meaning. The girl's lips formed an arch as they began to quiver.

"Please, Mademoiselle, Mrs. de Toi has gone. Fripon is cook, now."

"What?" I started from my bed with a suddenness that must have frightened her for she left me at a run. Throwing on my dressing gown, I went after her. But by the time I reached the dining room, I realized my illness had overtaken me. I felt dizzy and had to cling to the sideboard just inside the doors to keep steady.

Christian and Dr. Afreet were seated at the table as I entered. Both men rose when they saw me. Coming forward, the doctor looked genuinely alarmed.

"My dear girl, you look dreadful. The change of air has given you a turn for the worse. Anyone can see you are burning with fever. Go back to bed. I'll have a tray sent up and examine you myself."

"That won't be necessary," I cried as I made my way to the table and stood clinging to a chair. "Mrs. de Toi will assist me. Where is she? I want to see her now."

Both men stared at one another without speaking. At last, the doctor was the one to break the silence.

"I'm sorry, Rachel, but Mrs. de Toi left us in a pique two days ago. She and Fripon had a stupendous quarrel which I was unable to mediate. She packed her bags and left with the gardener. Neither of them told us where they were going. It was very unpleasant, I assure you. Still, we've managed in their absence," he ended brightly.

"Mathiam's gone, too?" I glared at Christian with a look Caesar might have given Brutus. "How could you let this happen? Why didn't you do something?"

"I-I couldn't stop her, Rachel. She was very angry..."

"She loves you. You know that. And Mathiam loves you, too. If you'd have asked them to stay, they would have. Did you even try?"

Christian stared down at his hands and said nothing.

Stunned by what I took for his betrayal, I began to shake. "I want them back. And if you refuse to find them, I will."

Afreet took hold of my arm, looking apprehensive. "You must go back to bed, Rachel, or I can't answer for what might happen…"

"Excuse me doctor," I said, shaking him off. "But you forget yourself. You're a guest in this house."

"And it's a good thing I am here," he said, blowing off my insult as if I were a petulant child. "If you don't calm yourself, you are in danger of collapsing. Is that want you want, Mademoiselle? I urge you to be reasonable and let me take care of things. As you see, you've been gone what…a week? Yet, the house hasn't fallen around our ears. I, for one, have had an excellent breakfast."

My throat was too sore to shout, nor did I wish to waste my energy. I looked past the doctor at Christian. "Help me find them, please. Please."

I shouldn't have been surprised that Afreet answered for him. "Yes, yes. Rest assured, my dear. We'll do our best for you. In the meantime, I'm happy to report we've already found a new gardener. Chanson comes to us with excellent recommendations."

"Chanson? The mute?" Again my eyes flew to Christian's but I could read nothing there. "You can't hire him. I won't have it. I won't." I made an effort to head for the kitchen where I intended to fire Fripon on the spot; but I proved to be so unsteady, Afreet again took hold of my arm.

"My dear girl, you must go to bed. And I insist upon a sedative—"

"Keep your powders, Doctor. Given the state of my partner's continuing poor health and his lack of backbone, I doubt they will benefit me."

My verbal slap had been meant to summon Christian's anger, if not his courage, but when I peered into his sapphire eyes, I saw a haunted look that made me regret my words. If ever a soul needed rescuing, it was his. That pale face, those eyes glistening with unshed tears…here was a man on the brink of collapse. I realized, in that moment, how much he needed me. And in that moment, I knew I could never care for anyone the way I cared for him. Love's bond isn't passion or even the need for security. Its bond is communion. We were both drowning. If we were to survive, I had to be strong. That was my thought as I collapsed into Afreet's arms.

* * *

I awoke in my bed as the mantle clock was chiming four in the afternoon. Despite my few hours of rest, my head was pounding and my throat felt like the scene of a violent crime. Attempting to sit made me dizzy so I rang the bell rope. I expected Claudine or Kathrine to appear but was in for another surprise. A tall woman entered, instead, dressed in white from her cap to her shoes. She glided forward, bringing with her the strong smell of disinfectant.

As if I were a rag doll, she propped me up against my pillows with a pair of strong hands and introduced herself as Nurse Verglas. When I opened my mouth to reply, she thrust a thermometer in it. Next she took hold of my wrist and started to count my pulse while starring at the watch pinned to her apron. In the silence that prevailed, I had time to observe her olive complexion and the wisps of mouse brown hair peeking from under her cap. I judged her to be in her mid-forties as faint lines appeared at the corners of her gray eyes and deeper ones marched like fence posts across her upper lip.

"I'm not really ill," I objected when I was at last free to speak.

The woman acted as though she hadn't heard me; her eyes were focused on the marks of the thermometer. "Your temperature is one hundred and three degrees," she said, as she popped her instrument into a vial and returned it to her pocket. "I'd say you were sick, wouldn't you?" Not waiting for an answer, she quick marched from the room without a backward glance.

Soon after, Dr. Cartouche appeared with a light rap at my door. I noticed his hair was wilder than before, almost as if he'd suffered an electrocution. For a few seconds, he stood shaking his head and saying nothing as if I'd been a naughty child.

"A temperature of one hundred and three? That's not good. Not good at all." He placed his medical bag on the nightstand beside me. "I'll need to look at your throat and take a swab. It could be strep throat. There have been a few incidents in the village." He was rummaging through his bag as he spoke and finally emerged with a tongue depressor. For several minutes, he poked and prodded, then took the swab as promised. "It doesn't look good, I'm afraid. The throat's quite raw. No doubt you're experiencing discomfort. I'll give you a shot now and have the pharmacy in Sainte Enimie deliver a prescription. I'm almost certain it's strep but I'll do the culture to be sure. In the meantime, follow the nurse's instructions and get plenty of rest."

"If it's important for me to sleep, why do I need a nurse? She can't help me with that, can she?"

The doctor smiled. "She's here for Monsieur de Hess, mainly. But should you need a course of injections, you'll be glad she's here."

I sat up against my pillows. "Why does Christian need a nurse? I thought he was getting better."

"A slight relapse, nothing serious. We'll soon have him right as rain." He was preparing a syringe as he spoke. "Now, if Mademoiselle would be so kind as to roll over on her stomach?"

"My stomach? Why?"

"Best given in the buttocks," he said, pointing to his syringe.

I did as he requested and while alcohol was being applied to the spot, I made the point that was burning on the tip of my tongue. "I guess his relapse can't be blamed on Mrs. de Toi, can it? She's gone."

"Yes, that is so," the doctor sighed.

"What's your theory now? Could it be that Dr. Afreet is inept at his job?"

"Or me, you mean?" The doctor told me I could roll back on my pillows again, which I did. "I can't explain it," he went on. "Tests can be wrong, I'm afraid." He started to reassemble the contents of his bag then paused to look at me. "Dr. Afreet mentioned your little quarrel earlier. I'm not certain I can say anything to convince you but the man strikes me as very competent. I admit he espouses a wild philosophy but his medical knowledge is remarkable, I can assure you."

"You think you know him well enough to make that judgment?"

Dr. Cartouche shrugged as he snapped his bag closed. "People don't have to know each other long to have opinions–"

"But in this case, you have known him longer than a matter of a few weeks, that's true isn't it?"

The doctor looked surprised. His eyebrows formed peaks above his eyes. "Did he tell you that?"

"He mentioned something," I lied.

Cartouche shrugged. "We may have exchanged a letter or two. He's a man of reputation as I've said. I probably wrote him on some professional matter. I don't recall."

"How long have you known him, then?"

"I've said, I don't remember how our paths may have crossed. But that's no concern of yours, is it? You must concentrate on getting better. Lots of liquids and lots of sleep. That's how you must apply yourself. I'll ask the new cook to make you some soup–"

"I'm not hungry."

He frowned, looking down at me as he picked up his bag. "I hope you're not going to be a difficult patient, Mademoiselle. You'll only prolong your condition or make it worse."

An hour after he had gone, Nurse Verglas entered my room with two bottles of medication. She opened both and from each shook a pill into a paper cup. "My instructions are to give you one pill every six hours; the other once a day."

"Why? What are they?"

"What difference does it make?" She poured water from my carafe into a drinking glass without looking at me.

When I hesitated to take them, the woman sighed and rolled her eyes toward the ceiling. "One pill is a light sedative to help you sleep. The other will relieve the soreness in your throat. Now, swallow, please."

I decided to do as she asked, as I was in pain. Despite the strange events going on around me, I doubted murder was part of the plan. Whatever game the two doctors were playing, I didn't imagine either of them wanted any more police underfoot.

When I awoke from a deep sleep, night had fallen and, to my surprise, my throat felt better. I had not been conscious long when Verglas appeared with soup and crackers. Seeing the tray, I realized I was hungry. I was not allowed to eat, however, until she'd completed her nurse's ritual—taking my temperature and counting my pulse.

Christian entered while she was still counting. "Is the patient awake?"

"You shouldn't be here." Verglas looked up and stopped counting. "Mademoiselle is infectious."

"I-I won't come near. I wanted to see how she's doing, that's all."

"She's better. Now I must ask you to leave." The nurse was reaching for a bottle of pills when Christian caught sight of them. "What's that? What are you giving her?"

Apparently unaccustomed to having her duties questioned, Verglas' back stiffened. "I'm not at liberty to say, Monsieur. If you wish information, you must ask Dr. Cartouche."

"Nonsense." Christian lurched forward as if he meant to snatch the open bottle from her but she evaded him and, in so doing, scattered several pills across my bed.

"Now, see what you've done," she cried with her eyes blazing. "You've no right to behave in this manner. I'm not a servant in this house. How dare you threaten me!"

An angry exchange followed which must have found its way into the hall for Afreet was not long in joining the fray.

"What's going on here? Why all this shouting?"

The moment he saw the doctor, Christian's face drained of color. His body went limp and he fell backwards into a nearby ladderbacked chair, collapsed like an abandoned marionette.

"I-I wanted to know what she was being given, that's all." His tone was sulky and child-like.

"Because?" Afreet persisted.

"Because I have a right to be told. That's why."

"I doubt that"—the doctor shrugged—" but if you must know, Rachel is being given an antibiotic and a mild sedative. With your enormous medical background, what regimen would you suggest?" As he spoke, Afreet collected the pills that had been sent flying and gave one of them to me while he returned the others to their container. Next he asked the nurse to accompany Monsieur de Hess to his room. When she started to object, he overrode her.

"He won't give you any argument. He knows better than to refuse to do what he's told." The doctor's eyes fell upon me, as if realizing his tone had been too commanding. "As you can see, my dear Rachel, Christian is still too emotional. He needs a firm hand."

To my surprise, Christian raised no objection, allowing himself to be led from the room like a lap dog. I was the one who became angry for him. This doctor at my bedside was more incubus than healer. He'd come into our midst like a cancer, taking over our lives by degrees, so that our desire to protests came too late. Christian and I, it seemed, had lost control.

Afreet pulled the ladderbacked chair closer to my bed and sat down. "What do you think of this new nurse? She lacks a bedside manner, perhaps. But Cartouche puts great store by her."

His calm was infuriating. He sat with his legs stretched in front of him as if the quarrel that had occurred moments before had never happened...as if his patient hadn't made it clear by his actions that he was frightened for me.

"You seem to have high regard for the man," I croaked. "Why do I get the feeling you and he are old friends?"

"Old friends?" Afreet's surprise brought me some satisfaction. "I wonder what gave you that impression. You and I are better acquainted."

"He mentioned something about your correspondence..."

"He says he wrote me? I wonder. It's possible. Over the years, I've been consulted by a number of doctors. But, the truth is, Rachel, I have no one close. I've led a vagabond's life. And you know what they say about a rolling stone gathering no moss?"

"Then you will have few mourners when you slough off this mortal coil?" My remark seemed to have piqued his vanity.

"Few mourners? Perhaps so. But I will have left my impression upon the world, I think."

"In what way?"

"By being of service, my dear girl. With the right intentions, one can alter the universe."

"Oh, yes, I remember. With the right intentions, one can walk through walls." Already, I was beginning to feel my eyelids grow heavy. I was conscious enough, however, to hear the doctor's chuckle.

"Mock me if you will. But I am confident it's only a matter of time before you come to see I am right."

"For once, I agree with you, Doctor. I am growing wiser. I've found you out, at least. You and Cartouche are more than acquaintances. You are...." I fell asleep before I could finish my sentence.

* * *

Although I remembered no images attendant with my drug-induced dreams, when I awoke the next morning, I did recall sounds: car doors opening and closing, voices and footsteps scurrying beneath my window. Curious, I asked Nurse Verglas if we'd had visitors during the night.

Her reply was acerbic. "My room is on the fourth floor with the servants, Mademoiselle. From those lofty heights, one hears nothing." She went on to say Dr. Cartouche would be informed of my restless sleep and he would probably want to increase the dosage of my sedative. I told her it wasn't necessary but, as usual, she ignored my wishes and left to place a call to the doctor.

I was sulking, with my head propped against the pillows, when Dr. Afreet looked in on me. Seeing I was awake, he came forward, rose in hand.

"A peace offering for anything I might have said yesterday to upset you. I hope I may be forgiven?"

Surprised, I took the flower from him and buried my nose in its red-black petals. The aroma was exquisite and yet I couldn't help thinking the blossom, although appearing at the peak of its beauty was already dead. A perfect metaphor for Afreet, I thought. He, too, was a deceiver. Trained as a man of science, he lived in the airy realms of sophistry and could rearrange the furniture of one's mind to make what was false seem true and what was true seem false. Either way, he could leave his victim smiling like an idiot. I despised him for what he was; yet I found him fascinating, also. "I am always happy to pardon anyone who is truly repentant," I said with a smile.

He looked pleased when he heard me. "I want you to know I walked all the way to the little flower shop in the village to find that beauty. The roses were imported, of course. It may be winter here, elsewhere, it is spring. We live in a world within worlds, as I have told you."

I placed the flower in my water glass and countered with my own observation. "Wherever this flower grew, I'm certain of one thing: the laws of nature everywhere apply. Once bloomed, the rose forever dies."

The doctor folded his arms and nodded as he looked down on me. "It's true. Life gives birth to death. But if we are to believe religious canon, the reverse is also true: death gives birth to life. Two ends of the same string, are they not?"

This was going to become another fatiguing conversation, I feared, so I was grateful when Christian appeared. His face broke into a scowl the moment he saw Afreet. The doctor, to the contrary, appeared ebullient.

"'Ah, how does my good Lord Hamlet? Well, I hope.' "

To my surprise, his patient refused to crumble as he usually did but answered in kind. "The problem is that 'I am pigeon-livered and lack gall to make oppression bitter.' "

Afreet, too, looked taken aback. What, he must have wondered, had come over the young man. Yesterday, he cowered like a child. Today, he seemed ready for a fight. When Afreet answered there was no mistaking the threat in his voice.

"My advice, good fellow, is to 'give thy thoughts no tongue.' "

"You advise me to put on an 'antic disposition?' "

"The role suits you."

"Then 'the play's the thing wherein I'll catch the conscience of the king.' "

The two men eyed one another with a contempt that was palpable. How long this literary joust could continue, I had no idea, but I was in no mood for theatre and haltingly attempted to redirect the action.

"Could you bring me another glass from the bathroom, Doctor? I'm parched and, as you see, I've used my current one for your lovely rose."

Afreet failed to respond, at first. His eyes remained fixed upon his antagonist as if he hoped to pin him to the wall like a butterfly. I had to make the request a second time to move him.

In the few seconds we had together, Christian rushed to my side. "Listen to me, Rachel. Don't take your sedatives. I want you to stay awake. You must get out of here tonight. Don't bother to pack or do anything except get away from here as fast as you can."

Naturally, I was alarmed. "W-why? What's going to happen?"

"I haven't time to explain. Just do as I ask…"

Afreet reentered at that moment and, seeing us huddled together, a grimace colored his expression. "Rachel looks tired, Christian," he snapped. "You must allow her to rest. We don't want any harm to come to her, do we?"

Chapter Twenty-One

Rain and wind rattled at the windows that evening as my ormolu clock struck ten. Rising from my bed, I saw my reflection in one of the panes—a portrait worthy of a place in Poe's House of Usher. A pale face surrounded by wild hair stared back at me; an image made more ghostly by the distortion created as drops of water slid down the window. Given that shadows draped over the furniture like shrouds, one might have supposed I'd been transported to that house of horrors, already. Except for the fire, the room showed little sign of cheer.

I tossed another log onto the fire and hurried back to my bed. Nurse Verglas arrived not long after, her face fixed with a no-nonsense expression as she carried another paper cup with my pills.

"Dr. Cartouche has increased your sedative so please don't make me stand here listening to arguments." She dropped the antibiotic into my hand and I swallowed it as I knew it was doing me good. My temperature had lowered and my throat no longer felt like a slab of raw meat. The sedative, however, I tucked under my tongue to be disposed of later.

As I'd given her no reason to suspect me in the past, the nurse looked satisfied. "I suggest you turn out the light and get some sleep." That said, she left me.

The minute the door closed, I leapt to the window, threw it open and spit the pill into the shrubbery below. Given Christian's admonition, I suspected I had something to learn by staying awake. As to stealing away under the cover of darkness, I was in no condition to consider that possibility, however tempting.

Even without the sedative, it was a struggle to stay awake. Reading made me drowsy and staring at my walls was anything but stimulating. From time to time, I stumbled to a window and opened it to receive a blast of cold air. I don't know how many times I made that journey from my bed to the window but when the ormolu clock struck midnight, I had left my bed yet again and was breathing in the air of a bright, moonlit night, the rain having abated.

What attracted me on that occasion was a splash of light flicking on and off at a distance. At first, I thought it was the beam of a passing car on the road to Sainte Enimie, but when it continued to flash at the same location, I knew that couldn't be the case. So, what was it? Not a harbor light, certainly. The Mediterranean was too far away.

My thoughts were interrupted by the footsteps I heard crunching on the gravel path below. Someone was moving in the shadows— more than one person, for I could hear voices. Soon, shadowy figures emerged from the shrubs and a person holding a torch situated himself in the driveway. On-off, on-off, the two points of light—the one in the distance and the one shining beneath my window— flickered like evening moths in a candle's glow. The patterns repeated themselves several times before they stopped. What followed soon after was the sound of whirring engines, trucks advancing toward the chateau, becoming loud enough to disturb the owl that made its home in a nearby tree. I watched as it spread its great wings and ascended into the moonlit sky. How I envied that creature's flight.

Eventually, six or seven trucks came to a stop directly below my window. It occurred to me then that the light from my table lamp might make it easy for me to be seen. Hurriedly, I ran back to switch it off and pulled the brown quilt from the foot of my bed to wrap around my shoulders. By the time I'd returned to the window, the drivers from the trucks had descended from their cabs and formed a circle with the men who had been waiting for them. I could hear their murmurings but make nothing of their words.

One man lit a cigarette. In its light, I saw a scar that ran from his left ear to his lower lip. Safe to say, this was no parish priest. Why he or any of the men were standing in the driveway was a puzzle. I was wracking my brain for a reason when Afreet appeared among them with Chanson trotting at his side. Even in the shadows, the humpback was unmistakable.

Both men gestured for the others to follow and, except for the man with the scar who remained on guard, they did. He stood with his back to me, looking out across the grove as he puffed on his cigarette. By now I'd leaned so far forward, I would have been seen if he had turned and gazed up in my direction. Mercifully, he didn't.

A short time later, Afreet, with his cadre of men, returned from the direction of the grove. I heard their voices before I could see them. Their slow, steady footsteps suggested they were carrying a heavy burden. When they came into view, the eight men had divided into two groups of four, each group balancing long crates on their shoulders. Even Chanson had put his strength to the task. These burdens, whatever they were, they deposited onto the back of the trucks then disappeared and reappeared with more crates, several times over until the tires of the vehicles bit hard into the gravel.

Finally, their work completed, the men scattered, some of them by climbing into their cabs and driving away, while the others drifted into the shadows from which they'd come. Only Chanson, with his broom, lingered a while longer, sweeping the path to erase all traces of their activity. Then he, too, disappeared.

With the silence returned, the great owl reclaimed its perch in the nearby tree. All was as before, so much so, that if the night air had not chilled me to the bone, I might have thought what I'd witnessed was a dream.

But I knew it was not. I was conscious of who and where I was and the year. My name was Rachel Farraday, a recent graduate of Mills College and part owner of the Chateau l'Ombre which was designed by Girolamo della Robbia in 1575 outside the village of Sainte Enimie. The day was December 3rd. The year was 1961.

This recitation I deemed necessary to keep me safe from being carried away by the deceit surrounding me. I knew too well Afreet's power. Already, he had gained a foothold into Christian's mind. He had driven away my allies, Mathiam and Mrs. de Toi, and had filled the chateau with hostile forces. And all this had been accomplished in the guise of a healer. What would he do to me if he knew I'd penetrated his disguise—seen through his flights of mysticism and other worldly claptrap—to discover nothing more than a common arms smuggler who was aiding the rebels of Algiers? For that was what he was doing. I had no doubt of it.

How he had ensnared Christian into his plot, I didn't know, but given my partner's warnings, I knew he was no innocent. He had some role in these nefarious dealings but as to the degree of his involvement, I had no notion. My only concern was how to save him. There were rights and wrongs to this war, certainly. But Afreet's methods were repugnant to me and he, at least, had to be stopped.

The grandfather clock in the foyer was striking two when I rose from my bed one last time and, leaving my room, headed downstairs without the benefit of a light of any kind except that pouring through the moonlit windows. The portraits hanging along the walls seemed to follow me with their eyes as I descended. Except for their company, I was alone. I didn't know what I was looking for or what I might find, but I knew, somehow, the tunnels were involved. I headed for them, still in my night clothes but with a shawl thrown over my shoulders for warmth. My slippers proved to be unsuitable, for the cold from the foyer's marble floor easily penetrated the soles. I could have been better prepared for my venture but how does one prepare for the unknown?

By the time I reached La Salle de Persephone, I was shivering and might have turned back, but I stopped when I thought I heard voices coming from the library. Moving forward, I stood with my ear to the door. Hearing nothing, I turned the handle and poked my head inside. The room was empty and, given that it was icy, seemed to have been without a fire for some hours. Puzzled, I retraced my steps.

In La Salle de Persephone, I heard the sounds again, this time coming from the area of the caryatids. A close inspection allowed me to see the latch had been sprung, so I pulled the panel a few inches wider and stepped inside.

Upon reflection, my behavior was foolish but I wasn't thinking at that moment, merely following my instincts, confident that in the blackness of the tunnel I wouldn't be seen. I was wrong in my assumption. To my surprise, a light did shine, a glow that spilled out into the passageway from what appeared to be an alcove. Although the source was at a distance, I could see enough of my surroundings to note a change since my first exploration. The path was no longer littered with rocks and stones but had been swept clean, and although the walls remained damp, the temperature was warmer than that of La Salle de Persephone.

I crept farther into the tunnel to listen to what the voices were saying, careful to hug the wall to avoid being seen. What I heard were male voices in high spirits. They were congratulating one another on a good night's work. I heard phrases like, "well done," or "it will soon be over," repeated several times. If I harbored any doubts about a smuggling operation, they were dispelled by their talk of munitions.

Finally, I'd heard enough. With my suspicions confirmed, I turned 'round, intending to call the police in St. Enimie, but gasped, instead, to find my way blocked.

"Mademoiselle couldn't sleep?"

Fripon grabbed hold of my wrists before I could react and began dragging me deeper into the passageway. No effort of mine, not kicking or scratching or digging my heels into the soft earth, impeded his progress. In a matter of seconds, I was hurled unceremoniously into the center of a brightly lit room and found myself being stared at by six or seven men—their eyes reflecting no more understanding of what had happened than the vacant windows of an abandoned building.

In the time it took them to come to their senses, I'd had a good look at their faces and learned I was not among strangers. Christian was there, standing shoulder to shoulder with Afreet. Chanson and Cartouche, too, were of that number, as one might expect; but to my horror the Vichy detectives, Tromperie and Boueur, were present, as well. As if it were a formal occasion, they all wore black. Defiant, I glared at them with the righteousness of the betrayed.

Afreet was the first to come to his senses. "My dear Rachel, this is an unpleasant surprise. You should have taken your sleeping draft this evening. Your presence, I'm afraid, poses a problem."

"Not much of one." Fripon disagreed as the ash from the cigarette in his mouth spilled to the ground. "I can deal with her."

"I think not." Afreet raised his hand in a forestalling gesture. "Another death coming so soon after Madame de Villiers…"

My eyes sought Christian's. "What's this about Odeil? Do you mean to say she was *murdered*?" A pair of blue eyes gazed at me in anguish but the man addressed made no reply. I had my answer. My hands flew to my face. "My God! How could you be a part of *that*? How could I have ever imagined I loved you?"

Christian moved in my direction with his arms outstretched. "It isn't what you think, Rachel. I can explain–"

"Explanations are unnecessary, my dear boy," Afreet said, placing himself between us. "However you proclaim your innocence, you played your part and took your reward."

"You bastard!"

The doctor ignored his patient and turned instead to me. "The birthday party was his idea, you know. What a teratological mind he exposed with that, didn't he? The cocaine helped, I suppose. Still, I confess I was sorry to have missed the evening. Everyone here thought it went well. No one imagined you'd stay after that. Of course, we knew nothing about the provisions of the will. That was unfortunate."

"You mean the men in this room came as guests?"

"Oh, surely, you've figured that out, by now. Chanson's not likely to be overlooked, is he?"

"No. His nature is an open one, at least. He's incapable of your depth of deception. He doesn't claim to be a healer and then use Christian's addiction against him. That was his reward for his co-operation, wasn't it: drugs and his release from the institution?"

"My dear girl," Afreet gasped, looking at me with owl eyes. "You can't blame me for Christian's habit. I did try to help him, at first. But he had no wish to be cured. And then, when I learned of the estate with its tunnels so ideally situated near Marseille... Well, let us say, he and I came to an arrangement."

"You mean, he became dependent on you as his source."

Afreet examined his fingernails before answering. "Something like that, yes. But that doesn't absolve him, does it? You'd like to think so, as you've already admitted you're in love with him..."

"Don't throw that in my face. It's got nothing to do with what you've done to him."

"Doesn't it?" A smile played about the doctor's lips. "You absolve him but you wish to accuse me. Are you not playing with the facts? Arranging them according to your private wishes? Bravo, my dear! I admit it. We are all shadow shapes. Remake us as you will."

"When I look at you, I see a murderer and a traitor. Christian is a drug addict. You can't compare the two."

Afreet's eyes softened instead of becoming angry, almost as if he pitied me. "You have much to learn, my dear, so much. But what matters now is what we are to do with you. We could confine you to this chthonic world, but how could we explain your disappearance? In a small village like St. Enimie, people would notice. We certainly can't afford a police enquiry, not a real one, at least." He turned to his cohort, Cartouche. "What do you think, Doctor? Have you any suggestions?"

The older man had been studying me the whole time Afreet was speaking. "An induced coma?" he said, at once. "That way she could be seen but would be rendered harmless. We could tell visitors she'd taken a tumble down the stairs. Or that she's had a stroke. It's rare in someone her age, but it does happen."

"And you can supply the means?"

"Oh, yes. No problem there, but…" The doctor paused with his lips pressed in further thought. "I suggest we dispense with pills. Forcing her to take them would be difficult. Injections are surer, much surer."

The thought of being reduced to a zombie horrified me and so, despite the odds, I tried to break through the surrounding circle. Tromperie, who was nearest, took hold of my arms and held me fast despite my struggles. "Why use not arsenic?" he grumbled as he wrestled me to stillness. "The history's been laid for it. Get it over and done with."

Afreet's eyes flashed his impatience. "Let go of her, Jacques. She can't get away. And no more talk of arsenic. You haven't been listening. We don't want the police snooping around. No, Cartouche's suggestion is best."

Tromperie turned me loose but continued to scowl as he stayed close. My eyes sought Christian's. Was there any kernel of decency left in him? Would he raise not one finger in my defense? Apparently not, for his gaze avoided mine.

Afreet turned to his colleague again once order was restored. "If you would be so kind as to make the arrangements, Doctor?"

The man addressed acknowledged the request with a bow. Then casting what seemed a small, apologetic smile in my direction, he drifted into the corridor and disappeared.

"I'd like to clarify one point for you," Afreet said, as we waited for Cartouche's return. "It shouldn't matter to me, but it does. Your employer's blood is not on my hands. The credit belongs to Chanson."

At the mention of his name, the hunchback bowed as had the doctor before him.

"The act was foolish," Afreet went on. "It could have destroyed our plans had the police investigated thoroughly. Fortunately, they didn't. My view is that we could have dealt with Madame de Villiers some other way. Everyone has their desires…their weaknesses."

"If you think she could be bought, you're wrong. She'd never betray her country."

The doctor shrugged as he looked at me. "You may be right. But I'm inclined to think you are wrong. Everyone has an Achilles heel. Even you, my dear."

"Oh? And what is mine?"

"Too trusting, perhaps? That would be one. Certainly you took much of what you saw at face value. You must forgive us our little game. But when you came on the scene so suddenly and unexpectedly, we had to explore the connection between you and your former employer. Christian couldn't enlighten us and we were afraid there was the slightest chance the French authorities might be on to us. You could have been a spy. A bit far-fetched, I agree, but then, to give one's estate to a total stranger seemed far-fetched, as well. That's where Tromperie and Boueur came in. I thought they were rather convincing as Vichy detectives, didn't you?"

I pressed my lips together as a sign I refused to answer.

"You were such an innocent," the doctor added softly. "And it all went off so well...except when Chanson found you in the tunnel. I was afraid he'd given you too severe a crack on the head."

"It was Chanson who found me?" That bit of information loosened my tongue.

"Yes. He carried you to the grove where Mathiam found you. The gardener wasn't one of us, by the way. Christian got him to draw a diagram of the tunnels, but the man had no idea why. He wasn't a sympathizer, after all, and once we ascertained that fact, we had to get rid of him along with your precious Mrs. de Toi. Fripon did a good job with her, I thought. They left you a note, by the way, to say where they were going but somehow...it got lost."

The tall man, with yet another cigarette dangling from his mouth, tossed a crooked smile in my direction. If he'd been close enough I would have spat on him.

"It's a pity you found us out," Afreet sighed. "Drugging you on the nights when there was a shipment seemed such a simple, nonviolent solution."

"I apologize for upsetting your plans."

Afreet shook his head. "Not much of an upset for us. But I'm sorry for what's about to happen to you. I wish it might have been otherwise. If you had not been so intractable in your thinking... If you'd have been more malleable, like Christian, we might have come to some accommodation. This isn't your fight, after all."

"Why don't you just shut up, Afreet? Don't you get it? She's not like you and the rest of us. She's got scruples."

"Ah. Prince Charming awakes. A little late for chivalry, isn't it?"

The blood vessel throbbing in Christian's temple should have alerted anyone to the level of his rage. He took a sudden leap, arms outstretched, in the doctor's direction, as if intending to throttle him. Despite his girth, the doctor proved to be too agile for him. His evasive action took him out of harm's way, leaving his assailant to fall into the arms of Fripon and Boueur. The pair managed to pin him by his shoulders but not before he'd landed a blow on the pastry cook's nose that sent blood spurting in all directions.

He was still struggling amidst a flurry of yells and cursing when Chanson unbuckled the leather belt at his waist and wrapped it around Christian's ankles. His quarry shackled, it was easy to slam him to the ground with a yank. A few swift kicks were administered until the bloodied captive was subdued.

Tromperie took hold of me when I tried to run to Christian's side. With no other vent for my anger, I cried out, "Murderers! Traitors! Murderers!"

Afreet put an end to my tirade with a slap across my face. "You accuse us of being criminals? We are the patriots whom France has betrayed, Mademoiselle. We have no choice but to free ourselves."

"Don't pretend what you're doing is noble," I bawled back, unrepentant. "You can't justify the deaths of so many innocent people. It's murder, pure and simple. And you won't get away with it. You may have driven Mathiam and Mrs. de Toi away, but what about Kathrine and Claudine? They'll get suspicious..."

Afreet chuckled as if I'd said something amusing. "I promise you, Kathrine won't care a fig what happens to you. She only has eyes for Christian, not for a woman she believes is her rival.

What's more, she trusts me. We became friends in Mende. And as for Claudine, dim-witted or not, she's one of us."

"So, you're all imposters!"

"Not entirely true, my dear. Cartouche and I are medical men and Verglas is a nurse working with her husband in the resistance forces. But enough said. Here come the accused now."

I swung around to see Verglas and Dr. Cartouche enter the room. The latter clutched his little black bag in one hand.

Chapter Twenty-Two

I CAN'T BE SURE ABOUT THE conditions under which I lived over the next several days. As I recall, my life was a cycle of temporary awakenings followed by drugs that put me to sleep again. Michael came to see me, I think. He and Dr. Afreet had an altercation and I thought I heard him shout that he wanted a second opinion concerning my condition. How like a Galahad, I cheered in my stupor before drifting off again. Still, I can't be sure any of it was real for Odeil came to me as well, flanked by the two suns that had come to mark her presence. Oddly enough, there were no elaborate dreams: the masque balls, the Elysian fields of earlier times. Instead, I swam like a mermaid in an endless sea of fog.

At some point, however, my thoughts began to clear. Fortunately, I had the presence of mind to hide the fact from Verglas or anyone who roused me to eat and to attend to my bodily needs. Although these visits always ended with the needle's prick, the drug seemed to be losing its effect. Why, I had no idea. Nevertheless, I was becoming lucid. Finally, I reached a point where I was awake for hours at a time. The drawback to my reawakening was that I remained helpless as an infant in its crib. If the sun was too bright or the room too cool, I could affect no change. I was a prisoner of my body. Little wonder that my increasing consciousness sometimes struck me as cruel. My thoughts could travel wherever they liked but the body was unwilling to respond. The schism was enough to drive one insane, although in time that, too, began to change. One day, I discovered I was capable of movement.

Nonetheless, the night Christian appeared in my room, I still doubted my sanity. My drapes had been left open and I was gazing at the stars when I heard the click of the door handle. Thinking it was Verglas, I shut my eyes and listened as footsteps approached my bed.

"Rachel? Rachel, wake up."

At the sound of his voice, my eyes flew open. "Christian," I cried, flinging my arms about his neck and refusing to let go. "Tell me, is it really you? Am I awake or dreaming?"

"I'm real, Rachel. I'm here."

"But how…?"

"I've been sabotaging Verglas' vials a little at a time, watering the dose, hoping to bring you back to me."

"So, that's why I've been regaining consciousness and why I can now move. But how did you manage it? It couldn't have been easy."

"It wasn't. I'm a prisoner the same as you. The only reason I'm given freedom of movement is that Afreet doesn't want to raise suspicions in the village. It wouldn't do to have both of us in a coma. But I'm seldom left alone."

"Then how is it you're here with me? Is no one watching your room?"

Christian's smile revealed he was pleased with himself. "Afreet has been generous with the cocaine, of late. He wants me in a stupor and I've been playing along. But I haven't been taking his drugs…at least, not all of it. I want to be strong enough to help you escape."

"Escape? Can we? Is it possible?"

"Not 'we,' Rachel. You."

"No!" I tightened my grip around his neck. "I won't leave without you."

Christian pulled away so that he could look into my eyes. "Listen, if you love me, as you said back there in the tunnels, then I beg you to do exactly as I say."

"I will, but why can't we escape together? Afreet thinks you're incapacitated and everyone's asleep. We could go now."

Christian shook his head. "Not by the front door, if that's what you mean. People are guarding the grounds."

"How, then?"

"You must leave through the tunnels. There's one that leads into the trees–"

"Yes, yes. I know it. Mathiam showed me."

"Excellent. I'll lead you to the exit. From there, you'll have no trouble reaching the village. But you must hurry, before they discover you're missing."

"But what if I can't manage on my own?"

"You must, my darling. I can't go with you. There's something I have to do and you can't be with me."

"Why can't I help?"

"No. It's too risky. Once the men discover either of us is missing, they'll disappear like rats into the sewers. I have to prevent that."

"Let them go," I pleaded, trying to pull him to me. "I don't care what happens to them. I want us to be together."

"But I *do* care, Rachel." Christian pulled away from me hard this time. "All my life, I've been selfish and now, because of it, I've endangered you and I've destroyed Odeil…"

"You couldn't have known…"

"Stop making excuses for me. For once, let me be honest. You should know the truth. I did poison my cousin."

"*What?*" I couldn't help being shocked. I sat up and stared at Christian with disbelieving eyes.

"I wasn't trying to kill her," he hurried on. "I wanted to make her ill, that's all. I wanted her to turn to me so I could care for her. But she was too clever. She found me out, told everyone I was crazy and stole my freedom. That's when love turned to hate. In my perverted mind, I blamed her. I couldn't face the truth. I couldn't admit she was right. I must have been mad. How else can one explain my impulse to hurt the person I loved? And I did love her once, even though she pushed me away. When she rejected me,

I thought drugs might ease the pain. They didn't, and I despise what I've become."

Christian's eyes grew misty as he examined me with a long, lingering gaze. "You're so kind, so gentle. When you told Afreet you cared about me, I felt my heart begin to thaw. I heard it beating as for the first time in years. Don't you see? You brought me back from the dead. I can't explain how or why you did it, but I am grateful. I don't want to go back to being what I was. Helping you escape will be the best thing I have ever done. You must give me a chance to redeem myself, Rachel, please."

He dropped his head into his hands and I knew he was crying. Although appalled by what he'd confessed, I couldn't deny the depth of his repentance. I couldn't reject him. I couldn't... He needed me, and what I felt at the moment was tenderness so expansive, it almost hurt.

Taking his face into my hands, I kissed away his tears. His eyes remained closed, almost as if he were receiving absolution. "I love you, Christian." I brushed my lips against his. "I love you."

Slowly, his arms encircled me and our kisses became more passionate and transforming. Our lips, our hands, our bodies ate hungrily of one another as if we meant to devour our corporeal existence. I was his. He was mine. And this co-mingling was sweeter than the sweetest music, purer than the breath of innocence. I could sense myself rising like smoke into the night sky and in that endless space where everything is real and nothing is impossible, Christian and I became one. Words cannot describe it, but rapture comes closest to the feeling.

Later, when we'd regained a portion of our senses, we lay exhausted, locked in one another's arms, satisfied that nothing could destroy our love. I dared to think we could have a future together. And then the ormolu clock struck four.

Time and place flooded into the room like the hint of daylight peeping through the exposed windows. When he heard the hour, my lover shot up and implored me to get dressed. With great tenderness, he helped me to stand, for I was so weak I could barely keep my equilibrium. Once I was steady, he rifled through my closet, tossing garments here and there until he found clothes warm enough for the cold night air.

"Hurry, Rachel. We've delayed too long. It's almost morning."

I tried to do as he asked but I was all arms and elbows. He had to help with the zippers and buttons of my garments. Getting me into my parka seemed to take forever. Finally, there was the matter of my feet. Christian had chosen a stout pair of walking shoes but I couldn't put them on by myself so he knelt down and tied the laces for me. As he did, I bent forward to kiss the back of his head. He looked up in surprise and there I saw not a smile but the look of beatitude. That moment in his life he was truly happy.

All that was left was for him to put on my mittens. I stood before him like a child being made ready for her first day at school and drunk in love with her care giver.

My head rested on his shoulder as we stumbled toward the staircase. The silence that greeted us in the corridor was reassuring. Below, the hall clock was ticking, but nothing else stirred.

We began our descent and, as we made our slow, steady way, my eyes fell upon the familiar portraits hanging along the wall, faces reduced to pigment that had once been capable of expressing joy, anger and love. Did they make note of our escape and wish us well? I imagined they did and in my thoughts, I said goodbye to them as if to old friends.

Christian saw my smile and mistook it for the lingering effect of the drugs. "You'll think more clearly once you hit the cold air," he said, trying to sound encouraging.

We'd made modest progress but froze in mid-flight when voices rose from the downstairs foyer.

"He's not in his room," said the first voice that I identified as belonging to Afreet. "I thought he might be in the kitchen but there's no sign of him. I'd better check the library."

"I'll come with you," said a second voice.

"No, Cartouche. We'll cover more ground if you search the upstairs. He could be in the girl's room."

"I don't have a torch."

"There's one in the kitchen, in the cutlery drawer."

"Which one's that?"

Sounding irritated, Afreet cut him off. "Never mind. I'll show you."

Their shadows disappeared in the direction of the kitchen. Once they were gone, Christian reached into his overcoat and chuckled. "I'm ahead of them for once. Here, take this," he said, handing me the torch. "You'll need it for the tunnels."

His amusement evaporated as his thoughts returned to business. "It may be that we'll have to separate, so listen carefully. Once you've reached the tunnels, don't wander off into the smaller corridors but follow the main path. About two hundred or three hundred steps from the entrance at Le Salle de Persephone..." He stopped in mid-sentence to ask, "Do you know how to open the passage?" I nodded that I did. "Good," he said, and hurried on. "When, you come to a branch that forms a T, take the left fork. The distance will seem endless but eventually you'll come to the exit that Mathiam showed you. From there, you can find your way to the village and the police station."

"But we won't get separated. We can't. I'm not certain I can make it on my own. Why don't we wait until tomorrow? I'll be stronger then."

"We can't wait. Rachel. Tomorrow another arms shipment is scheduled to leave for Marseille. The tunnels will be full of people loading munitions on to trucks."

"In a few days, then? What does it matter?"

"Because the shipment leaving tomorrow will be huge. It mustn't reach Marseille. I have to stop it."

"But how can you? You'll need help..."

"That's why you must make it to the village. You've got to inform the police."

"But I want to..."

Afreet and Cartouche had returned to the foyer, forcing me to silence. The older man was scratching his head.

"Where do you suppose the torch went to?"

"I don't know," Afreet snarled. "We'll forget the library for the time being. He's probably with the girl. Let's check upstairs."

Hearing Afreet, I tugged at Christian's arm intending for us to retreat to our rooms; but he resisted. "Remember, take the left fork." Before I could reply, he stood up and began to descend the stairs.

"Cartouche? Afreet? What are you doing up at this hour? I thought the shipment was set for tomorrow." He sounded almost jocular in his greeting.

The latter replied with suspicion in his voice. "It is. The doctor and I were checking the crates. Why are you up at this hour? And fully dressed? Are you expecting company?"

"I couldn't sleep. I thought perhaps a brisk walk…"

"But it's not fully light yet," said Cartouche, his voice also laced with suspicion. "Aren't you afraid Chanson might shoot you? You know what a nervous fellow he is."

"Is he on duty? I'd forgotten. Then I'd be advised to have a change of plans, wouldn't I? But I must do something. I'm wide awake. Perhaps, I'll cut myself another slice of Fripon's excellent cake… Would either of you care to join me?"

Never one to resist temptation, Afreet followed his charge into the kitchen with Cartouche close behind. The foyer fell silent. I knew I must either make my move or suffer defeat.

I reached the marble foyer in better time than I would have imagined, given my unsteady condition. The adrenaline coursing through my veins, apparently, was giving me strength. I would need more of it to cross the foyer and reach La Salle de Persephone without the aid of a railing. What's more, my sturdy shoes were proving an impediment. They created such an echo in that empty space, I had to proceed on tiptoe.

Halfway across the foyer, a light flashed through one of the windows. Terrified, I froze, waiting for someone to enter from outside. There was nowhere for me to hide, so I held my breath as the endless seconds ticked by. Finally, when nothing stirred, I screwed up my courage and scuttled toward La Salle de Persephone, giving no further thought to the sound my shoes were making on the marble floor.

Once inside, I closed the door behind me and dared to take a breath. No sooner did I congratulate myself on my success, however, then the same light flashed again and this time closer to the windows. With my back to the wall, I watched as the beam darted from floor to ceiling like a giant moth and, behind it, I saw Chanson's deformed silhouette as he pressed his face against the glass. All I could do at that moment was pray.

What passed for hours were only seconds but it seemed a lifetime before he moved away. By then, I was so terrorized my limbs refused to move. Like the caryatids, I'd become immobile. Not until I heard voices emerging from the kitchen did I find the will to scurry across the room toward the winking statue.

With moonlight streaming through the windows I found the latch and I heard the familiar click as the passage opened, a click that on that night and at that hour sounded like cannon fire. One look 'round to be certain no one was following and I plunged into the awaiting darkness and closed the panel behind me.

In that inky space, where no light shone from any quarter, I gave myself permission to take stock of my situation. What struck me first was that my unsteadiness had dissipated. I seemed to have regained much of my strength. Muscles which had earlier had been sluggish were remembering their function. Once I was satisfied I was no longer in danger of collapse, I began to hope.

Pulling off my mittens, which were bulky, I stuffed them into one pocket and withdrew my torch from the other. The light clicked on as required and produced a beam that carried a good distance into the darkness.

Creeping forward, I heeded Christian's admonition to stay on the path. Even so, by the light of my torch I could see a few alcoves had been carved into the walls. They didn't appear to be new and I marveled that I hadn't noticed them before, although during my two previous forays, I had to admit my attentions had been drawn elsewhere. I didn't stop to explore any of them but kept to my purpose, hoping against hope, no one was lurking in the shadows.

I had passed a fourth alcove beyond the munitions room where, earlier, Afreet had decided my fate, when I had reason to freeze. The outline of a man appeared in the periphery light to my left. Having nowhere to hide, I was at the mercy of whichever smuggler was standing there, although I was determined his efforts to subdue me would be at his cost.

The seconds ticked by and when no one rushed forward nor was there any sound except the beating of my heart, I came to the conclusion I was alone. Aiming my beam into the room's interior, I discovered no man but an airy space filled with *reliquiae* together with *memoria* designed for a graveyard.

How these objects came to be forgotten in this catacomb was a mystery, but never, I suspect, has a person been so happy to be confronted by the accoutrements of the grave as I was at that moment. From the condition of the bones and the dates chiseled on the statuary, many of them were centuries old, some of them dating back nearly four hundred years.

This cave, for that was its appearance, was somewhat narrow at the entrance but broadened toward the back, as more dirt had been scooped away, apparently, to accommodate larger objects: monuments and sepulchers and sculptured angels meant to memorialize the departed. These, in turn, were further ornamented by cobwebs and tracings in the dust left by insects that thrive upon decay.

Having nothing to fear from these tributes to the dead, I should have been glad to leave and hurry on my way. But I was lulled by the solemnity of the place and felt almost as if I'd reached a timeless portal between two worlds. I even imagined, if I listened hard enough, I might hear the final whispers of the departed for whom these replicas were created. I wandered among the coffins and marveled at their beautifully painted effigies. The skulls of the old, their transparent flesh barely covering their bones, seemed to stare with relief upon eternity. They'd labored and loved as was expected of them, had known the best and worst of their fellowmen and having satisfied their obligations, they'd drawn their last breath with an exhausted sigh.

Others, too young to have tasted much of life, stared out through their likenesses with wide-eyes and rounded features. "Pity us," they seemed to say. And I did, although I thought them worthy of envy, too. Despite their brief duration, they had been loved.

"She opened her eyes for a moment," one epitaph read, "but in that moment she stole our hearts forever."

In the midst of these forgotten images, my heart swelled with compassion and feelings of great tenderness. Existence was so fragile, so transitory.

Then my mind whirled with remembrance...I had been in this chamber before, had I not...?

"I agree. Death has it fascination."

Startled by a voice behind me, I spun 'round so that my torch cast a mosaic of light and shadow across the face of the man who'd spoken. In that fractured beam, he might have been wearing a joker's mask, but I saw no cause for laughter.

"Chanson saw you, if you are wondering how I came to find you here. But you needn't worry. I am alone. See?" Afreet held up his hands, one of which carried a torch. "No weapons. I merely wish to speak to you."

"Where's Christian? What have you done with him?" My voice betrayed my anxiety.

"Done with him?" The man opposite me lifted his eyebrows as a form of protest. "My dear girl, no harm's come to him. He's always been given the best of care. Were that not true, Cartouche couldn't have saved him from his last bout with pneumonia. I should have thought you realized that, by now."

"You must pardon me, Doctor. But it's difficult to have faith in a man who administers drugs to enslave his patient."

"Enslave?" The accusation rolled off his back like water. "It's a matter of perspective, isn't it? Christian has never objected."

When I made no reply, Afreet continued. "I see your point, however. It's a view the righteous might embrace. But I ask you to consider mine. Can you not conceive of a time when an individual's conscience must be silenced for the greater good?"

"What *good*, greater or otherwise, can exist without conscience?"

Afreet moved to a nearby coffin and sat on its edge." Let us simply agree that there are gradations of conscience. If a man comes to you for shelter from a storm, it would be a matter of conscience to let him in. You might even give him food as well as shelter. But if, during the course of your conversation, you learned he was a wanted criminal who had brutally murdered several of your neighbors, where would your obligation lie then?"

"You're wasting your breath if you think I'm interested in your word games. I asked about Christian. What's become of him?"

"He's where any sane person would be at this hour, in his bed. And please, Rachel, be so kind as to lower your torch as I have done mine. I am beginning to feel like a bug under a microscope."

I did as he asked.

"Thank you. Now, if you'll come back to the chateau, you'll see that all is well. I will even allow you to speak to him."

"Come back with you? Do you think I'm still in a miasmic stupor?"

"Frankly, you look better for the rest. It's only been a few days—"

"A few days, a week, a month? I'm not going back."

"Not even if I can show you it would serve both our interests?" The man opposite me smiled as if he knew he held a winning poker hand. My heart sank, but I lifted my chin higher, intending to make a brave stance.

"I doubt we have any interests in common."

"No? Not even Christian?"

"I-is that some kind of threat?"

Afreet shook his head. "Of course, not. I assure you, I have no wish to see anyone harmed. As a matter of fact, I've become fond of you both, especially you, my dear. Under different circumstances, I might even have taken your side, stood ready to cheer you on, as who would not, you being a pretty little thing and your righteous passion so touching. Yes, I would like to see a time when innocence prevails. That time is not now, I regret, if such a time ever existed in this world, or will in the next." My nemesis let his eyes wander about the room. "I wonder what these men and women would say if they could speak?"

"If you could hear them you might not like what they'd tell you."

"Really?" Afreet peered into my eyes as though to read some message there. "I suppose you've heard them then...? Yes. I believe you have. I've long suspected you of being an empath."

"A what?"

"Someone with a rare faculty to embrace the feelings of others as one's own. Not sympathize, mind you. Nothing so ordinary. No, I mean getting into their heads. Take Mrs. de Toi for example. You passionately defended her rights to the kitchen. It wasn't because you feared she would quit. You felt the pain of her rejection as deeply as if it were your own. It's true isn't it? That's why you went to such lengths to defend her."

"That's ridiculous. If I had that capacity, I'd have unmasked you long ago."

"I didn't say 'mind reader,' my dear. I refer to empathy. You receive emotions the way a radio receives sound waves. Don't pretend you fail to understand me. You may not have had a name for your talent but I venture to say at times, it left you feeling strange."

"I don't feel strange," I bristled. "You're imagining things. Maybe you could benefit from some professional analysis."

I heard a chuckle. "Why deny your talent and insist upon peering at the world through the peephole of commonsense? Perhaps you're afraid you will be overwhelmed by your perceptions? That is possible. But closing your mind to your abilities won't keep you safe. Your talent is too great. I warn you, if you continue to deny this gift of yours, you might even drive yourself into madness."

His words pricked at my flesh like needles. I could feel myself growing agitated as if a door was about to open and some hideous form would be set free. I needed him to stop talking. I needed to get away from him, but how?

As if aware of my anxiety, Afreet threw more gasoline on the fire. "Tell me, truthfully, have you never confused dreams with reality? Never awakened in your bed to wonder if you were asleep? Or had the queasy feeling, even for a moment, that you had penetrated another's sensations, maybe even someone not immediately present?"

I shook my head vehemently, as if trying to clear water from my ears. The gesture made him chuckle again. "Yes, yes. I knew I was right. I knew it."

A fury I had not seen coming ignited within me. I raised my torch above my head as if I intended to use it as a weapon. "Stop playing the fool. I can't be manipulated like Christian. You have no hold over me."

The doctor continued to look amused rather than threatened. "No, of course, not. Christian is an addict with an overwhelming need for approval. You are a greater challenge. The only reason I've gotten as far as I have is that you've crippled yourself. You've built a wall to keep intruders out because you're afraid of being discovered for what you are."

Now, it was my turn to be amused, but my laugher was harsh, even frantic. His words had an effect and I could no longer hide it, even from myself. As if the doctor had applied paint remover to my psyche, his words penetrated the defenses I had built up over years. Truth was threatening to bubble to the surface and I could feel my façade begin to peel away.

Perhaps it was my pallor or the fact that I was shaking that stopped Afreet from continuing with his hectoring. When he spoke again, his voice was gentle. "I can be a friend to you, Rachel, if you'll let me. This gift of yours is nothing to fear. Everyone has it to varying degrees. Some ignore it. Others, like you, attempt to kill it. But when the gift is as fine as yours—"

"Stop it. Don't say anything more." I threw my hands over my ears, dropping my torch. It rattled to the floor. "I won't listen. I *won't*."

Afreet came forward. "My dear girl, I wish you could trust me. I want to help. When our war is over, perhaps I can. All I ask is for your silence a little while longer. Then Chanson and the rest will disappear and you will never see them again."

He took hold of my shoulders and forced me to look at him. "Can't you see I would like to help?"

His expression was kind, almost fatherly. If this was another of his mind games, it was the cruelest one he'd played so far. That tenderness opened a vein in me that wouldn't stop bleeding. Back home, Dr. Devane had described my isolation as neurotic. Afreet proposed it was more: a power that was neither good nor evil in itself, but like a singularity hungry for light.

He was stroking my hair when Christian found us.

"Get away from her, Afreet. What have you done? Why is she crying?"

Surprised, the doctor did as he was ordered. "I've done nothing, dear boy. She needed consoling. I should think that was obvious."

"With you, nothing is obvious." Christian addressed his next remark to me, inquiring if I was all right. When I told him I was, he took hold of my hand and pulled me to him.

"It seems a bit late to play the white knight, doesn't it?" Afreet attempted to sound amused but there was no mistaking the growl in his voice.

"Early or late, what matters is the outcome." My champion was on his metal and, for the moment, I felt safe.

"You might get past me, dear boy. But what then? My men have the grounds under heavy surveillance. When you surface from the tunnels, they'll catch you."

"Don't worry about us, Afreet. We'll manage. First, we need to take care of you. Rachel, look for a rope or some rags. Anything we can use to tie him up."

I retrieved my torch from where it had rolled but my search proved fruitless. The strongest bonds I could find were cobwebs.

The doctor seemed to enjoy my desperation. "Perhaps, I can help. You'll find ropes in the munitions room. Oh, but I forgot, Chanson is probably there by now, searching for you."

"Shut up, Afreet. A couple of belts will do. Hand yours over." Christian was unbuckling his own as he spoke.

"Not in front of a lady, surely…"

"Stop playing the fool and do as I say."

"And if I don't?"

The doctor's tone had lost its mirth and taken on a steely challenge. Christian's body grew tense. "Take care, old man. I've nothing to lose."

Ignoring the threat, Afreet sat down once more on the edge of the coffin. "It's a pity you never took an interest in chess, dear boy. The game teaches one to conceive of a number of strategies for winning. If you attempt to bludgeon me with that torch of yours, for example, I can defend myself in any number of ways. I could shout for the others to come running. Several of my men must be in the tunnel, by now. Chanson knows Rachel is here, you see. Or, I could use the poor girl as a shield against any harm you might wish to settle on me…though if it came to fisticuffs, I think I might… No matter. The point is, you can't get away. I have you trapped like rats in a maze."

Here, Afreet paused and I saw in him again an almost filial tenderness. "But if you and Rachel were to return to the chateau with me, I can promise no one will be harmed."

Christian raised his torch as a weapon, as I had done minutes before. This time, there could be no doubt he intended to brain his caregiver. The doctor braced, preparing to defend himself, but in that moment, the game changed. People were in the tunnel and heading in our direction.

Afreet had played his part well. He had gambled for time and won. The stalemate was over. Christian and I had to run. But when I said as much, he reached for my shoulder and gave me a push. "Get out of here, Rachel, now!"

"What about you?"

"Run, I say!" His second shove was almost brutal and, once my feet were set in motion, they refused to stop. Without my willing it, I found myself dashing from the necropolis and into the main tunnel. Torches were flashing from the direction of La Salle de Persephone so I headed away from them, deeper into the tunnels.

I ran blindly with no light to guide me as I was afraid mine would be seen. Several times I stumbled and fell, but rose again, propelled by a fear that left my mouth feeling like tin. That fear helped me put distance between me and the voices pursuing me. Afreet's was the loudest. I could hear his shouts above the others. "She's in the tunnel! Fripon and Cartouche check the rooms along the corridor. Chanson, take a few men to search the passageways. She must be found!"

My lungs, my veins, ignited with fire. I was running now with a speed I hadn't thought possible. I knew more than my life was at stake. I had to reach the police station for Christian's sake. Before...before...

No time to think of that now. Run! Keep running!

At last, I arrived at the spot where the tunnel broke off into passages north and south. I should have been happy, but I was in too much pain. Pushing through it, I took the south fork, and then switched on my torch, satisfied I would be out of my pursuers' line of sight. The way seemed endless but I could move faster now that I could see.

Despite being drugged for days, the more I ran, the more energized I became. I was experiencing what runners called a second wind. My sturdy shoes seemed to be propelling me without my volition. Tears sprang into my eyes but I didn't need to see. I was using the mind's eye in what might be called a "hyper body." The experience was euphoric, despite the terror that fueled it.

How long I could have remained in that dimension, I don't know but when I encountered a second fork in the tunnel, I crashed. Christian had said nothing about a second fork. I was confused. Which way was I to go? All my elation evaporated and I crumpled forward, gasping for air.

Frantically, I considered how to regain my bearings. I'd come west from La Salle de Persephone, and then veered south. That had put me somewhere near the rose garden. A right turn would set me in a westerly direction again, out toward the rolling hills. I wanted to head east, back toward La Salle de Persephone, because from its windows one had a good view of the grove.

With this fragile map implanted in my brain, I took the left fork and headed in what I hoped was an easterly direction. My decision came none too soon as footsteps echoed in the corridor behind me. They were distant but gaining speed. I ran harder, hoping my pursuers would pause at the second fork just as I had done, giving me a little more time to put distance between us.

I was to be disappointed. When they came to the break, they didn't hesitate. They split up—one of them heading west, the other coming in my direction. The man behind me seemed impeded by a shuffle. When I heard it, I almost laughed at my good fortune. Chanson could never overtake me. I was too far ahead and, already, I could see a speck of light in the distance.

As I approached the exit, my jacket tangled on the root of a tree. Frantically, I struggled to set myself free while Chanson's footsteps drew closer. Determined not to be found like a plum dangling in midair, I struck at the root with my torch again and again until the light went out and I felt my hand bloodied. No matter. Once I heard the tear, I knew I was free. I dove through the hole into the light.

In that hour before dawn, I stood in the silent grove, gulping in the cold air like someone held for too long underwater.

By now, the crescent moon had almost completed its descent. This was the hour when the world lay wedged between sleep and waking and, for a moment, I felt as though I was alone on the planet and that time was endless. I knew what I felt was an illusion. I had to go on. I had to reach the police and save Christian.

I would arrive in the village within twenty minutes if I stuck to the road. But knowing Afreet's men would be looking for me, I decided to cross the fields in search of cover, even though that way would slow me down.

A faint glow had started to cap the trees on the horizon as I headed in the direction of St. Enimie. The light was so new, it had yet to reach the ground. Dew still covered the ferns at my feet. As I jogged along, their fronds swished against my pant legs—the only sound to be heard in that final hour of night. Already I was thinking of the well-lighted rooms of the police station. Soon I would be telling my story to amazed faces. Soon there would be arrests and Christian would be freed from Afreet's tyranny.

So deep was I in thought, I barely noticed the first short burst of light that came not from the east but from the west. Turning my head, a second flash almost blinded me, this one accompanied by a sound like the roar of a thousand race car engines starting at once. The third flash brought with it a thunder louder than the first, enough to shake the ground and force me to take cover.

Crouched beneath a tree with my hands protecting my head, I endured what can only be described as the tumult of Judgment Day. Globes of fire hurtled through the air, lighting the sky. Some of them were hurled far enough to ignite branches of the trees overhead. Soon the entire grove would be alight. Even the ferns were being transformed into a burning carpet.

With the air too hot to breathe, I had no choice but make a dash for the road, a clear space which promised safety. As I ran, a tongue of fire pursued me, but I managed to reach the area unscathed, except that my face and hair were singed.

From my vantage point, I had an unimpeded view of the terrain. The scene was horrific. I could only watch as the walls of Chateau l'Ombre disappeared and in its place stood a blackened hulk, little more than a skeleton, little more than a funeral pyre whose flames climbed into the night sky as if molten lava was being spewed from the earth's core. The moon and the stars were obliterated by its brightness and so was the world from which I had escaped, its structures, its people, reduced to ashes as surely as if a judgment had been decreed.

And the man I loved? What of him? Was this conflagration his doing? Is this why he refused to escape with me? I didn't know. I couldn't think. My endurance had reached its endpoint. I collapsed upon the ground, grateful for the darkness that overtook me.

* * *

So, that is my story, exactly as I've told you before. Surely, you can see why I've had bad dreams…why no identification papers exist?

You must have heard the explosion.

Has no one talked to the police? They can vouch for me. I'm the American who lived at the Chateau l'Ombre.

My attorney is Michael Allaire of the law firm Larouche, Gillard and DuBonnet. Has he tried to reach me? Yes? No?

I can hardly see your face. My eyes aren't damaged are they? I feel no pain. Why am I being kept in this darkened room? You said I've been in a coma, but that is past. I'm better now...aren't I?

What's that you say? I have a visitor? Who? Mrs. de Toi? Mathiam? No? Who then?

I must look a fright. A mirror please and a comb... No wait. Open the blinds first. There's nothing wrong with my eyes, if that's what you fear...

Stop! Stop! That's not possible. This is some trick Afreet is playing...some sick joke. Is Odeil here? No, that can't be right.

Where am I? Look at those twin suns gleaming through the window.

My God!

What's happening to me?

Am I awake...or dreaming...?

About the Author

CAROLINE MILLER IS A WOMAN of many distinctions. She writes short stories, plays, novels, and is a frequent blogger. *Trompe l'Oeil* is Ms. Miller's third novel and she is putting the finishing touches on her fourth novel while crafting the structure of her fifth novel. Caroline's short story, *Under the Bridge and Beneath the Moon* was dramatized for radio in Oregon and Washington.

Her work is rooted in literature: strong character-driven storylines, descriptive imagery, and multi-layered meanings. But her work is also often categorized as "Sensational" or "Gothic" because she enjoys painting her situations with a paranormal shadow and her endings are harrowing rather than romantic. She is a first-rate storyteller.

Caroline Miller was head of the Portland Federation of Teachers and is enshrined in Oregon's Labor Hall of Fame. She taught English in high school and at the university level. Ms. Miller holds degrees from Reed College and Northern Arizona University, where she graduated with honors in Literature.

Other Books by Caroline Miller

Caroline Miller's first book, *Heart Land*, is a fictional memoir of a boy growing up in rural Ohio between 1939 and 1940. During a time of social and historic importance that still resonates with Americans, Miller draws a humorous and sometimes poignant tone. The story is brilliantly driven by distant memories evoked from photographs found in an album as the family gathers for their mother's funeral during the height of the Vietnam War. *Heart Land* is destined to be a true classic of American literature.

> "...*Heart Land* wears the triple crown of literary genius: it is profound, beautiful and arresting from the first page..."
>
> - *Writerface.com*

At the center of Caroline Miller's second novel, *Gothic Spring*, lives Victorine Ellsworth, an intelligent and beautiful Victorian girl. Because she is plagued by epilepsy, her maiden aunt deems her to be too fragile to attend school and Victorine is brought home to live under very strict rules.

Increasingly anxious, Victorine struggles under her restrictions until her aunt relents and allows the new vicar to tutor her charge. He is charismatic, mature, well educated, and interested in his young student, which turns Victorine's head. The vicar is far more appealing than the lovesick constant attentions of Jeremy, a local boy, who is dotes upon her. Victorine's adolescence sexuality explodes into provocative flirtations. The vicar's wife does not take this rival completely serious. Then the vicar's wife has a fatal accident that shocks polite society. Victorine has becomes a force to be reckoned with.

Ballet Noir, Caroline Miller's fourth novel, clearly demonstrates her impressive mastery of the Paranormal Goth Romance genre. Experiencing her first tour in Europe, Tara Bentley is a young prima ballerina with a small Seattle dance company who watches her excitement turn to horror when she's haunted by the voice of her deceased dance teacher, Yelena Natilova. She fears she might be going mad until she meets a necromancer who assures her the voice is real. Is he a charlatan? Or, has he the power to guide her through this nightmare as she struggles to hold her career together? Their dash through the great theaters of Europe becomes the performance of a lifetime with death waiting in the wings. Another terrific read from the pen literary imagination of Caroline Miller, *Ballet Noir* is an original and compelling read that is consistently entertaining from beginning to end. Very highly recommended for community library collections and personal reading lists, *Midwest Book Review 3/2016*

About the Cover Art

The cover art of *Trompe l'Oeil* is a collaborative, mixed media work by John Legry and Slaven Kovačević.

* * *

John Legry is a San Francisco native whose creative output includes illustration and serious artwork. His oil paintings and drawings are in private collections across the United States and western Canada. His pen and ink sketches and cartoons have appeared in professional, trade, community, and general publications. John is also the writer-illustrator of several books, including Oregon history, young people's tales, and underground comics.

His on-line gallery is at: http://www.zazzle.com/jlegry

* * *

Slaven Kovačević is an independent who worked for fourteen years as lead graphic designer in small publishing company. He is a specialist in Adobe InDesign, Photoshop, Illustrator, Acrobat, PDF, and all aspects of desktop publishing, including the production of traditional books, e-books, brochures, photo-manipulation and photo-editing.

He can be contacted via email at: slaven980@gmail.com